Praise for
Rossio Square N.°5>

"Through her compelling characters and deft storytelling, Jeannine Johnson Maia takes the reader into the suspenseful and dangerous world of Lisbon 1941, when the city served as an escape route for Jews and others fleeing the Nazis and the Second World War."

-Richard Zimler, author of *The Last Kabbalist of Lisbon* and *The Gospel According to Lazarus*

∂ ∂ ∂ ∂ ∂

"Jeannine Johnson Maia's novel is a breath of fresh air on a theme that is never exhausted. I read it from beginning to end, hardly putting it down. The subject of refugees in Portugal during WWII has been addressed in various historical essays, such as those by Irene Flunser Pimentel and Esther Mucznik, among others. But what this book brings us is something new. Through a fictional account, it transports us back to a Lisbon in turmoil, full of spies on both sides, the capital city of a provincial country that suddenly finds itself invaded by tens of thousands of people fleeing the Nazis who look to the United States, the destination of most refugees, as a new promised land. This is a Lisbon with few available rooms, but still space for a love story between two young people."

-César Santos Silva, author of *Antonio, the Other Salazar*

∂ ∂ ∂ ∂ ∂

"World War Two Lisbon was a hub of intrigue. Spies, refugees, Nazis, disappearances, and a murder affect the lives of two young people, Claire and Antonio, trying to survive in the city. This carefully researched, well-written, engaging historical novel tells a wonderful story set in this difficult time and place."

-Phyllis Hall Haislip, author of *Lottie's Courage: A Contraband Slave's Story*

ROSSIO SQUARE
N.º 59

ROSSIO SQUARE
N.º 59

Jeannine Johnson Maia

To Daniel
For traipsing around Lisbon without getting too impatient,
and for the strength and inspiration you give me

To Anne and Lynn
For the lifeboats, and the laughter

CHAPTER 1 – LISBON
SATURDAY, APRIL 5, 1941

ANTONIO WOVE THROUGH the crowd, eyes alert for the best target. Maybe a suitcase, not too big. Not one belonging to a haggard refugee stumbling off the train from Madrid, or to a mother with clinging, crying children. No. Better to find one owned by a man with a smart suit and hat, who was certainly better off than Antonio and his grandmother would ever be. All along the platform, men handed bags out the open doors, calling "Make way." Beside them, tired passengers and grumpy children climbed down.

Antonio's foot hit a pair of glasses, the lenses still intact. They skittered ahead of him. No owner in sight. Antonio bent down and slid them into a pocket. They'd be worth a few *escudos*.

Further along, among the jumble of luggage on the platform, a small leather suitcase lay on its side. Not too new, and unattended. A 17-year-old could carry it out of the station without attracting attention. Antonio knelt beside it, pretending to adjust his shoe, and gripped the handle. He started to stand, then froze.

From a few yards away, a slim girl about his age stared at him. Her clothes were travel-worn but stylish, and thick, shoulder-length hair framed a pale face. Her eyes narrowed.

Merda. It wasn't even her bag. Antonio set the suitcase upright, as if that had been his plan all along, and pushed himself to a standing position. The girl tossed her head, still glaring. She wasn't buying it. Antonio hadn't been caught yet, and he wasn't risking it now. Pulling his beret over his forehead, he edged away into the crowd, trying to look unconcerned. He was too old for this.

From the window of a train car ahead, hands passed a parcel wrapped in brown paper down to a heavyset, bearded man on the platform. Thomas. The German refugee who had become his friend sat at one of Antonio's tables in the café almost every evening. Antonio didn't want Thomas to see him here. He tugged his beret further down and turned away.

"Boy, can you give me a hand?" A man with haunted eyes reached out to him, speaking in French. Beside him, a tiny, ancient woman swayed on her feet. "Stay with her while I fetch our luggage, will you?"

Antonio tucked a hand under the woman's birdlike arm. She was even frailer than his grandmother. But she'd made it this far. Tough old biddies. Had to admire them.

"*Ça va?*" He'd picked up more than enough French at the café to ask how she was. Since the war had begun, he no longer tried to count the number of languages he heard at the Chave d'Ouro.

"*Ça va.*" She managed a wan smile. "But I'm tired. So very tired."

Antonio shifted to steady her better, and saw the girl out of the corner of his eye. She was pretty. Definitely not Portuguese. And still watching him.

"Don't worry, Mother. We'll rest here." The old woman's son was back. "Look, I've brought someone to help us." A lady with red lipstick introduced herself as Gina from the refugee assistance agency. She picked up one of their bags.

The man turned to Antonio. "Thank you, son. We'll be fine now."

"It's nothing." Antonio squeezed the old woman's hand and got another half-smile in return.

Around him, the platform teemed with passengers and aid workers. "Red Cross, this way," a woman called. A group of refugees surged in her direction.

"Unitarian Service Committee," a man bellowed in Antonio's ear. Antonio jerked back, almost knocking over a boy holding a sign that read "American Jewish Joint Distribution Committee."

Anxious men and women flocked to all of them.

"Where will we stay?"

"When can we eat?"

"Where's the post office?"

Antonio elbowed his way out of the crowd, angling toward an exit. From behind a stone column, he saw the girl, still on the lookout. And a policeman in gleaming black boots, coming his way. Time to go.

Claire

Claire scanned the hall. She'd lost sight of the boy who'd tried to steal a suitcase.

A gentle hand squeezed her arm. "My dear, we have to say goodbye."

Claire smiled at the woman who'd watched over her since they'd boarded the train together in Barcelona. Mrs. Deauville's two young daughters wedged themselves between their skirts.

"The refugee people are taking us to our boarding house." Mrs. Deauville kissed Claire's cheeks, then gave her a searching look. "Are you sure you won't come? What if your parents don't arrive before your ship sails? You can't travel to America alone."

"Don't worry. I'll be with my uncle." Claire heard her voice waver. He wasn't there to meet her. Surely her parents had managed to send him word. Four days had passed since she'd been at home, in Marseille, staring at a visa that gave her six hours to leave France. Barely enough time to throw clothes and her sewing kit into a bag before Father bundled her onto the train for Spain. His last words had been a promise he'd let Uncle Vincent know she was on the way. The rest of the family would catch up with her in Lisbon, he'd said. Claire prayed they were somewhere behind her, and safe.

"We'll be staying at the Europa boarding house." Mrs. Deauville brought Claire back to the present.

"You'll come see us?" her youngest daughter asked. "Soon?"

"I'll try." Claire bent to give her a quick embrace, the child's wiggly body reminding her once again of her own small brother. She hoped he'd weather the voyage on the train as well as these two girls had. They trailed behind their mother, waving goodbye until the crowd hid them. With them went two worn sheets, the only defense the four of them had had against bedbugs on the trip across Spain. Mrs. Deauville, her finger tracing an ornate "D" embroidered on the fabric, had told Claire they were among the few possessions she'd salvaged the night the Gestapo took her husband away. Without them, Claire felt as if she'd lost a layer of protection. And she was so hungry her legs wobbled.

She looked around for a bench, then shook herself. The station was emptying out. From somewhere above, a clock struck five. She had to find her uncle. Near the end of the platform, a porter rolled an empty cart. Claire forced her feet into movement and hurried to head him off.

"Please sir, can you…?" Her voice caught in her throat, and she started again. "Can you tell me how to get to the Colonial boarding house?"

The porter shook his head. "*Não percebo.*"

"Do you speak English? *Parlez-vous français?*" She held out a piece of paper. "*Pensão Colonial?* Rossio 59?"

The porter peered at her father's scribbled handwriting. "Rossio? *É perto.*" A string of directions followed. In Portuguese. Claire didn't understand a single word. Her confusion must have been obvious because the porter beckoned her down a flight of stairs to the station's main entrance. With his fingers, he mimed walking straight ahead and then turning right. Not far, he seemed to say.

"*Merci, monsieur,*" Claire said. The man tipped his hat and returned to his cart.

Claire took a deep breath, tightened her grip on her suitcase, and willed herself to step out alone into this strange city. At the threshold she halted, squinting. The late afternoon sun blazed in a cloudless sky, reflecting off bright facades and pavement stones inlaid with white and black designs. The light stung her eyes, but its warmth contained a welcome. She inhaled the sweet smell of pastries and strong coffee. It had been ages since they'd had such things in Marseille.

Whizzing along in front of the train station were lines of cars, more in a minute than she'd see in an hour back home. The Portuguese must not be rationing petrol. The cars stopped to let two women cross. They walked arm-in-arm, chatting merrily. Claire followed, pulled along in the wake of their laughter. No one in Marseille laughed like that now.

On the far side of the street, Claire turned. From the outside, the train station's entrance was a double horseshoe of ornately sculpted stone. Breathtaking. As she took in the details, she noticed a boy with a beret peering at her through a side window. The thief, again.

Claire whirled around and took off in the direction the porter had indicated, bemoaning her unsteady legs. Columns rose in front of an imposing building to her left – yet another facade of blinding white. To her right stretched a long square bordered by cafés and shops, with a tall statue in the middle and fountains at both ends. Behind her, there was no sign of the boy. She searched for the name of the square. *Praça Dom Pedro IV*. That wasn't right. Had she misunderstood?

Tears pricked the corners of her eyes. She blinked them away. It couldn't be far. Outside a café, a waiter in a long black apron smoked and chatted with a customer. Claire held out the paper with her uncle's address.

"Please sir, how can I find Rossio Square?"

"You've found it, miss," he answered in accented English. "This is Rossio."

"But it says Dom Pedro."

"Same thing, miss." The waiter ground his cigarette into the pavement with his shoe.

Number 59. Claire looked up and let out a sigh of relief. The *Pensão Colonial* sign hung above a tobacco shop on a five-story building, just steps away. The front door was locked. She leaned forward, trying to see through the grimy pane, then jerked back as a bearded man opened the door from the inside and nodded at her to enter. Claire slipped past him and took the stairs to the first-floor landing. The concierge, an old fellow with a two-day stubble and watery eyes, shuffled out from behind heavy wooden doors.

"Yes?"

"Vincent Lemoine," Claire said. "Does he live here?"

The old man held up five fingers and pointed at the dingy ceiling. "At the end of the hallway."

Claire stifled a groan. Of course Uncle Vincent would live on the very top floor. "Is he in?"

The old man nodded. Claire picked up her bag and trudged upstairs, trying to ignore the hotel's musty smell and her thudding, uneasy heart.

Antonio

From the center of Rossio Square, Antonio looked up at the boarding house where the girl had disappeared. He'd surprised himself by following her. She'd ruined his heist. Normally he'd be angry. But no refugee his age had ever locked eyes with him so defiantly, as if he were the one who didn't belong. In his mind, he sketched her face. As soon as he got a chance, he'd capture her spirited toss of a head on paper.

The sun angled lower, turning the buildings around the square a warm yellow. *Merda.* He'd lost track of time. He saluted Scrappy, the shoeshine boy, and jogged over to the Chave d'Ouro café.

His boss was at the entrance, barring the way with a beefy arm. "You're late. Again. Keep it up and you'll be looking for a new job." Mr. Silva's dour expression could hide a biting wit, but Antonio sensed no humor today. "Get to work."

"Yes, sir." Antonio ducked under the outstretched arm. No job meant no rent for the cramped rooms he shared with his grandmother. That wasn't a risk he was going to take.

Inside the large, smoke-filled café, dozens of tables teemed with customers. José was the only other waiter in sight. In the back, Antonio pulled on the Chave d'Ouro uniform – black jacket over a white shirt, black bow tie, black trousers. At least he only had the main floor today. No running upstairs to the gallery, or to the restaurant above that. He might be the youngest waiter, but he was fast and the regulars liked him. And Mr. Silva knew it. Antonio made sure of that.

A man hailed him. "*Um café de máquina.*" His three friends nodded for the same. Antonio signaled to the bartender – four fingers for four small cups of strong coffee. Then he moved on to two tables of Germans, a couple of French girls smoking at a window table, and a newly arrived Polish refugee who clutched his bag and gazed about as if the café were a wondrous thing. Back at the Portuguese table, Antonio handed around the drinks.

"Can't your boss do something about those girls?" one of the men grumbled. His friends nodded but didn't take their eyes off the two French women near the window. "No respectable lady goes out without a hat or..." He stopped, and Antonio grinned. He knew what the man was thinking. No respectable Portuguese woman would wear skirts that slid up her legs that way, or sit down in a café without a male companion. More's the pity. Antonio watched as one of the girls, her knees showing, leaned forward to light another cigarette.

"If my daughter did that, she'd not leave the house until her wedding day," the man said in a loud voice. The French girls chatted on, oblivious.

"Doesn't do any good to yell," said one of his friends. "They've no idea you're going on about them."

Which was just as well. Antonio left them to pick up another order. It'd be a sad day when a bunch of grumpy old men scared the pretty girls away.

"*Olá, Tó!*" From his customary seat along the wall, Thomas grinned at Antonio over a newspaper.

Antonio smiled at the accented use of his nickname. "*Olá, Thomas. Como está?*"

"*Bem, obrigado,*" Thomas answered, enunciating carefully.

"*O seu português está a melhorar.*"

Thomas blinked. "Sorry. What?"

Antonio switched into English. "I said your Portuguese was improving."

"Humph." Thomas grinned ruefully. "I wish I picked up languages as quickly as you do. When's my next lesson?"

From the bar, Mr. Silva glowered in their direction.

"*Quer uma cerveja?*" Antonio asked hastily.

"*Sim.*"

Still smiling, Antonio went to fetch a beer. They'd been doing this for months, mostly during long walks around Lisbon. When he wasn't fretting about what he'd left behind in Germany, Thomas was a good companion. And he understood a lot more Portuguese than he let on in the café. Antonio brought the beer and a glass to the table. "Tonight the theme of our lesson will be…" Something lighthearted. "Women and song."

Thomas chuckled. "Women and song – in the movies."

"Right. Anything to get your mind off those newspapers."

"Impossible." Thomas poked a finger at the front page. "Look at this. Another ship sunk by a U-boat, another bombing raid…"

"But you're out of it. You made it to Lisbon. Stop looking back." They'd had this conversation a hundred times. Knowing

Thomas, they'd probably have it a hundred more.

"I'm not," Thomas retorted. "I'm looking around, and finding no good news anywhere." He glanced at the German customers and lowered his voice. "Serpents are running my country. How would you feel if it were Portugal?"

"Which is why you left. So you'll be around to pick up the pieces when it's over." Trying to convince Thomas he'd done the right thing was like lifting a mountain. "Stop feeling guilty."

"It's not…"

"Antonio!" Mr. Silva barked from across the café. "Work!"

Claire

At the end of the dim, fifth-floor corridor, Claire knocked a second time. Silence, except for her own breathing. The man downstairs had said her uncle was home.

She rapped harder.

"Who is it?" It was her uncle's deep voice.

"Me. Claire. Let me in."

"What?" A second later, the door flew open. Uncle Vincent pulled her into a hug, smiling hugely. "Welcome! I was wondering when you'd arrive." He stuck his head into the hallway. "Where's everyone else?"

"I came alone." Claire looked at him in alarm. "You didn't get a telegram?"

Vincent's smile disappeared. "No. Should I have?"

She'd been damping down fear and fatigue for days. Now they threatened to envelope her. "Uncle, please. I need to sit down."

"Of course. Come in." Vincent ushered her into a cluttered room overlooking Rossio and bolted the door behind them. Paper covered almost every flat surface, except for a corner of the table where a battered typewriter sat. In the corner was a sink, with plates and glasses on a shelf above it. Vincent cleared off an armchair, then crouched down in front of her. "What happened? Is your family all right?"

"I don't know." Her words came out as a croak. "May I have something to drink?"

Vincent poured a glass of water and pushed it into her hand.

"Talk."

Claire took a grateful sip. "As soon as our tickets for America arrived, we got the transit visas for Spain and Portugal. But our French exit visas – the ones we needed to leave Marseille – didn't come. We started to worry we might not get to Lisbon in time."

"Understandably," Vincent said. "Our ship leaves in eight days. You're telling me Michel couldn't think of another way to get your family out of France?"

"Leave without the visas, you mean? Father didn't want to risk it, not with little Frédéric and Grandpa. What if we got arrested?"

Vincent ran his fingers through his graying hair, standing it on end, but didn't say anything. Claire knew a guide had helped him escape on foot over the Pyrenees Mountains one foggy night, but that was different. He was a grown man traveling on his own.

"When the exit visas finally came, they were only good for six hours. No time at all. And Father's was missing." He'd been so relieved, at first. Then she'd seen his whole body tense.

"Michel wasn't given an exit visa? Why?"

"We didn't find out before I left. The only train for Spain that day was leaving two hours later."

"But…why didn't Michel send the whole family? Surely he could have made it across the mountains by himself, and met you somewhere in Spain."

Claire bristled. "He would have. But Mother was out with Frédéric, looking for food, and Grandpa refused to leave without them. So Father made me come alone. I didn't even say goodbye." Her voice shook, and she stopped.

"I'm sure they're fine." Vincent patted her shoulder awkwardly, then began to put the papers scattered around the room into piles. "I'll take you to the post office tomorrow. Maybe the letter will be waiting for us." He paused. "Where have you arranged to stay?"

"With you, of course. Where else would I go?"

"Ah." Vincent shifted uncomfortably. "That might be problematic."

"Why would it be? You're the only family I have in Lisbon."

"There's only one bedroom. And I work here."

Claire stared at him fiercely. He couldn't be thinking of turning her out.

He glanced away. "I'm busy with my work, you see. I can't keep you company..."

"I'm seventeen. I don't need babysitting. You do realize that I just traveled across three countries – during wartime – by myself?"

"Indeed you did." Vincent gave her a thoughtful look as he moved a jumble of papers into a glass-fronted cabinet. "Are you hungry?"

"Very."

"We won't have dinner for a while. I'd suggest you go downstairs to one of the cafés while I tidy up. Ask for a *torrada* – that's toast with butter, quite filling. It'll carry you over until we eat." Vincent untied the cord of his change purse and pulled out a coin. "This should do. Unless you brought *escudos* with you?"

"*Escudos?*"

"Portuguese money."

Claire shook her head. She wasn't taking the money or going downstairs. It was irrational, but she was suddenly afraid her uncle wouldn't open the door when she came back. "Don't you have anything here? I'm too tired to go downstairs." Which was true.

"Bread and a bit of cheese from this morning. That's all, I'm afraid. I expect Esther will be here shortly with something for dinner."

"Esther?"

"My...a lady friend." Vincent moved the typewriter to a chair. "From Belgium." He put a plate and knife on the table with the food and gestured at her to sit down. "I'll be with you shortly. *Bon appétit.*" Arms overflowing with papers, he disappeared into the bedroom and nudged the door closed with his foot. Claire stared after him, feeling more alone than ever.

Antonio

"Antonio, go find the shoeshine boy for Mr. Thaler, will you?" Mr. Silva indicated a well-dressed German with thin lips and cheekbones that protruded like knuckles under his skin. Antonio studied him as he put down his tray. It was the second time the man had come in. He wasn't a refugee. Maybe a diplomat. Or a spy. There were enough of those around, all trying to figure out what the others were doing. Antonio suspected some of the Chave d'Ouro waiters were trying to get in on the action too.

"While you're at it, get me some Gauloises." The man held out a coin.

"Yes, sir," Antonio said. "Back in a minute." The nearest cigarettes were a few doors down. Antonio glanced up at the Colonial boarding house before entering the tobacco shop, wondering where the girl was. Maybe she'd come into the Chave d'Ouro one day, and he'd wait on her. Hear what her voice sounded like. Find out where she was from. Inside, the shopkeeper rang up a packet of cigarettes and gave Antonio the change. He jingled it in his hand. Mr. Well-Dressed had better give him a tip.

Back outside, he searched the darkening square for the shoeshine boy. Scrappy never went more than fifty yards away from Rossio, and he defended his territory like a fierce little dog. The streetlights came on, dropping pools of light on the pavement. His cousin Rita was standing under one at the far end of the square, but Antonio didn't go over. He'd socialize with her the day she stopped claiming she couldn't chip in for their grandmother's medicine. And when she shut up about how no foreign girl would stoop low enough to be seen with him in public. He finally spotted Scrappy, finishing a job on the other side of the statue. Antonio skirted an oncoming tram and jogged over.

Behind him, tires screeched. Antonio spun around and saw a black Citroen skid to a stop outside the Chave d'Ouro. Two men ran inside, leaving a fellow with a needle-thin mustache behind the wheel. Inside the café, someone yelled. The men reemerged, dragging Thomas between them. He was fighting, trying to pull away. One of the men punched him in the head. Thomas crumpled forward into the car. The men jumped inside and the vehicle raced away, trailing exhaust. Too late, Antonio sprinted after it. The car turned a corner and was gone.

"*Merda.*" Antonio ran back to the Chave d'Ouro. It was abnormally quiet. At least half of the customers – including the recently arrived Polish refugee, whose eyes were now wide and terrified – were gathering up their hats and purses and making for the exit. Mr. Silva stood by the door, his jaw clenched, looking like he wanted to hit something himself. Thomas's table lay on its side, his glass in shards around it.

"What happened?" Antonio asked. "Who took him?"

"I'm not sure. But they knew who they wanted. Went straight

for Mr. Schiller." Mr. Silva signaled to José to clean up the mess. The waiter righted the table, then bent down again.

"He lost these." José held out a pair of glasses.

"And these." Antonio found Thomas's keys on the floor beside his newspaper.

Mr. Silva placed the items on a shelf behind the cash register. "Until he returns," he said.

"You think…" Antonio began.

"Boy, did you get my cigarettes?" Mr. Thaler interrupted. He was sitting calmly, watching the exodus.

"Yes, sir." Antonio handed him the cigarettes and his change, then waited with his palm outstretched.

"What about the shoeshine boy?"

"Couldn't find him." Antonio kept his hand out. The German grunted irritably but gave him a small coin.

"*Danke.*" Antonio went back to the cash register. He hadn't finished his conversation with Mr. Silva. "When are the police coming?"

His boss didn't answer.

"You called them, didn't you?"

Mr. Silva shook his head.

"Why not? He's a good customer."

"I saw the driver. He's an informant for the PVDE. I'm not getting involved."

"The secret police? What would they want with Thomas? I thought – he thought – the Nazis might be looking for him. Not the Portuguese."

"Keep your voice down." Mr. Silva looked around the café. "You know as well as I do that some of them are working for the Gestapo."

"So what will you do?" Antonio asked. Someone had to start the search for Thomas.

"Nothing that will cause problems for the Chave d'Ouro. Same goes for you. Understand?"

Antonio nodded. Because Mr. Silva wouldn't accept anything else.

"Good. Now get back to work. You've got customers waiting."

Antonio started taking orders again. But his mind was outside, trailing the black Citroen through Lisbon's dark, narrow streets.

The soiree at the *Coliseu* in support of cyclone victims
was a *'festa brilhantissima'*

Diário de Notícias

CHAPTER 2

SQUEALING TIRES JOLTED Claire awake. Across the room, Uncle Vincent shied away from the open window and yanked the curtains shut.

In the sudden dark, Claire sat up, dazed. "Uncle, what's wrong?"

"I'm not sure." He turned on a light, double-checked the curtains, then dropped heavily into a chair. "I think a man just got kidnapped. Right here, on Rossio."

"Oh no." Claire clutched the edge of the sofa so tightly her finger poked through the worn fabric. People disappeared that way in France. They weren't supposed to here. "Do you know who it was?"

"I hope it wasn't…I couldn't see very well." Vincent's knuckles were white where he gripped the table, but his voice, when he resumed speaking, was calm. "The best thing to do in this city is keep your head down. That's my advice as long as you're here. Don't get noticed."

"I wasn't planning to," Claire said. The menace beneath his words was clear, and puzzling. "Who would notice me?"

"Don't be naive. Every second person you'll see is a refugee, a diplomat, or working for some country's secret service. Information is precious, especially in wartime. And especially in a neutral country like Portugal." Vincent checked his watch and sighed. "It doesn't look like Esther is coming tonight. She's usually here by now. We'll have to have dinner out."

"After what just happened? Is it safe?" Claire's stomach was growling. But leaving his rooms was the last thing she wanted to do now.

"You just got here. They won't be after you yet." Vincent gave her a lopsided grin that was only half-joking. He flicked the curtain aside a careful inch or two and peered down at the square. Claire waited nervously. "It seems all right now. Besides, I'm a rotten cook, and we share the kitchen with all of our neighbors on this floor." Vincent grimaced. "Although Esther doesn't seem to mind."

Esther again. Claire waited, but he didn't say more. "Aren't you worried about her being out alone?"

Vincent gave her an odd look. "Esther can take care of herself. She helps new refugees get settled. Some days she's so busy I don't even see her." He pulled on a jacket and opened the door. "Come along. We're going to the Negresco. It'll be a nice change from your usual fare." He smiled, but the worried look didn't leave his eyes.

Light was spilling from the front windows of the restaurant when they arrived. Claire stopped outside and gazed in silence at the stained glass, the gleaming fixtures, and the customers flitting in and out.

"What is it?" Vincent asked.

"We can't have lights on in France after nightfall."

"There's no war here." Vincent took her elbow and ushered her inside. "Or maybe I should say it's conducted in less obvious ways."

Yet another comment that hid more than it said. Had her uncle always talked that way? Claire hadn't noticed it before. Maybe she just hadn't been paying attention. They settled into a corner table, away from the windows. Vincent ordered for both of them in a mix of French and stumbling Portuguese.

"Uncle, if my family doesn't arrive before the ship sails, what will we do?" Claire asked after the waiter left.

"Let's hope that doesn't happen. I'm sure Michel went off to request new visas the minute your train left."

Claire picked at a loose hem on the tablecloth. "There's more I need to tell you."

A tall, slim man appeared beside the table, interrupting their conversation. "Vincent," he said as they shook hands. "I didn't expect to see you here tonight."

"Nor did I. I had a surprise visitor. This is my niece, Claire. She just arrived from France. Claire, let me introduce Paul Gray, who runs a gallery not far from here. He's got lots of art and other nice items the Nazis haven't managed to confiscate yet."

"And never will, if I have anything to do with it. It's nice to meet you, Claire." Mr. Gray gave a little bow. "Will you be in Lisbon long?"

"Until the thirteenth."

"I hope you'll be able to enjoy the city while you're here. You must come by the gallery."

Lisbon was a refuge. Not a holiday. She wouldn't enjoy anything until her family arrived. "Thank you. I'll try," she said politely.

He smiled. "I look forward to it. Have a nice evening." He nodded goodbye and left.

Vincent turned all his attention back to Claire. "What were you saying?"

"The day before I left, we learned that Father was on a Gestapo watch list."

"Because of his work at the newspaper?"

Claire nodded. "If they arrest him, he'll be sent to an internment camp." She bit her lip. "People starve in those, you know. Or worse."

"And even that wasn't enough to make Michel take the mountain route? I don't believe it!" Vincent brought his hand down on the table, making the silverware jump and clink. The diners at the next table glanced their way.

"It's not easy with a young child and an old man who can hardly walk," Claire shot back. "But yes, that's what they were going to do if he couldn't get the visas. Maybe they're on their way now, and that's why you haven't heard from them." She had to believe that.

The waiter arrived. He set plates of cod, potatoes and green beans on the table with a flourish. "*Bom apetite.*"

Claire leaned forward, inhaling until her lungs couldn't hold any more. Bliss. Then she grabbed her silverware and dug in.

After a moment, Vincent set down his fork and sat there,

watching her. "You haven't eaten well in a while, have you?"

Claire swallowed her mouthful of fish and leaned back. She'd been impolite. But she couldn't remember ever having a meal that tasted so good. Guilt swept through her. Wherever they were, her family certainly wasn't feasting like this. "No one in France eats much these days. But after Father lost his job, it got worse. There are so many refugees in Marseille now, and food prices keep going up."

When they finished, the waiter came to take their plates. "Dessert?" he asked.

"May I?"

Uncle Vincent nodded, and minutes later a creamy egg custard arrived. Claire forced herself to spoon it up with more restraint. They made their way back to the boarding house soon afterwards, each lost in thought. In her gut, Claire knew there was no way Grandpa could make it across the Pyrenees on foot. If her family had even gotten that far.

Antonio

The Chave d'Ouro stayed quiet for the rest of the evening. Tables slowly filled again, but the boisterous crowd they usually got on Saturday night had stayed away. And the refugees were missing. Antonio could usually pick them out easily, but now he didn't see a single one. He took orders and carried drinks and wiped tables mechanically, his mind on Thomas. A friend who talked about a book or a piece of music as if it were a living thing, whose laugh came from somewhere deeper than his chest. Who, more than once, had lent Antonio money when his grandmother needed medicine. The only person who hadn't laughed when Antonio dreamed out loud about going to New York to become an artist.

"Antonio, can't you see you're wanted?" His boss cuffed him on the head as he walked by. Mr. Thaler had left and come back. Antonio made his way over to the table where the German was deep in conversation with a Portuguese man who sat with his legs stretched out, blocking the aisle. Antonio had seen them both before, but never together.

"Two beers," the Portuguese man ordered. Antonio skirted his outstretched legs and went to get them.

"…been searching for a week," Mr. Thaler was saying, in English, as Antonio came back. He pressed his lips into a thin line as he waited for Antonio to place their glasses on the table and leave. Antonio stationed himself behind them. The waiter's distance, he called it. Far enough away that customers would think their conversations were private. He'd lost count of how many plans he'd overheard about assassinating Hitler, sabotaging the British war effort, or forcing the Italians to switch sides. Lisbon was full of wishful thinkers.

At the table, Mr. Thaler started speaking again. "They're in Portugal, Bruno. A refugee brought them."

"There are thousands of refugees here. How…?"

"Oh, we know who," Mr. Thaler said. "But it seems he no longer has them. And he won't say where they are. We can't let them get beyond our reach."

"Beyond your reach how?"

"They can't leave Portugal. And the Americans can't get their hands on them."

"America isn't in this war."

"They're aiding the British." With his protruding cheekbones, Mr. Thaler's pale, intense face made Antonio think of a skeleton. "That's not being neutral."

"What's so important that the Americans would want them?" The man called Bruno stretched his legs out even further. "Without knowing more, I can't be of…"

At that moment, a man at a table across the room signaled. Antonio headed his way, inwardly cursing the timing. Those two, he'd bet, were in a league the wishful thinkers could only dream of.

Above the bar, the clock showed five minutes to midnight. Antonio's next customer, one of a handful still remaining, was a tall, angular Englishman named Gray who ran an art gallery up on one of Lisbon's hills. Antonio had gone there once or twice. At the Chave d'Ouro, Gray usually spent his time trying to draw the waiters and other customers into conversation, like some of those foreign reporters who came in from time to time. But tonight Gray drank his beer silently and was the last customer to go. Twenty minutes later Antonio and the other waiters were out the door too, with Mr. Silva locking up behind them. No one had come in with news of Thomas. To Antonio's fury, Mr. Silva acted like nothing had happened.

Antonio glanced one last time at the Colonial boarding house, wondering if the girl slept behind one of the darkened windows, then set out across the square. If he had a clue where to go, he'd look for Thomas himself. But he didn't. Ahead, the stone castle of São Jorge loomed high on its hill above the city. Below it, steep, narrow streets wound upward through Mouraria, where he lived with his grandmother.

Streetlights illuminated Rossio and Praça da Figueira, the next square over, but the daytime bustle of pedestrians, cars, and trams had died down. Antonio was almost alone. Usually it didn't bother him, but tonight everything felt unsettled. He'd never thought how easy it would be to make someone disappear in Lisbon. And how hard it would be to track them down, especially if the PVDE had something to do with it.

High above, a window slammed. Antonio jumped, then shook his head. He was worse than a nervous seagull. He turned into the first of many alleyways that led toward home, and almost collided with a tall, dark figure. Antonio reeled backwards, and felt a hand clamp around his wrist. He wrenched it free.

"Calm down, kid. It's me." Gray's voice was low and unruffled.

"Are you mad? What was that?"

"Didn't mean to startle you. I wanted to talk."

"This is how you go about it? You were just at the Chave d'Ouro."

Gray shook his head. "Too many people. Let's walk, shall we?"

Antonio hesitated, trying to remember how much the man had had to drink, then nodded. If he kept acting strangely, Antonio would disappear into Mouraria's winding alleys. A foreigner would never find him. "What is it?"

"What do you know about Hitler's plans to invade Portugal?" Gray asked.

"Rumors. Everyone talks, but nobody really knows anything."

"We think it's more than speculation. Portugal has to be ready to defend itself."

"Who's 'we'?"

"People who don't want Portugal to fall under German control. Your own countrymen, and others like myself."

"And you wanted to talk to me about…?" Antonio let the

question hang as they climbed a long flight of stairs.

"I've been watching you. I thought you might want to join us."

Antonio almost tripped over a step. "Join you? Doing what?"

"Keeping track of what the Germans here in Lisbon are doing. Watching the movements of their ships. Making it hard for them to move around the country if Portugal is attacked."

Antonio stared at him warily. "How?"

"Think about it. What would happen if rail lines were cut? If there was no electricity?"

Antonio could imagine. He could also imagine the trouble they'd be in if they got caught. "Why me?"

"You seem like a smart lad, you've got languages, and you work at the Chave d'Ouro. Everyone talks there. Especially when they're drinking. It's a good place for us to have someone."

Angry yells echoed suddenly through the deserted street. From somewhere ahead, punches and kicks thumped against flesh. Someone moaned. Antonio crept to a vantage point behind a low wall, Gray following him. In the small square below was a fight, two groups of kids going at it. Not Thomas then. Antonio backed away from the wall and chose another street.

"This isn't our war," Antonio said as the scuffle faded away behind them. "Portugal's neutral. I'm neutral. We don't take sides." It was the safe response. But he meant it too. There was no point in getting involved.

"You think that's what I'm asking? You'd be defending your own country if it's invaded, that's all."

Gray was calling this patriotism? It sounded more like a fight that couldn't be won. "What's in it for me?"

Gray stopped. "If you don't know, perhaps you're not the right person after all. Forget I said anything." The tall man turned abruptly and left.

Bemused, Antonio watched him go. The Portuguese government would call what Gray was suggesting treason, whatever the motive. Antonio wasn't getting involved. No way.

German warship sinks British auxiliary cruiser and transport ship

Diário de Notícias
April 6, 1941

CHAPTER 3 – SUNDAY, APRIL 6

"CLAIRE, WAKE UP."
Uncle Vincent stood over her, waving a small bundle above her nose. Through the paper wafted the heady smell of just-baked bread. He'd fed her twice now, and let her sleep on his couch. Were these peace offerings after his reluctant welcome? She sat up, rubbing a crick in her neck. Sunlight streamed through the open window, making her blink. The couch was lumpy and too short, but it hadn't stopped her from sleeping.

"I brought breakfast," Vincent said. "We'll eat, and afterwards you can explore Lisbon."

"I can explore? You wouldn't come?" She'd never expected to end up in Portugal without the safe cocoon of family. Even in Marseille, walking around on her own in wartime had been discouraged. Striking out alone in Lisbon was even less appealing.

"We'll go to the post office this afternoon, as I promised. But I have work to do." He waved a hand around the room.

"You're a printer. What can you do with no equipment?"

Vincent looked pained. "We'll talk about it later." He set out the breakfast things and waved her to a chair. "Do you have your exit visa with you?" he asked as they began eating. "I'd like to see it."

"I have all my documents with me." Either he hadn't noticed she hadn't agreed to a solo outing, or he was ignoring it. She pulled her passport and boat ticket from a beautifully embroidered pouch she'd made herself, in more carefree times. It had been hidden under her blouse since she left Marseille.

Vincent turned the passport from side to side, examining the French visa that had been stamped onto one of the pages. "Not difficult," he muttered. "But there's no time."

"Time for what?"

"Nothing. I was thinking aloud. Do you mind if I hold on to it for a bit?"

Claire hesitated. "Father told me not to let it out of my sight."

"He was talking about strangers. I'll keep it safe." He held her gaze until Claire nodded. "Oh, and keep your boat ticket well hidden. It's like gold these days."

"Why?" She turned it over. Nothing seemed out of the ordinary.

"The main operator running ships across the Atlantic has stopped selling tickets. Too big a backlog. You should see the lines of desperate people outside their offices."

"I'll be careful." Claire tucked the pouch back under her blouse.

Soon afterwards, she let herself out of the boarding house. Alone, again. Her uncle had practically pushed her out the door after drawing a rough sketch of the city that showed Rossio, a crisscross of streets, and a wavy line that represented the Tagus River. Not a very precise map, considering it was coming from a printer. At least she had a good sense of direction.

Rossio was bustling. At café terraces around the square, customers nursed small cups of coffee and scanned the headlines. Hunched over his stool beside a fountain, a shoeshine boy polished as fast as he could, his gaze flitting occasionally to the line of impatient men in front of him. Tram bells clanged and taxis honked, clearing the way of pedestrians.

In front of a fancy women's clothes shop, Claire paused. The designs in the window could've come straight from Paris. Trim waists, full skirts, narrow high heels. A year ago she'd been training to make clothes like these, and dreaming of studying dressmaking in Paris. Instead, here she was at the end of the continent, her future in America utterly uncertain. She raised her fingers to the glass, itching to touch the beautiful fabrics, then balled her hand into a fist. Why torment herself?

She walked on, passing a busy café with big keys painted on

both sides of its entrance. *Chave d'Ouro.* The Golden Key. At another café, Nicola, customers took their orders standing at the counter and then left, making way for more. And the food. Through restaurant windows, she watched waiters deliver plates of meat, potatoes and vegetables, savory rice dishes, and carafes of wine. In the air hung the slightly burnt smell of grilled fish and garlic. She wasn't hungry, but her mouth watered anyway. In France, a simple meal of bread, cheese, mushrooms, and sardines had seemed a feast.

Beyond Rossio train station stretched a wide, tree-lined avenue. *Avenida da Liberdade.* Liberty Avenue. A good place to start a new life. She quickened her pace, feeling a rush of freedom. No fear of anyone watching her, no one eavesdropping. No boy thief. In this tranquil, sun-dappled spot, her uncle's stern words of warning seemed out of place. For the first time in days, Claire started to relax. For a while, her feet followed the flowery black and white designs inlaid into the stone pavement. Finally she stopped and looked up. This was a city of hills. She wanted to go higher.

She retraced her steps to a narrow street that climbed upward, straight and very steep. Claire puffed her way to the top and found herself alone in a public garden with palm trees, statues, and a carefully manicured lawn. A sign said *São Pedro de Alcântara.* Beyond a low wall, downtown Lisbon spread below her, the tile roofs a patchwork of red and gray. On the hill opposite rose an old stone castle, like a remnant from a fairy tale. Flying seagulls made tiny slits against the wide Tagus River, shimmering silver in the sun. Claire leaned against the wall and took it in, relishing the warmth on her arms and face. Frédéric would love it here. She could see him sneaking behind the fountain to splash her if she came too close, then running away with a giggle. Her little brother was always running.

A young couple entered the park, holding hands and whispering to each other. They gave Claire barely a glance, but stopped further along the wall and entwined their bodies in an embrace. A moment later, a man in a suit sat down on a bench behind them and started reading a newspaper. For the heart of a busy city, it was remarkably quiet.

"Catarina?"

Claire jumped. A skinny old fellow holding a cream-colored envelope had appeared at her side.

"Catarina?" the man repeated.

"No." Claire shook her head, in case he didn't speak English. "You've got the wrong person."

The man backed away quickly, then headed tentatively toward the couple. They separated before he reached them. The woman stepped forward and put out a hand.

The old man slowed. "Catarina?"

She nodded.

Suddenly, the man on the bench lunged at them. He shoved the boyfriend to the ground, snatched the envelope, and sprinted toward the park exit. The old man yelped and ran after him. Back on his feet, the boyfriend followed, soon overtaking the elderly messenger. The girl darted away in the opposite direction. In a moment they were gone. Claire stared after them, dazed. The garden had gone quiet again, but it was no longer the tranquil place of before. She left in a hurry, checking over her shoulder and hoping no one would remember she'd been there. Whatever had happened, she wanted absolutely nothing to do with it.

Uncle Vincent had been right about the need to keep their heads down. She could – there was nothing especially remarkable about her – but what about Father? He'd always been outspoken. And Lisbon certainly wasn't the safe haven they'd dreamed of. She'd needed less than twenty-four hours to confirm that. Claire checked the street behind her again, not quite sure what she was looking for. But surely it would be all right. Her family would be there only a few days before moving on. She wrapped her arms around herself, pressing the pouch with her boat ticket in it tight against her stomach, and kept walking.

The road she was on sloped downhill between cafés and shops. She was one person among many, thankfully. At the bottom end of the street, water glittered beyond another square with a statue of a standing man in the middle. Seagulls circled above it, their cries somehow both nostalgic and belligerent. It was an uneasy, unsettling sound. Claire tried to shake it out of her head, but couldn't.

On the bank of the river, a small crowd had gathered to watch a fishing boat that was idling a short way out. Three men dropped a net over the side. Claire stopped. They wouldn't fish this close to shore. One of the sailors yelled something and the crowd leaned forward, watching intently as the men worked to position the net under something in the water. It was big, and they struggled to pull it out.

"That's no fish." The voice was right beside her, speaking in English.

Claire jumped. It was the boy from the train station. Without thinking, she folded her arms over her pouch and backed up a step. His hair was darker than hers, his eyes a piercing green. He was still wearing his beret and had slung a stubby cardboard tube across his back.

His brief smile at her reaction didn't reach his eyes. "Do you know what's happening?"

Claire shook her head. She should just leave, ignore him. Mother had always said good girls didn't talk to strange men. But he didn't look at all threatening. Just preoccupied. And his hands – for now, at least – were in plain sight. Not reaching for someone else's property. She gave in to her curiosity. "What is it then?"

"Not what. I think it's a person."

"A person?" She looked back at the boat. The fishermen were raising something long and heavy. Red stained the quiet water below it. Claire's stomach looped queasily. "Who?"

The boy shielded his eyes with his hand. "Don't know."

The fishermen pulled the limp form into the boat and motored toward the quay.

The boy turned to Claire again. "You arrived yesterday, didn't you? On the train from Spain?" He paused and added, "I'm Antonio."

Claire narrowed her eyes and studied him. Was he bluffing, pretending he didn't know she'd seen him about to steal a suitcase? Or could she have been mistaken? She couldn't read him.

"And you?" he prodded. "Your name?"

"Claire."

"Are you alone?"

Alone could mean vulnerable. She hesitated. "I'm here with family."

"Are you staying long?"

"No. We sail to New York in a few days."

"Too bad. You need more time than that to get to know Lisbon."

Claire gave him a puzzled frown and changed the subject. "Your English is good. Where did you learn?"

"From my mother. She was an English teacher."

"Was?"

The boat thudded against the quay. They watched as the fishermen lowered the body over the side into the arms of two waiting men. They placed it carefully on the ground. There was a gust of wind, and the tarp covering it flipped open.

Beside her, Antonio went rigid.

Antonio

"No. Oh, no." Antonio used his elbows to push past the people in front of him, barely hearing their angry mutters. He dropped to his knees by the still figure and shook it gently. "Thomas?" There was no response, no warmth when he touched his friend's clammy hand. Below Thomas's head, blood seeped onto the concrete. This sodden body bore so little resemblance to his friend. Antonio stared down at it. He couldn't get his brain to equate the two.

One of the fishermen came to stand over Antonio. "Who is he, lad? Do you know?"

"Thomas Schiller," Antonio said in a monotone. "A German refugee." The description explained nothing. It left out Thomas's hearty laugh, his decision to choose generosity over bitterness. And so much more.

Antonio didn't know how long he'd been there, bent over Thomas, when he felt the fisherman grip his shoulder and pull him to his feet.

"Move aside, son. They're taking him away."

Someone knelt and checked for a pulse, then pulled the tarp back over Thomas's face. Antonio watched, his vision blurring, as two men placed him in a long black vehicle. There was no hurry, no urgency. In the face of something so wrong, their calm seemed obscene. Antonio turned and ran for the docks. He needed something to hit, something to stop the trembling that had nothing to do with being cold. He picked up an empty oil can and flung it as far as he could into the river. It bubbled as it filled with water, then sank. None of his anger went down with it.

Further along, a jumble of truck tires stood chest-high beside a warehouse. Antonio found a metal bar on the ground and went at them, kicking and pounding. The tires didn't budge, didn't care. Their indifference – the whole world's indifference – infuriated him. Antonio kicked a tire so hard it jarred all the way up his spine. He cursed and limped away, still clutching the bar.

Why? Why? Why? The word beat in his skull like a headache. Thomas hadn't been writing. At least he'd told Antonio he wasn't. He'd wanted to put an ocean between himself and the country he'd lost. Why would someone kill him now? Why? Why? Why? The pounding didn't let up.

Ahead, parked cars lined the side of a long warehouse. German, Spanish, French, Italian. Foreigners, getting Portugal mixed up in a war it didn't want. Antonio lifted the bar and smashed the windshield of a shiny black car. It shattered with a loud, satisfying crack. He took out the side window of another car, and more glass flew. The destruction only fueled his anger. He brought the bar down on the gleaming hood of a third car, similar to the one that took Thomas away. Then the yelling started. Men were racing out of the warehouse. Antonio dropped the bar and sprinted away. He didn't regret what he'd done. But he would regret getting caught.

Ahead on the avenue, a tram's bell clanged. It was just leaving a stop. Antonio looked back. One of the younger, fitter men was gaining on him. Antonio pumped his legs harder.

"Anda! Anda!" A boy was hanging onto the outside of the tram, hollering encouragement. Antonio put on another burst of speed and leaped for a handhold. He swung himself up beside the boy, breathing in gasps. The tram gathered pace. His pursuers fell behind, then stopped in the middle of the road, shaking their fists. A car swerved around them, its horn blaring. The street boy doubled up with laughter. Antonio didn't look at him, or at the men. He was drained, hollowed out.

"Got a light?" The boy held out a cigarette.

"No."

The boy stuck his head in the open window. "Light?" he asked a smoking passenger. They touched their cigarettes together. The boy smoked in silence, eying Antonio. He jumped off at the next stop.

Antonio rode for another few minutes, parallel to the river, until the tram slowed in front of the sprawling Jerónimos monastery. Its elaborately carved façade of kings and saints and exotic plants found by Portuguese seafarers drew his eye. If she'd been there, his grandmother would've told him to go inside and pray. Antonio turned away. Churches didn't comfort him. The last time he'd been in one had been for his mother's funeral. Another day when there was nothing in the world but pain.

He crossed a garden and went to sit on the riverbank. Too bad he couldn't sail away to a new land, like the mariners in the old stories. Shaking his head, he pulled the cardboard tube off his back and slid out several sheets of paper and a pencil. Using a patch of flat, hard dirt for support, he began drawing, capturing in a few quick lines Thomas's wide nose, his messy beard. The refugee had encouraged Antonio to draw, when no one else cared, and told him flying high wasn't just for birds. Words Antonio's father might have said, if he'd lived long enough. Probably not, though. Papa's art was making good shoes. Creativity on paper or canvas was for children. Dreams had to be useful. Antonio focused again on Thomas, sketching quickly, his hands remembering the details more clearly than his mind did.

A shadow fell over his drawing. Antonio looked up. A British seaman in his blue uniform, one arm linked in that of a giggling girl, was leaning over his shoulder. Antonio started to roll up his sketch, but it was too late.

"Wait. That isn't bad." The seaman grinned at him. "In fact, it's quite good. Could you do one of my lady here?"

The girl pulled back, still laughing, her dress swishing around her. "That's not necessary. Leave the boy alone."

"I'm serious," the seaman insisted. "Will you? Make me a souvenir of my Beauty? I'll pay." He caught her around the waist and stole a kiss. She pushed him away playfully.

Antonio thought a moment. "Five *escudos*." A high price. Maybe now they'd leave him alone.

The girl widened her eyes, but the seaman didn't flinch. "That's fine." He rooted around in a pocket. "With the monastery in the background, all right?"

Antonio slid the drawing of Thomas into the tube, then bent over another piece of paper and started sketching. Brown hair flipped up at the ends, flirty eyes. He added an arched eyebrow, the glint of a filigreed earring. The seaman grunted approvingly. In ten minutes Antonio was done.

The seaman handed him the coins, then clutched the drawing to his heart. "Now we'll never be apart, even on the endless sea," he said dramatically. The girl laughed and wrapped her arms around him. "Silly boy," she said. They'd already forgotten Antonio.

Then the girl tilted her head, and for a second her profile reminded Antonio of Claire. He hadn't said goodbye. For reasons that had to be obvious. But he probably hadn't made a good impression. Although he wasn't sure why he wanted to. There were plenty of nice-looking girls in Lisbon. He wasn't sure why she seemed different. Maybe because she had the courage to travel alone, and wasn't afraid to talk to strangers. That alone made her exotic, and unlike any Portuguese girl he'd ever met. Antonio stood up, his back still sore from kicking the tire, and found a more comfortable spot on a bench beside two old men sharing a newspaper.

"We're next in line," said one. He thumped his cane on the ground.

"You really think so?"

Antonio gazed at the river, trying unsuccessfully to tune them out.

"Yep. Hitler is going after Yugoslavia. It's a matter of days, I'll wager. Portugal will be next."

"I don't know." His friend drew out the words until they held a world of doubt. "He's got Belgium and the Netherlands. And half of France, and Poland and Czechoslovakia. The Germans must be stretched awfully thin."

"Maybe. But Portugal is an escape route. Out of Hitler's control. He's not going to tolerate that for long."

"We're neutral."

"So was Belgium. Neutrality won't save us. The Germans would slice through us in a second."

"And the British? We have a treaty with them. They have to help us."

"Don't be a fool. Look at this newspaper. They're in a bombing war with the Germans, on land and on sea." The man nodded at a big cargo boat steaming toward the ocean, the Union Jack flying from its bow. "U-boats are torpedoing their ships all the time. You think the Brits have men or equipment to spare for us?"

To Antonio's relief, both men lapsed into a morose silence. Their conversation was painfully like what Thomas would've said if he'd seen the day's paper. He wondered what Prime Minister

Salazar would do if Germany invaded. Neutrality wouldn't mean anything then. And maybe Gray and his group would be seen as heroes.

The men started up again.

"So it comes down to whether Salazar will be able to keep us out of the war, doesn't it?"

"He's wily, but I don't know." The old man pushed himself upright with his cane. "I don't know what anyone can do to protect us now."

His friend stood too. "Here tomorrow?"

"As usual."

They shook hands and went off in different directions. When they were gone, Antonio pulled out his drawing of Thomas. He'd told Gray he wouldn't take sides unless his country did. But now he had a better reason to eavesdrop on people in the café, as the Englishman had suggested. He was going to do his damnedest to find out why Thomas had been killed.

Claire

Antonio had forgotten her completely. Claire couldn't blame him. Her stomach roiled every time she remembered the body, and the hot sun drilling down on her head as she followed the river made it worse. Her uncle's scrawled map was useless. He hadn't expected her to walk this far. All she wanted was to get back to the boarding house so he could reassure her that kidnappings and drownings and chases in public gardens didn't happen every day. Even then, she wasn't sure she'd want to go out again.

It was almost lunchtime by the time she made it back to Rossio, still feeling queasy.

"Uncle, are you there?" She knocked, and again heard the faint rustle of paper.

Vincent cracked open the door. Behind him, plates and silverware for three sat on the corner of the table. Papers and the typewriter covered the rest.

"Ah, you're back." Vincent stepped into the hallway and locked the door behind him. "I'll take you to meet Esther. She's making lunch."

"Uncle, wait," Claire protested. "I wanted to tell you…"

"We'll talk in a few minutes. During lunch." Vincent bustled her down the dim corridor toward the back of the building. Halfway along, a doorway to the right opened onto a large kitchen. The first thing Claire noticed was the heat. A floor-to-ceiling fireplace took up most of the far wall. Two pots hung over the flames, their contents burping meaty smells. A slender woman with a braid down her back was cutting potatoes into tiny chunks beside a stone sink. At the back, a glass door led to a small patio, surrounded by walls but open to the sky, where clothes had been hung to dry.

"Esther," Vincent said. "I'd like you to meet Claire."

Smiling, the woman wiped her hands on her apron and kissed Claire on the cheek. "Welcome to Lisbon," she said, "although I know it's not how you wanted to arrive."

"Thank you. I hope you'll meet the rest of my family soon."

"I'm sure I will." She smiled again, briefly.

"Claire, can you help Esther here?" Uncle Vincent asked. "I'll finish what I was doing and we'll eat." He was gone before she could react.

Claire sighed and picked up a knife. "Shall I cut the carrots?" Her hand shook slightly, and she pressed the heel against the counter to steady it. The last thing she felt like doing was making small talk.

Esther nodded and tossed the potatoes into one of the pots. "Thin slices, please. I want them to cook quickly."

For a few minutes, they worked in silence. Then a stooped old woman in black entered the kitchen. She acknowledged them with a nod, gave the second pot a sniff and a stir, and exited as quickly as she had come. Somewhere on the other side of a wall, a baby wailed.

"We share the kitchen with the whole floor," Esther explained. "There are three other families living here."

Claire sliced and nodded, her attention caught by the word "we." "Have you been in Lisbon long?"

"Quite a while. I arrived a few weeks after France fell."

"But…I thought you were Belgian."

"I am." She rested thin, graceful hands on the counter. "It's a long story. Let's say that neither France nor Belgium are good places for Jews right now." She scooped up the carrots Claire had sliced and dropped them into the stew.

"How did you meet Uncle Vincent?"

"Helping other refugees. Each in our own way." She stirred the pot. "I work with HICEM. It's one of the refugee relief agencies."

Claire remembered Mrs. Deauville and her daughters marching off behind a sign that said "USC." "You meet the trains?"

"It's more than that. Most refugees arrive with fear, loss, and anxiety – and with very little luggage. They can't afford nice hotels and aren't lucky enough to have family here, like you. They're the ones we try to help." She stirred the pot again, then dipped a spoon in the stew. "Mmm. This will do. "

"When will you leave Lisbon?" Claire hoped Esther would answer her silent question: *Are you coming with Uncle Vincent to New York?*

"I can't." Esther's mouth set in a grim line. "We're done here. Let's see if your uncle is ready to eat."

"What's he so busy with anyway?"

"You'll have to ask him yourself." Esther wrapped a rag around the handle of the pot, lifted it off the hook, and left the kitchen. Claire followed, unanswered questions floating behind her. They opened the door to find the table cleared and neatly set. Vincent waved his hand, inviting them to sit down.

"You cooked. I'll serve," he said, and ladled the thick stew onto their plates. "Claire, you must have worked up an appetite walking around. How did you find Lisbon?"

"Well...." Her upset stomach came back with a rush. She blew on a spoon full of vegetables, then placed it back in her dish without tasting it. She didn't want to ruin their meal. "The restaurants and shops – they have everything. It hardly seems like there's a war on."

"The wounds people carry to Lisbon are mostly inside," Esther said. "But they're very real. I see it every day."

"I know." Of course she did. Suffering and uncertainty had traveled with every person on Claire's train, never giving up their seats, never letting go. She took a tentative mouthful of stew.

"Eat, girl," Vincent urged. "Where's that healthy appetite I saw last night?"

Claire shook her head. "It's delicious. Really. It's just..." She hesitated, then plunged ahead. "In Marseille, everyone thought that if you get to Lisbon, you'll be safe. It's not true though, is it?

It's sunny and bright, but it's frightening too."

"What do you mean?" "What happened?" Vincent and Esther asked at the same time.

Claire took a shaky breath. "I saw someone attacked. A couple who'd just been given some documents."

Vincent and Esther exchanged a glance.

"How terribly unlucky." Esther bit her lip. "And on your second day here."

"That's not all. Afterwards, I walked to the waterfront, and saw some fishermen pull a dead man out of the river."

Under his tan, Vincent turned pale. "Did they know who it was?"

"A boy said he was a refugee from Germany. Thomas something."

"Not Schiller?"

Claire nodded. "I think so."

Vincent set his glass on the table with a thud.

"Did you know him?"

"He was…a friend of your father's. Michel's going to take this hard. Do you know what happened?"

"His head was bleeding. I don't know more."

There was a pause.

"This complicates things." Vincent's voice trailed off. He surveyed the messy room.

"You'll have to…" Esther began.

"I have to keep working until the very last minute. You know that."

"Not if it puts you in danger."

"I'm careful."

"Is that enough?" Esther shoved her chair back irritably and carried her dishes to the sink. Vincent followed.

Claire looked from Esther to her uncle. "What are you talking about?"

"Nothing that concerns you," Vincent said. He kept his back to her.

Nothing that concerned her. Claire gritted her teeth. He thought she was still a child. She was sorry she'd shown her distress.

"You have to tell her," Esther said, so quietly Claire could hardly hear.

"No, I don't. I'm not going to put her in more..." Vincent turned and saw Claire was still listening. "...in a more awkward situation than she already is, staying here."

"It's worse not knowing." Esther put her hand on his sleeve.

Vincent shook it off impatiently and picked up his jacket. "I disagree. Claire, shall we go to the post office? We'll see if there's any word from your parents."

At the post office, long lines wound from outside the door to three frazzled clerks behind a tall counter. Most people filed out silently, their hands as empty as before. Ahead of Claire, a clerk handed a crumpled envelope to an old man. He said thank you and cradled it in bony, shaking arms, like a child. A roomful of envious eyes followed him out.

When it was their turn, the clerk checked and said no, there was nothing for Vincent or Claire Lemoine today. Claire gripped the counter, her fingernails carving little crescents into the wood. Father had said he'd write.

"Don't fret. You have to expect disruptions in the mail service during wartime," Vincent said. "It's a miracle anything gets delivered at all."

"That really doesn't help."

"I have an idea. Let's send your parents a telegram." Vincent asked for paper and scribbled out a terse message.

The clerk read it back to them: "Claire safe in L. Stop. Send latest on your arrival. Stop. V."

"That should do." Vincent recited the address and handed over a coin, and they emerged into the bright sunlight of the Praça do Comércio.

Claire blinked. Minutes ago, she'd been hoping for news. Now she prayed that no response meant her family was on its way. The alternative... She stopped herself. No alternative was worth thinking about.

"Let's have something to drink."

"I don't want anything."

"You can't give up." Vincent steered them to a crowded café on the other side of the square. Claire sat listlessly, looking out at the people strolling around the square. Maybe one of them had crossed her family's path somewhere during their travels. She'd never know.

"Why don't you go with Esther later?" Vincent broke into her reverie. "You can't stay in the boarding house moping."

"To do what?"

Vincent shrugged. "Esther can tell you more than I can. The refugee folks can always use an extra pair of hands."

"Can't I help you instead?"

"No."

"Why not? You said you're busy."

"What I do is printing-related."

"There must be something I can do. It would be better than spending time with people I don't know."

"You know Esther. And no, you can't help me. You don't have the skills."

"Can't I learn?"

"Don't be ridiculous."

Claire leaned back in her chair, her small rebellion defeated.

"That's settled then," Vincent said. "We'll talk to her when we get home." He looked relieved.

Claire wanted to find out why.

Intense military preparations in Yugoslavia
The government is ready to abandon Belgrade,
says American radio

Diário de Notícias

CHAPTER 4

"YOU'RE HERE EARLY, Antonio." Mr. Silva looked up from counting out the cash drawer.

"Forgot something last night." Antonio rummaged beneath the counter.

Mr. Silva turned back to the drawer, his lips counting silently. Behind him, Antonio closed a hand over Thomas's keys and slid them into his pocket. He waved his own key in Mr. Silva's direction.

"Found it," he said. "Had to wake up my grandma to get in last night."

"Idiot." Mr. Silva looked disgusted. "I hope she chewed you out."

"You would," Antonio said under his breath. "Did you hear about Mr. Schiller?"

"Yeah. They're saying it was a reckoning between refugees."

"And you believe them?"

"Better for my health if I do. Same goes for you."

"Right." Antonio left his drawing tube in a corner of the back room and headed out the door, grabbing a custard pastry from the dessert display on the way. "Later."

"That's out of your pay," Mr. Silva called after him. "And be back on time." He patted the gleaming wood of a big radio he brought out every time Benfica played in a soccer championship. "We'll have a big crowd tonight."

Antonio raised a hand to show he'd heard. So far, so good. He headed uphill along the Avenida da Liberdade, following the path he and Thomas had taken a couple of months ago. The evening his friend got a telegram from his sister, informing him that their brother had been killed. Antonio had snuck Thomas drinks behind Mr. Silva's back all night, then kept him upright as he staggered home.

Within fifteen minutes, Antonio was standing across from the Pensão Astoria. A refugee who looked as rundown as the boarding house exited, shutting the door carefully behind him. Antonio scanned the street. No unusual activity. Thomas had told him refugees' addresses were given to the PVDE. There was no telling when they might show up. If they hadn't already.

As he approached, a woman plodded up, bags hanging from both arms. Behind her, a little boy kicked at loose paving stones.

"Hurry up," she ordered in French. "Come get the door."

By the time she'd turned around, Antonio had pushed it open for her. "May I help?" he asked. "I'm going to the third floor."

She measured him with her eyes, then shrugged and gave him the biggest bag. "*Oui*," she said. "I'd appreciate it."

Her son sidled past them and ran ahead to the stairs. Antonio and the boy's mother followed. The concierge, a scarecrow with beady eyes as black as her dress, stopped sweeping to watch them pass.

At the second-floor landing, the woman stopped and took her bag. "*Merci, monsieur*," she said.

Antonio touched his beret and continued up to Thomas's floor. Below, a door slammed. Antonio leaned over the railing. No one was in sight. He took the remaining steps two at a time, fumbled the key into the lock, and slipped inside.

Thomas's room was a mess. Bedclothes trailed onto the floor, a couple of dishes lay in a tiny sink, and newspapers were everywhere. Antonio thought back to his last visit. Had it looked any better then? He didn't think so. Maybe he really had beaten everyone else here.

The wardrobe door stood ajar. In it hung two pairs of trousers, two shirts, and a worn jacket. So little for a man who had been a successful writer in Germany. Before Hitler. Antonio rifled through the pockets but found nothing except a notice announcing a concert with American starlet Josephine Baker. He let it fall to the floor and turned to the cabinet beside the sink. Two hardened rolls and a half-finished bottle of red wine. Thomas must eat at the refugee food kitchens. *Must have eaten.* Putting Thomas's life in the past tense felt wrong. And he had a sister who didn't even know he was gone.

He circled the room again. The only personal items were a couple of well-used books in German on the seat of a chair. Had Thomas suspected he was in danger? Antonio remembered his friend's good humor in the café the evening before and shook his head. Thomas hadn't expected death to come so soon.

Where was the parcel from the train station? Thomas hadn't had anything with him in the Chave d'Ouro last night. Antonio sifted through a pile of newspapers and found some articles that had been torn out. He set them aside, then checked under the mattress. Nothing.

He crouched down, trying to get a different perspective on the room. There had to be something in it that would help him make sense of Thomas's murder. Under the bed, he saw more newspapers. As he pulled them out, he heard a soft thump. Antonio reached further back, and his fingers touched a thin book. He pulled it out. It was some kind of journal, full of writing. Antonio stuffed it into his jacket pocket and pulled the bed away from the wall. Still no parcel. Standing again, he surveyed the room. What was he missing?

On the other side of the door, someone knocked.

"Senhor Schiller?" A woman.

Antonio froze.

"Senhor Schiller, are you there?"

Antonio tiptoed to the window. It was too high to jump out. He heard the woman muttering. Keys jangled, and his heart stopped. The concierge was coming in.

In three giant steps, he was across the room, leaning all his weight against the door and praying she was alone.

The door handle tilted down, and Antonio felt a push. The door barely shifted. She shoved again, and let out an unladylike stream of curses. She withdrew the key and stomped toward the stairs. They weren't the steps of someone who had given up.

Interminable seconds ticked by. Antonio cracked open the door. The hallway was empty. He slipped out, eased the door shut, and was almost to the stairs when the scarecrow appeared. A man twice her size was one step behind. Keeping his face expressionless, Antonio stepped aside to let them pass.

The concierge's watchful eyes went from him to Thomas's room. "You don't live here, young man."

"Visiting friends, *senhora*." Three other rooms opened onto the same hallway. Antonio hoped they were occupied. He touched his hand to his beret and took the stairs at a normal pace – until he turned the first corner. He flew the rest of the way down and out through the entrance hall. A black Peugeot was parked outside, the man with the needle-thin mustache resting his elbows on the wheel. Antonio averted his face and made himself stroll calmly to the nearest corner. Whoever had killed Thomas wasn't done yet. And that had been too close a call. Antonio rounded the bend, and ran.

Claire

"Where are we going?" Claire's voice came out grumpy, but she couldn't help it. One finger – if that – was all she needed to count the important things in life that were still under her control.

"To Rossio station. We have a train to meet." Esther shut the boarding house door behind them.

"Coming from where?"

"Madrid."

"A refugee train? Like mine?" Claire felt an upswing of hope.

"They're all refugee trains, one way or another. Unfortunately."

"Do you know who's on it?"

"Don't get your hopes up. We're expecting a group from Italy. Who knows whether there will be others. We'll have to find housing for them, get them settled in." Esther gave Claire's hand a sympathetic squeeze. "Are you sure you're all right coming with me?"

"Of course." Although she wasn't. Not at all. She tried to picture her parents at home, busy packing, or already on a train, trying to keep Frédéric in a seat and occupied. Both images were fuzzy, unreal.

"Remember not to talk about anything personal. Not about Vincent, your parents, nothing. No matter how friendly a person seems. All right?"

"Yes." Uncle Vincent had already gone over this.

A group of refugee aid people was already on the platform when they arrived.

"Claire, meet Timmy and Gina," Esther said. "Timmy's with the Unitarian Service Committee and Gina helps out at HICEM."

Gina pushed a strand of straw-colored hair into place and smiled at Claire, her mouth framed with bright red lipstick. "It's always good to have more help," she said. "What brings you here?"

"It's a long story," Esther said shortly. "Save your questions for our new arrivals." She peered at the telegram she was holding. "We've got at least fifteen people coming in today, and we all know what that means."

"That we'll be finding homes for thirty," Gina answered. "We didn't house you though, did we, Claire?"

"No. I'm staying with fam—"

"Work first," Esther interrupted.

Claire pressed her lips together, feeling chastised. How much vaguer did Esther want her to be?

"Gina, look here," Esther continued. "I want you to take charge of these two families. They've got seven kids between them, if this list is to be believed. The last thing we want is all of them underfoot. Can you show them to the Europa, then bring one adult from each family along to HICEM?"

"Of course."

"What a luxury having two – or three – of you," Timmy said. He was holding a sign that said USC. "What I wouldn't give to have someone to order around."

"I'm not—" Esther stopped when she saw the smile on his face. "Joker. How you manage to keep a sense of humor in all this, I'll never know."

"Practice, my dear. Practice."

Claire watched their easy banter, wondering once again about Esther's relationship with her uncle. Then she stopped listening and let her eyes roam around the station.

Several uniformed policemen had stationed themselves further down the platform, between the refugee workers and the exit. A group of five or six younger boys peeked out from behind big columns the refugees would have to pass to leave the station. Claire frowned and they ducked out of sight, only to reappear moments later. Antonio wasn't with them. Claire wondered what he was doing now. Mourning his friend, maybe.

A whistle sounded and the train pulled into the station, brakes squealing. With it came the familiar stench of oil on hot metal. Claire wrapped her arms around herself, feeling slightly dizzy. Coming here today was like arriving a second time herself. It was too soon.

The train doors opened.

"Hold this, please." Esther handed Claire the white sign that said HICEM. "Up high. I'll help people off the train."

"Wait. What if they start asking me questions?"

But Esther was already off, swinging a little boy off the stairs. Then she took a suitcase tied shut with rope from his mother, who was holding a squirming toddler in her other arm.

Claire closed her eyes. Yesterday's chaos, all over again.

"I'm supposed to look for you, miss."

Claire opened her eyes to see a gap-toothed man in front of her.

"Where do we go now?"

"I...I don't know. But wait with me. The lady in charge will be here in a few minutes." Claire hoped she would. Now she couldn't see Esther or Gina anywhere, and more people were gathering around her. Then, in a space between dark coats, she saw a face that looked familiar. Could it be?

"Hold this." Claire shoved the sign at the gap-toothed man and plowed into the crowd, weaving between suitcases and people and trying not to trip. The girl she'd seen had disappeared. Then the crowd shifted, and she got another glimpse.

"Eleanor," she called. "Wait for me."

The girl turned, and suddenly Lisbon felt a tiny bit closer to home.

"Claire?" Her best friend's face lit up. "You're here too?"

Claire hugged her. "I'm so glad to see you."

"Me too. Although it was awful leaving Marseille."

Claire felt a jolt of anxiety. "You're not here alone, are you?"

"I'm with Mother and Father. But it was terrible. We left without exit visas, on foot. The border guards in Spain caught us, and threatened to take us back if we didn't pay them." She took a shaky breath. "What about you? I didn't see you on our train."

"I arrived yesterday. Father sent me ahead, and now I don't know where my family is. Have you seen them?"

"I'm so sorry. I haven't."

"Eleanor, dear, we must go. People are waiting." Her father nodded formally at Claire, then steered Eleanor away.

"Wait!" Claire called after them. "Where are you staying?"

Eleanor tugged her arm free and turned back. "I don't know," she said. "At a boarding house. Somewhere in Lisbon."

"I'll find you."

Eleanor nodded. Her father was calling her again. She ran to join him. Claire watched her go, amazed at the relief that washed over her. She'd left without saying goodbye to any of her friends. If she could help it, it wouldn't happen again.

"Claire!" Esther called from the other side of the platform. "Get over here. You're supposed to be helping, not running off."

"I saw a friend from Marseille." Finding out that Eleanor was in Lisbon was well worth a scolding.

At least twenty people had gathered around Esther. Most sagged where they stood, their baggage at their feet, too tired even to look around. Claire wasn't surprised. Whether they'd like their new home wasn't important. They'd made it to Lisbon safely, and that was all that mattered.

"Good afternoon." Esther raised her voice above the noise in the station. "Can everyone walk?" She waited for murmured translations and nods to die down, then continued. "We're going to the HICEM office first. There, we'll help you find lodging. I'm Esther and this is Claire. Please follow me. Claire will make sure nobody gets left behind."

"Of course I will," Claire muttered to herself. If they got separated, she'd be as lost as the rest of them.

The refugees gathered their children and possessions and plodded after Esther up the Avenida da Liberdade. Claire, trailing alongside, noticed the stragglers shooting glances at her. She was the only one with empty hands. She caught up with a woman who was clutching a thick cardboard suitcase to her chest.

"Shall I carry your bag?"

With a hesitant smile, the woman handed it over and rubbed her wrists. "Thank you."

As they walked, some of the refugees talked quietly. Others gazed around silently, saving every ounce of strength. A few kept their eyes down, focusing on nothing but their next step. They'd be the ones in need of the most help, Claire guessed. Them, and a couple of dazed-looking children drifting along at the back, holding hands.

"Can you take your bag now?" They'd covered three long blocks. The woman sighed but took her suitcase, and Claire headed for the children. They drew closer together as she approached.

"Hello. *Bonjour.*" Claire crouched down beside the little girl and pulled up one of her stockings.

"*Bonjour,*" they answered shyly.

"What's your name?" Claire continued in French.

"Alicia," the little girl said.

She looked about five. Frédéric's age, with the same dark hair and big eyes. Claire suddenly missed the enthusiastic bear hugs he gave when she got down to his level. She forced her attention back to the present.

"Are your parents here?"

Alicia shook her head and pointed at the boy. His smudged face didn't seem much older. "That's my brother. Serge."

Claire looked for Esther. She was leading the rest of the group steadily away from them.

"Alicia, why don't I give you a ride?" Claire hoisted the child onto her back. Her hair smelled like it needed a wash. She bent again to take Alicia's small satchel. "This is all you have?"

Serge held out the one he was carrying. "This too."

Time for questions later. "Let's catch up with the others," she said, and sped up, making Serge almost run beside her. The little girl was heavier than she looked. They followed Esther's group into a side street and up another hill to a narrow, five-story building.

"Time to get down." Panting and sweaty, Claire slid Alicia off her back. The child clung to her hand. "Where are your parents?"

"I don't know." Serge clutched his satchel more tightly.

"When did you last see them?"

"The train stopped a long time ago and some men made Papa and Mama get off." His little boy voice wavered. "Papa said to pretend we weren't with them. They didn't come back." Tears made tracks through the dirty smudges on his face. Beside him, Alicia sniffed.

"What happened then? Did you know anyone else on the train?"

"An old lady took care of us. But when we got off, we couldn't find her."

Claire's heart sank. Children her brother's age, here on their own? "May I look in your satchels?" Serge nodded. Claire rooted through the small bags but found no identity cards or addresses. She sat back on her heels. "Why did you come with us? Did someone tell you to?"

Serge and Alicia shook their heads, their small faces tense and wary.

"You won't make us leave, will you?" Serge asked.

"Of course n…." Claire stopped. Who was she to promise anything? "I…I'm sure you'll be taken care of."

The children reached for each other's hands and looked at her beseechingly.

"Don't worry. You'll be fine," Claire said hastily. "And I'll come to see you. I promise. But first you've got to tell me: Why did you come with us?"

Alicia pointed a finger at Esther, who was urging the newcomers over the threshold with a gentle smile. "We followed the nice lady. She looks like Mama, a little."

Claire sighed. A good reason, from a child's point of view. But it didn't get her any closer to figuring out how to help them.

"Come with me." Claire slung the satchels over her shoulder and took Alicia's hand again. "Let's see what the nice lady will be able to do for you." Claire herself had no clue.

Antonio

Antonio made it back to the Chave d'Ouro on time. Barely. His favorite soccer team was playing tonight, but he felt so jittery he waited outside a moment before going in. It was obvious someone wanted something Thomas had had, and would kill to get it. If he'd gotten caught…

In the back room of the Chave d'Ouro, he took a few deep breaths, got into his uniform, and knotted the obligatory red Benfica scarf around his neck. All the staff had been instructed to wear one, but Antonio would have anyway.

When Antonio came back into the main room, Mr. Silva tossed

him an apron. "Here. We're already filling up. You've got the gallery."

"Right." Antonio went upstairs. At least he wouldn't have Mr. Silva looking over his shoulder constantly. From there, he had a view of the entire ground floor. It was a growing sea of red. Familiar faces crowded in, filling the downstairs and quickly overflowing to the gallery. Antonio greeted the group of grumpy Portuguese men, then other regulars who never missed a game. Foreigners either noted the red influx and made a U-turn, or settled in to enjoy the excitement. They didn't care who won. And Academica fans? None of them would show their colors tonight.

For a time, the café resounded with clinking glass and loud voices. Antonio moved effortlessly through the haze of tobacco smoke, taking orders. No one had to signal him more than once. Then the game began, and the crowd went silent. Not for long.

"Gooaall!" the man on the radio yelled. Benfica fans leaped up, clapping and shouting and pounding each other's backs. Antonio pumped his fist in the air, almost unbalancing his tray. He recovered just in time.

From the other side of the gallery, Mr. Thaler beckoned. "Over here, boy." The German with the jutting cheekbones sat at the railing, eying the packed room below. "Bring me a coffee." He turned his attention back to the crowd.

Antonio followed Mr. Thaler's gaze, but couldn't tell whom he was watching. At a table near the bar, Antonio spotted Gray, cheering for Benfica like a native. Had he heard about Thomas's death? He didn't seem bothered. But he'd said he had a network. People in networks know things. Antonio looked around at the crowded gallery. He'd have to find a moment to get downstairs. He brought Mr. Thaler his coffee and left to take another order.

"Gooaaalll! Two-zero, Benfica!" The café exploded in cheers again. Amid the noise, the German sat calmly, eyes going from the clock over the bar to the front entrance. As the cheering died down, a small man in a dark coat entered. The brim of his hat hid his face. Mr. Thaler straightened in his chair.

Customers called from elsewhere in the gallery, but the German soon hailed Antonio again. He was no longer alone.

"What can I serve you?"

The new arrival looked up. Antonio forced his face into a mask. It was the man with the skinny mustache, the driver of the car.

Antonio had never seen him before, and now they'd crossed paths three times in two days.

"*Uma cerveja.*" There was no flicker of recognition.

Antonio nodded and threaded his way to the bar, taking orders along the way. "Six beers, two coffees," he said to the barman. He leaned against the counter and watched the man Mr. Silva had called an informant. He wanted to shake him until he got the name of whoever killed Thomas.

"Ready to go." The bartender pushed a fully laden tray at him. Antonio picked it up and made his rounds. He served the German's table last, then stationed himself behind them.

"Back to work, boy," Mr. Silva growled in his ear.

Antonio jumped. When had his boss come upstairs?

"We're too busy for you to just stand there. Get going."

Antonio circled the gallery. His boss followed him, shaking the hands of the Chave d'Ouro regulars. As soon as he went back downstairs, Antonio started maneuvering to get behind the two men again.

"Gooooaaaalllll!" The radio announcer's yell went on forever. Everyone in the gallery was on their feet yelling, their fists punching the air. Antonio held his tray of drinks with both hands, trying to keep it stable.

"Three-zero!" A man near the railing spilled his beer, sending most of a full glass onto the crowd downstairs. Someone below bellowed angrily.

Antonio fetched the mop and cleaned up the mess. When he looked up, the informant was gone. *Merda.* Mr. Thaler was still in his seat, twisting a cigarette to shreds between his fingers. It wasn't a night for eavesdropping.

The announcer finally called the end of the game. Amid the celebrations, the grumpy Portuguese men began a loud post-game analysis. Even the foreigners smiled and ordered more to drink.

As Antonio worked the gallery, he saw Gray watching from below. Antonio jerked his chin toward the exit. Gray frowned, not moving. A few minutes later, though, he pulled a cigarette from a case and went outside. Antonio emptied his tray, then pushed his way down the stairs and followed him.

"Nice win for Benfica," Gray said when they were away from the cluster of people at the entrance. From everywhere on the hills around them, people were celebrating with firecrackers that popped and sizzled.

"They're the best." Antonio's response was automatic. But that wasn't what he wanted to talk about. "Someone killed Thomas Schiller. The refugee who was taken from the Chave D'Ouro last night."

Gray lit his cigarette. "And?"

"You said you had a network. Can you find out what happened to him?"

"Why?"

"He seemed like…a decent fellow." Antonio wasn't giving him anything more. "And things like that shouldn't happen here. Portugal is neutral for a reason."

"Ah. Your Portuguese neutrality again," Gray said. "I'm afraid I can't help you."

"Can't or won't?" Antonio shot back. "Seems like someone in your group must have heard something."

"Have you thought about what we discussed?"

"You do know something, don't you? But you won't tell me unless I do what you want? Is that it?"

Gray locked eyes with him but didn't answer. Antonio held them, hoping the man would give. He didn't.

"*Merda.*" Antonio spun around and stalked back to the café. He'd have to find out on his own. He thought of the diary in his jacket pocket. Maybe reading it would give him a clue.

Gray didn't reappear, and the crowd slowly thinned. By midnight, only a few tables were occupied. Antonio's shift was over, but Mr. Thaler was still at his table, as unperturbed now as he had been when Thomas was hauled off. He and the informant had been there to talk, not for the game. He had to know something. Antonio changed out of his uniform but stuck around, helping half-heartedly with the clean-up. Finally Mr. Thaler dropped a few coins on the table and stood up.

As soon as he was gone, Antonio headed for the exit. "I'm off."

"Antonio." Mr. Silva's tone held a warning.

Antonio pretended not to notice. "See you tomorrow," he said.

The German was already crossing Rossio. Antonio hung behind, keeping him in sight at a distance. Mr. Thaler stopped once, at a crossroads leading up into the Chiado neighborhood, and Antonio slipped into the shadows of a doorway. The man continued onward until he reached a quiet cross street. He stopped in front of a darkened store, scaring a skinny cat sleeping in the entranceway. It yowled and dashed away. Mr. Thaler swore, then let himself in.

Outside the building, a sign said *Moreira – Sales*. Sales of what? Antonio went closer. A curtain across the big front window blocked any view of the interior. Mr. Thaler hadn't turned on the lights.

The cat yowled again, this time from a narrow alley beside the building. Antonio walked into it, trying not to breathe in through his nose. There was cat pee. Lots of it. Where the building ended, a wall higher than his head began. He jumped but could see nothing. The second time he leapt higher and got a handhold. He pulled himself up, straddled the wall, then flicked off a bird dropping and lay on his stomach, as flat as he could get. In the back yard, there was nothing but a few overgrown bushes and some patchy grass.

A light shone through a second-floor door that was open onto a balcony, dimly illuminating an outside table. On it were thick black rods positioned to form a large three-dimensional diamond shape. Inside but out of sight, a man and a woman argued, just audibly, in German. Antonio couldn't make out a word. Moments later, Mr. Thaler appeared at the window. Antonio stopped breathing.

"Are you crazy?" Mr. Thaler hissed at the people behind him. "Get that off the balcony."

Mr. Thaler and the other man carried the black rods inside, and someone pulled a beige curtain across the window. Antonio breathed again. No one had seen him except the skinny cat. It sat at the far end of the wall, eyes gleaming. A few words filtered through the curtain, but nothing Antonio could string together into something meaningful, or link to Thomas. He shifted on the wall, trying to find a more comfortable position. Maybe he'd learn nothing here. But the night wasn't over yet.

The German army has invaded Greece and Yugoslavia
Belgrade and Thessaloniki bombed

Diário de Notícias
April 7, 1941

CHAPTER 5 – MONDAY, APRIL 7

"WHAT ARE YOU doing today, Claire?" Vincent stood up and cleared his breakfast dishes off the table. "Are you going with Esther?"

"Trying to get rid of us?" Esther tipped her coffee cup toward him. It was still half full. "Let us finish eating."

"Actually, Uncle, I was thinking of spending the day with you." Claire surprised herself. Until he'd asked, she'd been planning to find Serge and Alicia, and see how they were getting along. She'd kept them entertained at HICEM the day before while they were waiting for Esther. Patty-cake, patty-cake, and the kind of simple games she played with Frédéric. As she left, they'd wound their hands into her skirt and refused to let go. Claire looked at them, and saw her brother. And she'd promised to come back as soon as possible, to do something fun.

Vincent's cup clattered in the sink. He swore under his breath and examined it. "It's not broken," he said to Esther. "And no, you can't," he told Claire. "You need to find something else to do."

"We've hardly spent any time together." His reaction made her want to push back. Mother said stubbornness was her most unattractive trait, but it could come in useful. "I can keep you company while you work. I won't bother you."

"I told you I don't have time to babysit."

"That's not what I'm asking."

"Give me a hand here, Esther. Your people need help more

than I do, right? And didn't Claire do a good job yesterday?"

Esther raised her hands. "I'm sure she'd be useful wherever she is."

"She's too young. I'm not getting her involved."

"Too young?" Claire sat up straight. "For what?"

Esther crooked a finger at Vincent. "Can you excuse us, Claire? We'll be back in a minute." She shepherded Vincent into the bedroom and shut the door.

Their voices rose and fell, but Claire couldn't catch the words. She was tempted to put an ear to the door. She sighed. Curiosity was another of her less-than-ladylike attributes.

Instead, she washed her dishes and folded her few possessions into a neat pile. If she was going to stay here until her family arrived, she needed somewhere to put them. But where? The cabinet was stuffed so full its door was ajar. She pushed it shut, and it clicked open again. Something was blocking the latch. Claire opened the door wider and peered inside. A pair of scissors lay on a mound of newspapers. Beside it sat rubber stamps, razors, a ruler, and bottles of ink, all tools of her uncle's printing trade. The rest of the cabinet was filled with stacks of old playbills and papers in various sizes and shapes. Her uncle had been a packrat ever since she remembered, but this seemed excessive.

Claire glanced over her shoulder. Esther and Vincent were still talking behind the closed door. As she pushed a bunch of theater stubs and train tickets further inside, something fell to the floor. A French identity card. Ingrid Bannister. She picked it up and studied the serious blond woman in the photo. One of her uncle's old girlfriends? She'd met several, but not this one.

At that moment the bedroom door opened. Claire whirled around, pressing the identity card into the folds of her skirt.

Vincent's eyes went from her to the open cabinet. "What are you doing? I thought it was clear you weren't to poke around in here."

"I was just trying to..."

"What did you take?"

"Take? I didn't take anything." Stung, Claire held up the card. "This fell out when I was trying to close the cabinet. Who is it?"

Vincent snatched the card from her.

Claire's anger flared. "I'm the one who should be asking questions. What are you doing? What's so secret?"

"If she's going to stay here, Vincent, you have to trust her," Esther said.

"Michel will kill me." Vincent sat down heavily at the table, the identity card still in his hand.

"Father's not here."

"This is not a good idea."

Esther crossed her arms and didn't answer. Claire did the same, hoping she looked as decided as Esther did.

"Women." Vincent gave a bitter laugh. "I'll regret this. You mark my words."

"Tell me," Claire said.

"Only if you swear on your grandmother's grave that you won't breathe a word of what I say. To anyone. Lives depend on it."

"I swear."

Vincent took a deep breath and exhaled slowly. "What are the biggest problems most refugees face?"

"Finding a place to stay. Food. Money. Clothes," she answered instantly. And the worst one of all. "Being separated from their families."

"What else?"

"I don't know," Claire said, exasperated. "There are so many."

"Think. Of the future."

"Umm…They need a place to go next. After they leave Lisbon."

"And what do they need to get there? To travel at all?" Vincent answered his own questions. "They need passports, transit visas. Documents."

Claire sat down across from him and took Ingrid Bannister's identity card. "And you're doing what? Making them? Here?"

"Most documents require a printing press and other equipment I don't have. But I can do a lot of the detail work. Stamps, for instance."

"Show me." Even to herself, Claire's voice sounded less certain.

Vincent grimaced, then heaved himself out of the chair and went to the bedroom. When he reemerged, he placed a letter of transit and a passport in front of Claire. "This is what I do."

She flipped through the pages in the passport. "This isn't real?"

"Not all of it. There might be a new photo, a new date. A page that no longer marks a person as Jewish." He picked up the letter of transit. "See this? It gives Valéric Rembert the right to enter and stay in Portugal. Without it, she could be detained – or sent back to whatever hell she thought she'd escaped."

Claire put her hands in her lap. She didn't want to touch the documents. "It's illegal, isn't it?"

Vincent shrugged. "People are arriving here from Poland, Czechoslovakia, Italy, the Netherlands. From all over. Lisbon's the only open port. If they can't get out of here…" He didn't finish his sentence. "If it saves someone's life, does it matter if it's against the law?"

Claire hesitated. What was illegal in wartime was hard to define. And sometimes even harder to justify. "Uncle, what if you get caught?"

Vincent lifted his shoulders again. "I'd probably end up in a Portuguese jail, which I've been told is to be avoided at all costs. So I'm very careful. So is Esther." He paused. "Claire, do you understand now why I didn't want you involved?"

Under the table, Claire kneaded her hands, pulling the skin so tightly it hurt. A few months ago, in the middle of the day, the Gestapo had taken away an entire family who lived four doors down from them in Marseille. A warning not to get out of line, people said. But what her uncle was doing was more than out of line. And it put anyone who lived with him in danger. It was a selfish thought, and she tried to stifle it. "Yes. I understand."

Vincent regarded her thoughtfully. "Now that you know, can you handle it?"

"I…I guess so." Her family's whereabouts: unknown. Lisbon: a place of unexpected dangers. And now her uncle, forging documents in a city where demand was infinite. Another wall in this supposedly safe haven was crumbling before her eyes, and there was nothing at all she could do about it.

"You have to." Esther's face was stern. "And you can't say a word. Vincent is exposed enough as it is, going out for deliveries and pick-ups."

"I won't." Claire's answer was almost inaudible, but she knew they heard.

"So, do you still want to stay with me today?" Vincent asked. Beneath his words ran an unspoken accusation: *I knew you couldn't cope.* Maybe he was right, and she couldn't. Not now.

"I told those children I met – Alicia and Serge – that I'd come see them as soon as I could." Claire could've sworn she heard someone whisper *coward*. Esther and Vincent exchanged a look, but neither had moved their lips. "I probably shouldn't break my promise."

Antonio

Antonio gave the sidewalk table a final swipe, straightened up, and stretched his arms above his head. Last customer of the day for him. It had been a short night, followed by the morning shift. He'd have felt better if he'd learned something useful during his hours on the wall. He shook his shoulders, loosening them, and untied his apron.

Now the afternoon lay ahead, to do what he wanted. Like find a private place to look at Thomas's diary. He scanned Rossio. Nothing much going on here, except... Wasn't that the girl? Claire? A woman kissed her on the cheek and said goodbye. She shuffled in his direction, eyes on her feet, not noticing him. She could be interesting company for an afternoon, if he could get her to spend it with him.

"Good day, Miss Claire. How are you?"

She raised her head, unsmiling, and took in his apron and the damp dishcloth. "You work here?"

Antonio nodded. "But I'm finished for today. Are you busy this afternoon?"

Claire shook her head, her expression uncertain.

"Then don't go anywhere." He ran to the back room and tore out of his uniform, hoping she'd be patient. He slung his drawing tube across his back, pulled on his red scarf, and was off.

Claire was still standing outside, shifting from one foot to another.

"Would you like to take a walk?" Antonio asked.

"Umm...Sure." She eyed the scarf. "Are you cold?"

"What?" He laughed. "No. This is for Benfica."

She looked at him uncomprehendingly.

"Our soccer team. We won the national championship last night."

"The Germans invaded Yugoslavia yesterday," she said stiffly. "How can you care about a game?"

Antonio shrugged. "You should have seen the Chave d'Ouro. It was packed. I bet a lot of people think soccer is more important than the war."

Claire looked at him askance. "Really? Aren't they the lucky ones."

She wasn't Portuguese. He couldn't expect her to understand. Although she did have a point. An awkward silence enveloped them.

"I have an idea," Antonio said after a moment. "Have you been anywhere in Portugal? Besides Lisbon?"

"We got out to eat at a train station when we crossed the border from Spain."

"That doesn't count. Why don't I take you to Estoril this afternoon?"

"What's Estoril?"

"A little town along the coast." Antonio had a sudden urge to get out of Lisbon, to do something different. Something that would improve Claire's mood. She was too subdued. "It's pretty. You'd like it."

Claire looked down at her feet again. "I don't think…"

"You've got to see a bit of Portugal while you're here," Antonio interrupted. "We could be there and back on the train in a couple of hours. No one would even realize you'd gone. If that's the problem."

She gave him a wary look.

"Come on. What are you afraid of?" He was daring her, trying to force that spark of defiance he'd seen back to the surface. "Surely not me."

She straightened. He'd struck some kind of nerve.

"All right. Why not?"

Antonio blinked. A Portuguese girl would never have said yes. "But I have to be back before dark."

"Of course. Shall we go?" He couldn't believe his luck.

Claire

Claire cleared her throat. What had one moment of bravado gotten her into?

"Yes," she said, a little hoarsely, and fell into step beside him. An afternoon outing with a boy wasn't a crime. Nothing as bad as forging documents. Although her parents might disagree, especially if they found out how and where she'd first seen him. She pushed aside the thought that they wouldn't if they never arrived. She examined his profile, noticing for the first time the straight line of his nose and a small scar above an eyebrow. Besides, she'd caught the challenge in his eyes. Her courage had been tested once today, and she'd failed miserably. It didn't make her proud. She wasn't backing out a second time.

Antonio steered them toward the waterfront.

"Aren't we going the wrong way?" Claire slowed, her distrust returning. Maybe his face didn't have thief written on it, but appearances deceived. And she knew Rossio station was in the other direction.

"The train to Estoril leaves from Cais do Sodré."

She must have looked doubtful, because he continued.

"Not far from where we met last time." He didn't elaborate.

"Oh."

A few minutes later they passed the statue on the square. She paused. This place was indeed familiar. "I'm sorry about your friend."

"So am I." He kept his face averted from the place where the body had been brought ashore.

"Was he a good friend?"

"Yes."

Father and this boy both knew the murdered man. Three men, three countries, and apparently little in common. It was an odd coincidence.

"Do you know what happened?"

"No. Not yet." Antonio looked like he was going to say something, then stopped. "I'd rather not think about it right now."

"Oh. Yes. Of course." Although she wanted to know more.

At the station, they boarded the train and found empty seats. Claire tucked her skirt close around her legs, wondering if he'd sit beside her. At least there was no one to tell her parents about it. But Antonio slid the tube off his back and eased into the free place across the way. Claire felt a pinch of disappointment.

She pushed it away and pointed at the tube. "What's that?"

"Paper, pencils. I like to draw."

The train jolted into motion.

An artist? That wasn't what she'd expected from a café waiter. But it made him more interesting. She studied him again. Antonio carried his drawing materials around as if they were a part of him.

"May I see?"

"Later, maybe. Don't you want to watch where we're going?"

Outside the window, docks, warehouses, shops, and apartment buildings rolled by to the thrumming of the train's wheels. These soon gave way to an unobstructed view of the widening river, sunlight winking on its choppy surface.

Claire shaded her face with her hand. "I've never seen light like this before."

Antonio cocked his head. "Where do you come from exactly?"

"Marseille."

"It's on the water too, isn't it? What's different about the light?"

"I don't know." Claire touched the window glass. It was warm against her fingers. "Nothing shines as brightly when your country's at war."

"Why did you come to Lisbon?"

"The boat to America leaves from here."

"I mean, why did you leave home?"

Remembering Esther's warning, Claire chose her words carefully. "My father lost his job, and my mother's brother said he'd help us get to America. We'll live there with him until the war is over."

"You have family in New York?"

"My mother is American. My father is French."

"He can't find another job?"

"It's not that simple. He was the editor of a newspaper. They told him he'd never work in France again." Even to herself, her voice sounded strained. She forced it back into its normal range. "Staying in Marseille was impossible."

"But now you'll travel to America, and everything will be all right." Antonio eyed her curiously. "Won't it?"

"I hope so. As long as my family gets here. The problem is, I don't know where they are." Worry squeezed the air out of her lungs. No one had been able to tell her where Serge and Alicia were either. They hadn't been at HICEM that morning, and Esther had given her so much to do that she hadn't had time to find out where they'd been taken. It felt almost like she'd lost track of more members of her family. And they'd think she was abandoning them too. Claire gazed out the window, her fingers still spread against the warm glass, and took long, slow breaths. It helped, a little.

Antonio chewed his lower lip. "You came to Lisbon alone?"

"My uncle's here," she said briefly, then started to stand as the train drew to a stop, brakes screeching. A sign on the platform said *São Pedro de Estoril.* "This is it?"

"Not yet. Two more stations to go. This is where the refugee children get off."

"What do you mean?"

"There used to be a summer camp in São Pedro for kids. Now orphans and refugees stay here, until someone figures out what to do with them."

The train started moving again. Alicia and Serge hadn't been shuttled way out here to another strange place, had they? She'd have to find out tomorrow. They slowed again a few minutes later. This time Antonio stood up.

"Now we're in Estoril. Let's go." He led her out of the station, then made an expansive gesture with his arm, as if showing off his private domain. "What do you think?"

Below them was a wide beach with white tents staked into the sand. A building that looked like a big stone castle stood at the far end. On the terrace of a hotel called Tamariz, well-dressed customers occupied every table.

Claire stared, open-mouthed. "What is this? A holiday resort?"

"In a sense. But anyone can walk in the sand." Antonio offered her his arm. "Even us."

Claire shook her head and remained where she was, enjoying the briny, gusting breeze. Antonio kept having to push his hair out of his eyes, but his shoulders had relaxed and he was smiling. At her. His fingers, slender and tanned, were on the railing, not quite touching her hand. Claire almost reached out, wanting to see the contrast of her white skin over his. She made herself stay still. A proper girl wouldn't even be thinking about it.

On the beach, two ladies held their hats with one hand and clutched their skirts with the other, trying to remain dignified. Three little boys kicked a ball into the water, then plowed in to rescue it, shrieking with delight. This was indeed a different world.

"Who are these people?"

"Refugees mostly. From all over Europe. Waiting to leave, like you."

Two couples let small waves lap their toes. The women backed away. "How cold, how cold," they cried, laughing. The men plunged in anyway, then raced out, gasping and rubbing their arms.

"They're nothing like me," Claire muttered. If she'd ever been that light-hearted, it was a distant memory.

"Estoril is where the rich people come," Antonio continued. "Let me show you something."

He wrapped his fingers around her arm and led her away from the beach. His touch was firm and warm – and too forward. She pulled away, her skin tingling. Before them, a grassy park sloped gently uphill, crisscrossed with paths and flower beds. In an arcade of shops, a man was selling ice cream. Its sweetness filled the air.

"Mmm." Claire smiled. "I haven't tasted ice cream in ages."

Antonio raised an eyebrow but didn't say anything. They continued along a path that curved past red and white roses, then beside beds of bright yellow flowers whose heady scent Claire didn't recognize. In front of them, at the top of the park, stood a long building with a rounded façade and cream-colored awnings. A line of people wound their way toward it along the sidewalk.

"We're going there," Antonio said. "That's the casino."

Claire stopped short. Even from a distance, she could make out the women's stylish, jewel-colored dresses, the plumes on their hats, their perfectly coiffed hair. A hefty, black-suited man at the door was nodding them in with wide smiles.

"No, we're not. You…you can if you want. I'm not," she stuttered. Go in among that crowd in her worn traveling clothes? Absolutely not. "Why in the world would you want to?"

Antonio's lips had curled in a provocative grin. Claire caught her breath, and for an instant forgot what he was proposing. His green eyes were sparkling at her again. In Marseille, even innocent flirting had become a casualty of war. She forced her gaze away. Antonio might be a rogue. But he was a very attractive one.

"Relax," he said, and held out a hand.

Antonio

Claire tossed her head and ignored it. Seeing her discomfort, Antonio's grin widened.

"Come on," he said, and climbed the casino steps. "Don't you want to see the rich people?"

Claire trailed behind. "No."

By the door, the man in the black suit frowned and brushed his fingers along the side of his leg, front to back. A small, quick gesture, like wiping crumbs off a tablecloth. Antonio pointed at a low wall not far from the casino entrance. The doorman shook his head.

"What are you doing?" Claire asked.

"Wait here," he said, and approached the doorman, who was still shaking his head.

"Not today," the man said. "There's a big gala this afternoon. Best head out before the manager sees you. Don't want either of us to get into trouble."

"Are you sure?" Of all days to be turned away.

"I'm sure."

Merda.

"He's not letting us in?" Claire's expression lightened considerably when Antonio returned.

"Don't look so happy. There's a private event today. Invitation only." Antonio wasn't about to tell her now that his visits consisted of waiting near the entrance, offering to sketch portraits of the casino's guests. On a good day, before a boat was scheduled to leave, he'd go home with a satisfying jingle of coins in his pocket. But today… Well, he'd find another spot. "Let's go back to the beach. If you're patient, I'll get you that ice cream you wanted."

"Will you now?" Claire practically skipped down the steps. Antonio grinned again. He'd never met someone who flashed so quickly from one emotion to another, or who displayed them so openly. A human pendulum.

He stepped aside to let a woman in a silk dress and glittering earrings weave by, leaning on a fellow perhaps half her age. Maybe her son. Maybe not. He'd bet the price of those earrings would keep him and his grandmother going for a year. He clasped his hands tightly behind his back, no longer smiling, and watched as more men and women made their way to the casino from a nearby hotel, the gleaming Palacio. They were like a procession of rich ants. Who unfortunately wouldn't be providing him with a single *escudo* today.

Claire stared too. "These people can't be refugees."

"They are."

"They're not."

"Ask one of them."

"I don't believe you."

"Do or don't, it's the same to me." His tone was more impatient than he intended. Claire frowned at him. "They stay in fancy hotels, go to expensive shops, and lose piles of money at roulette." Antonio nodded at an older couple walking by, slow but dignified. She wore a double string of pearls and perfume so strong it made his nose itch. "Do they look like they've lost anything? They live better than anyone I know."

"Is that why you do it?"

"Do what?"

"Steal from the refugees. Because you think they're better off than you are?"

Antonio shook his head. He should've known that she wouldn't forget, even if he acted like a perfect gentleman now.

"I saw you at the train station. You know I did. How do you live with yourself afterwards?"

"You don't know what I live with." Antonio started walking again.

"You think you're worse off than people who've been persecuted?" The outraged expression he'd seen at the train station was back. "People who have lost everything?"

Antonio jerked his head in the direction of the casino. "They haven't lost everything. And you seem to be doing okay."

Claire flushed bright red. "You...I don't believe you. I'm going back to Lisbon." She turned and made for the train station. Not running, but almost.

Merda. He'd gone too far, and for no good reason. Except that she'd made him feel even more ashamed than before. He and his grandmother had barely scraped by after his mother died, and stealing had helped. For her medicine, nothing else. Now that he worked at the Chave d'Ouro, he only did it if things got bad. And last week, his grandmother had really been sick. But he didn't like it any more than Claire did.

He ran after her. "Please wait."

Claire ducked her head and kept going.

"Will you let me explain?" He put a hand on her arm. She shook it off and backed away.

"Doing okay?" she choked out. "Do you have any idea what you're saying?"

"Listen to me. Please. What I meant was that a lot of refugees who come to Portugal get help. They go off to better lives in America, or wherever. We don't. We have to stay here and manage."

"Manage what?"

"Things." He didn't want to tell her about the damp rooms that kept his grandmother coughing, or the parents he no longer had.

"Things? That doesn't mean anything." She turned away again. "Leave me alone."

"I'm sorry. I didn't mean to offend you."

"You did though."

They walked toward the train station in silence. Claire wouldn't look at him.

"I really am sorry," Antonio said again. "I promised you a nice afternoon. Can we start again?"

Claire sniffed.

"We'll go back to the beach. We can laugh..." He stopped before saying "at the foreigners." She wouldn't appreciate that either. "Please." She didn't answer, but let him guide their steps to the Tamariz restaurant. They stopped beside the terrace. "Give me a few minutes to earn some money, and I'll buy you that ice cream."

"Earn money?" she asked flatly. "Or steal it?"

"Watch." He held up a finger. "For a minute. Or two. All right?" She shrugged and went to sit on a wall overlooking the beach.

Antonio slid the tube off his back and made his way to the terrace. It was still crowded with customers. He carefully unrolled one of his best drawings and paraded it between the tables, holding it so everyone could see it.

"Ladies and gentlemen, a portrait in a minute? A souvenir of a beautiful day?" He started in Portuguese, then switched to English and French. He glanced over his shoulder and caught Claire's eye. She shook her head and turned back to the beach. Was it his imagination, or did a tiny smile tilt the corners of her lips? Maybe she'd let him draw her. After he got her to accept his apology. First, though, the ice cream.

But at table after table, people shook their heads and returned to their conversations. He glanced back at Claire. She was watching people on the sand, her back to him.

Then he saw a young couple, beaming and clinking glasses at a table near the wall. Their two small daughters, in matching white dresses, were kneeling on their chairs, giggling at the beachgoers below. Antonio headed in their direction.

"May I offer you a portrait? Of your lovely daughters? It's two for the price of one if they'll pose together." He winked at the girls. They giggled again.

"Mummy, yes, let him do our portrait," begged the older girl, who was perhaps about six.

"Well…" the father started to say.

"This looks like a special moment," Antonio broke in. "Wouldn't you enjoy having a picture to remember it?"

"Please, Papa, please." The younger sister clasped her hands and looked at her father beseechingly. Antonio stifled a laugh. They were doing his job for him.

"Why not? It'll be part of our celebration." A smile overrode the worry lines on the young mother's face. "Our papers came. We're going to America."

"Congratulations." Antonio pulled out his pencil and a clean sheet of paper before they could change their minds. "Girls, why don't you stand here, with the beach and the castle behind you?" He gently led them into place. "Good?"

Their parents nodded. Antonio set to work, his pencil flying over the paper, trying to capture the younger one's innocent stance and the other's dreamy stare before they started to fidget.

A gentleman at the next table set down his beer and leaned over to watch. Another couple stopped behind Antonio's chair. "How lovely," the woman said. Antonio hoped Claire was paying attention. There. A few more strokes and he was done. He turned the picture in a circle so everyone could see it, then handed it to the older child. She started to trace the image of her hair with the tip of a finger. Her mother took it away, scolding her.

"Thank you." The father handed Antonio five *escudos*.

He pocketed them with a small bow and turned to the rest of his audience. "Who's next?" But the couple had wandered off, and the gentleman had gone back to his beer. Antonio headed toward some new arrivals, his model drawing held high.

Behind him, the little girl who had so easily charmed her father flitted from table to table, her tiny hands holding the portrait out in front of her. "Look at this," she ordered complete strangers. "This is me. This is my sister. Aren't we pretty?" They laughed and told her she was.

"Come sit down," her mother called.

Instead, the little girl caught up with Antonio. She pulled on his sleeve. "Draw another one," she said. "Please. I want to watch."

"I need a subject," Antonio told her. "Can you find someone who wants me to draw their picture?"

She twirled around. "You do!" She pointed at a lady in a hat trimmed with lace. And got a shake of the head. "Do you?" she asked another table, then another. By now everyone around them was laughing.

"All right, all right," a man finally said. "Come over here, boy, and we'll give the little lass her wish."

"Will you wear your hat?" She pointed to a black fedora on the seat beside him.

"What do you think?" He put it on, then turned his head for her to judge. "Should I or shouldn't I?"

"You should," she said decisively, and went to stand at Antonio's elbow. He traced the man's head, his deep-set eyes, and made ticks that became a thick mustache. As each feature emerged, the child beside him let out a soft *oh*.

Antonio glanced at Claire, wondering if she was at all impressed. She wasn't where he had left her. He straightened up, flexing his hand. She'd come closer, to the entrance of the terrace, and was watching him. Antonio finished his drawing with a flourish.

"What do you think?" he asked the little girl.

She reached out to touch it. "His hair is darker than you made it."

"Art critic, eh?" Antonio smiled and passed the portrait to his client. More small coins joined those already in his pocket.

"Mummy, I want to draw," the little girl said as she ran back to her family's table. "Let's tell Papa."

From across the terrace, Claire followed the child's progress with twinkling eyes. It was the first time Antonio had seen her so serene. He slipped his pencils and paper back into the tube and joined her.

"I kept you waiting."

"That's all right. It was entertaining." The sparkle stayed in her eyes.

"Ready for that ice cream now?"

"With pleasure."

He offered his arm. This time she took it.

Claire

Claire regretted the gesture immediately. Here she was, being so familiar, and they hardly knew each other. She'd never have acted this way in Marseille. As soon as they reached the ice cream vendor, she dropped her hand.

Antonio ordered, then handed her a cone. "As promised."

"Thank you." He was on his best behavior now, but what he'd said earlier… That was hard to forget. She concentrated on the utter creamy wonderfulness of the ice cream, taking small licks so it would last. They walked toward the far end of the beach, past a man grilling sardines. One whiff, and she had fish in her nose and vanilla in her mouth. *Yuck.* Antonio laughed and took her upwind to a wall overlooking the beach.

Directly below them, a young couple sitting on the sand in their bathing costumes began to kiss. Claire tried not to stare. Two people in love, self-absorbed, seemingly worry-free. Antonio nudged her, and her face burned. He'd been watching the kiss too. But no, he was pointing at a man in a crisp black uniform, heading their way.

"Watch this," he said in a low voice.

The policeman planted his feet beside the couple, drew himself up, and cleared his throat. "A-hum."

They didn't react.

"Good afternoon," he said loudly.

This time they shaded their faces and looked up at him.

"That is not allowed on the beach," the policeman said.

"What isn't?" asked the young man.

"Intimacy. It's not allowed in public places."

"Well, isn't that odd. All right then." The man and woman put several inches between them and waited for the policeman to leave. Instead, he scrutinized them, then pulled a ruler from the breast pocket of his jacket.

"Miss, I believe your bathing costume does not follow regulations," he said. "Permit me to measure it." He moved the ruler toward her thigh.

"You must be joking." She clutched her dress in front of herself and scrambled to her feet.

Her boyfriend stepped between them. "What are you doing?"

"I am a member of the Beach Patrol Police. And you," he pointed at the girl, "are not allowed to wear such a bathing costume. It is prohibited."

"Really?" Claire whispered to Antonio.

He nodded, grinning. "It's against the law. They say it's an offense to dignity."

Claire had forgotten her ice cream. It dripped cold onto her fingers. She licked a circle around its base and turned her attention back to the scene below.

"But I bought this bathing costume here, in Estoril," the young lady protested.

"You may buy them, but you may not wear them. If you do, the fine is fifty *escudos*." The policeman gestured toward the stairs leading off the beach. "If you would please accompany me to the station."

"I will not." In one quick movement, the girl pulled her dress over her head and tugged it into place. "There's nothing to complain about now, is there?" she asked. "Let's go." Her companion grabbed her hand and they sprinted away, kicking sand up behind them. The policeman smiled in satisfaction and replaced the ruler in his pocket. Then he spied a man emerging topless from the water and marched pompously in his direction.

"Is he serious?" Claire asked.

Antonio nodded. "I told you it was funny to watch." He popped the last of his cone into his mouth and wiped his fingers on his trousers.

"Not funny for them though."

"Our prime minister is very serious about upholding Portuguese morals." Antonio sounded like he was reciting a lesson. "I guess he thinks you foreigners will corrupt us with your modern ways." He flashed her a teasing smile. "Then again, maybe I wouldn't mind it, just a little."

"I don't know what you're talking about." She stepped back. Coming so soon after their argument, his banter was unsettling. She shouldn't like it, but she did. "Shouldn't we be getting back to Lisbon? It'll be dark soon."

"We have time."

They squinted at the sun. It was still high in the sky, but clearly on its way toward the horizon.

"I should take the next train. Do I have to go alone?"

"No. Of course not."

He turned away, his familiarity gone in an instant. He'd been too suggestive and she'd cut him off, as a decent girl was supposed to do. He'd stopped, as a young man should. Now, as he walked away, Claire couldn't help noticing the fluid, graceful way he moved. She followed irritably, wishing she didn't feel so irrationally and inappropriately disappointed.

Antonio

The train was packed. Antonio pushed past mothers with whiny, sun-reddened children and men smoking and talking. Through a second car, then a third. In the fourth, he spied a seat in a compartment that was occupied only by a large leather bag.

"Is that place free?" he asked the small woman sitting beside it. She tensed, and Antonio pulled Claire forward. "For the lady?"

The woman relaxed and placed the bag under her seat. Wheels squealed, and the train pulled out of the station. Antonio gestured to Claire to sit down.

"And you?" Claire asked.

"I'll be in the corridor. Right there."

"You don't want to sit? After all the hard work you've done today?"

"Work?"

She mimed drawing a picture, and he grinned. For a moment,

by the beach, he'd been afraid he'd made her mad again. But now she was the one teasing him.

"I'm fine." In the corridor, he leaned his forehead against the window and watched the river flash golden in the lowering sun. The clacking and swaying of the car were hypnotic. He closed his eyes and, as always, the images came. Claire taking his arm, and being delightfully embarrassed about it. His mother running a finger along a page as he, a young boy, stumbled through a new book. His grandmother singing mournful, nostalgic *fado* music with all the energy of her earlier years. Thomas laughing, then falling forward into that black car. Enough. Antonio opened his eyes and stared unseeingly at the river. Why couldn't his brain keep the happy images and bury the rest? Even drawing them only made them go away for a while. He shut his eyes again and focused on nothingness.

"Yugoslavia. Greece. Where will Hitler go next?" An anxious voice to the left, speaking in Portuguese, fractured Antonio's concentration.

"Wherever the Brits have any kind of influence. Hitler wants to kick them out of Europe. Says they're the troublemakers." This voice was barely above a whisper.

"What a bunch of bullshit."

"Schht. Keep your opinions to yourself."

They quieted. Farther along, a discussion began in Polish. That was a language Antonio hadn't mastered at all, except to say *dzień dobry* to customers. To his right, two men began a quiet conversation in German. Antonio listened idly, surprised at how much he could understand.

"You found someone to do it?"

"Yeah. A dockworker."

"Good. But sending it to the bottom – that's nasty work. Does he know?"

Nasty work? Antonio kept his eyes on the river.

"The *Serpa*'s carrying war materials. Can't let any ship make it across with those."

"War materials? That's what you call refugees?"

Antonio forced himself not to move. They were planning to sink a ship full of refugees? He couldn't have heard right.

"That's not our problem," the second man continued. "But don't worry about the dockworker. He'll get good money. He won't talk."

"Not even afterwards?"

"Especially then."

Just then, three men further down the corridor broke into a loud argument. All conversations stopped, and Antonio pretended to shake himself awake. Along with everyone else, the Germans beside him craned their necks toward the ruckus. Antonio examined them out of the corner of his eye. One big, red-nosed and balding. The other with a strong, angular face, like a movie star. He'd remember what they looked like. The shouting escalated, like men on the verge of a fistfight.

"What's going on?" Claire came to the door of her compartment.

"Nothing that concerns us." Antonio could feel the men's attention shift his way, and turned his back to them. "A fight."

"Over what?"

"I don't know. Someone will break it up."

"Not you?" She smiled.

"Not me." He couldn't smile back. Hundreds of refugees crowded onto those ships. And some of them, for him, now had faces. Like the little girls in white, celebrating their departure. By boat. Like Claire.

Hitler issues a proclamation addressed to the people of the Reich

Diário de Notícias

CHAPTER 6

ANTONIO SAID GOODBYE at the corner of Rossio Square and left with a polite kiss on the cheek. Claire wasn't sure how she felt about that – or, after today, about anything related to Antonio. He could be attentive, amusing and entrepreneurial. He was definitely attractive. But he'd basically admitted to stealing, and that was inexcusable. Even if he somehow managed to justify it to himself. So why was the thought of seeing him again so appealing?

At number 59, she tugged on the bell pull and the heavy boarding house door clicked open. She trudged up the stairs. What made it worse is that she had no one to talk to. Certainly not her uncle. If she could help it, he'd never know how she'd spent the afternoon. She needed to find Eleanor.

In their rooms, Vincent was walking around barefoot, looking smart in a pressed shirt and suit pants. He stood still a moment to let Esther straighten his tie.

"It's dark, Claire," he said. "Where have you been?"

"Exploring. As you suggested."

"Alone?"

"I'm fine on my own."

Esther, her hands busy at Vincent's neck, gave her a sideways glance but didn't say anything. Claire wondered if she'd seen Antonio outside the Chave d'Ouro.

"Why are you all dressed up?" Claire asked.

"There's a gala tonight. I don't want to miss the opportunity to mingle with Lisbon's finest."

"Ha!" Esther inserted a world of scorn into one syllable.

Vincent gave a short laugh. "Those who consider themselves Lisbon's finest," he amended.

"Are you going?" Claire asked Esther.

Esther shook her head. "It's not wise for us to be seen together at that kind of event. Besides, it'll be crawling with Nazis and their agents. Smiling and making small talk with them..." She pressed her lips together. "No thank you."

"You know I have to do it." Vincent sounded reproachful. "One must keep up appearances."

"What appearances?" Claire dropped onto the couch and rubbed her feet.

"No one here knows what I'm doing. I want to keep it that way." Vincent sat beside her and pulled on a sock. "So I play jolly old Vincent. The man who shakes your hand, laughs at your jokes, and offends no one."

"That doesn't sound like you," Claire said doubtfully. Her uncle had hardly cracked a smile since she'd arrived.

"I'm a good actor. And that was me, kind of, a few years ago." He reached for his shoes. "You were probably too young to remember."

"I remember you had a lot of girlfriends," Claire said. Esther's eyebrows went up.

"Uh, yes. Thank you, Claire."

"So you go out even if you know you won't like the people you'll be with. That sounds like a waste of time."

"Some I do like. Besides, it's quite useful to see who is ignored, or who refuses to raise their glass for a toast. You learn a lot."

"But it's risky."

"If people go away from it convinced I'm not worth a second thought, that's an extra layer of protection for us." Vincent stood up, shrugged into his suit jacket and kissed Esther. "Don't wait up for me, ladies."

"Wait. Is there news of my family?"

Vincent paused with his hand on the doorknob. "I'd tell you if there was." The door closed behind him, leaving an empty silence.

Esther forced a smile. "I always worry when he goes out. He dives into a tank of piranhas and hopes not to be eaten." She took a quick, in-out breath. "So you and I are on our own tonight. Why don't we eat something simple, and afterwards we'll go for a coffee?" She started to take a wedge of cheese out of its paper wrapping.

"Umm…sure." Anything was better than sitting around. Claire washed her hands and set the table. "Why does Uncle Vincent do it?" she asked as they sat down. "The forging, I mean. He could certainly find a safer way to help."

Esther pressed her lips together. "How much do you know about why he left France?"

Claire cut a slice of bread while she thought. "He had to sell his printing business, and didn't want to stay after that."

"Do you know why?"

"He doesn't like the Vichy government." Claire's words came slowly. She'd been too busy studying the latest fashions with her friends to pay much attention to Vincent's conversations with her parents. "He said he couldn't live in France when it was governed by Nazi puppets."

"That's part of it. For years, he's been part of a group helping people get out of Germany. Mostly Jews, but others too. Communists, artists, journalists. Anyone who got into trouble with the Nazis." Esther paused, looking torn. "Vincent should be telling you this."

In her mouth, Claire's sandwich had turned to sawdust. She stopped chewing. "So he left France because of something he did with this group." That would explain his sudden, late-night departure over the mountains. From her bed, she'd heard muffled voices at the bottom of the staircase, but he hadn't even waited to tell her goodbye.

"He wasn't driven out, if that's what you mean. He managed to sell most of his printing equipment. To a Vichy collaborator – you can imagine how he regrets that – but at least he didn't lose everything. Vincent's always managed to stay a step ahead. So far."

"And he came to Lisbon to forge documents?"

"He came for the same reason we all did. It's the last open gateway out of Europe. And it's where your family was to meet him. He arranged your boat tickets, you know."

Claire fingered the pouch around her neck. She hadn't known.

"Vincent knew people in Lisbon who would give him a hand," Esther continued. "And that way he could keep doing what he'd been doing in France."

Claire put down her sandwich, no longer hungry. She should

be proud of her uncle. Instead, her overwhelming sensation was that she didn't know him at all. "He likes to take risks, doesn't he?"

"Yes. But he has a big heart too."

Antonio

Antonio heard his grandmother long before he saw her. He blew out a loud, exasperated sigh. Avó's wavering voice was a shadow of what it had once been. But when she sang the *fado* – when she wasn't sick – she still filled the small square where they lived with music. A week ago, every cough had been a struggle for breath. But here she was, standing outside their doorway, head thrown back, at it again. One wrinkled hand gripped the back of a chair. The other curved grandly in front of her, projecting her presence well beyond her small frame. In the twilight, only her face stood out, a pale oval beneath a streetlamp. As always, she was clothed in black, the only color she'd worn since Antonio's grandfather died.

She saw Antonio but kept on playing to her audience. Which tonight consisted of their landlady, a toddler bouncing a ball, and two neighbors who'd pulled their kitchen chairs out onto the square to listen. She finished the song with a regal nod, and the women clapped. "More, more," one of them called.

Avó hesitated.

"Don't let me interrupt," Antonio said sarcastically.

"Respect, young man," their landlady scolded.

His grandmother lifted her chin. "I'm fine, Antonio. I wouldn't be singing if I weren't."

That wasn't the point. Avó always felt fine – until she didn't.

"Did you take your medicine?"

"I've run out," she said lightly.

"What? Why didn't you tell me?"

"Oh, stop it." His cousin's voice came from their doorway. "She feels better when she sings. Isn't that enough?"

"So speaks Miss Rita, who's never around to help when it gets bad," Antonio snapped. "What would you know?"

"Antonio!" Avó's voice was sharp. "Don't use that tone under my roof."

Antonio looked up. "We're not under anybody's roof right now," he muttered.

His grandmother gave him a stern look.

"Enjoy your singing." If nothing else, that would keep them outside longer. Antonio gave a mock bow and pushed past Rita into the dark hallway. He took the steps to the second floor two at a time and entered their dim rooms with a sniff. No matter what Avó cooked, thanks to the neighbors it always smelled like boiled cabbage and fish. And damp.

His grandmother's room was in perfect order, the narrow bed neatly made, a crucifix on the wall over the headboard. In the tiny kitchen, two pots sat on unlit burners. He sniffed again. Definitely not cod and cabbage.

Avó started singing again, more quietly now. In the living room, Antonio crouched down before the heavy wooden china cabinet that doubled as their linen closet and ran his hand under the sheets on the bottom shelf. Thomas's diary was at the back, where he'd hidden it. Antonio dropped onto the couch and ran his fingers over the tattered brown cover. Only a few pages at the end were blank. All of the others were covered in small, dense handwriting. There were bits in German, English, Portuguese. As Antonio brought it closer to the lamp, a piece of paper fell onto his lap. He unfolded it. A telegram. From France.

Dearest Thomas, it read, *The baby is due on April 5. We are excited and nervous, and hope it will arrive safely. Think of us as the day wanes, and let us know how you are.* It was signed, *Stéphane and Aurélie.*

Carefully, Antonio tucked the telegram back into the diary. Thomas's friends would never know why he hadn't sent his congratulations. He turned to the next page. It was filled with Portuguese words and pronunciation notes. A smile tugged at his mouth. These were the first phrases they'd worked on together. Antonio remembered the day he'd doubled over, shaking with laughter at something Thomas had tried to say. Thomas left the café shortly thereafter, looking dour, and Mr. Silva had given Antonio an earful for offending a customer. He'd been relieved when Thomas waved at him from his table the next day and good-naturedly asked for help.

Antonio flipped over another page. Here was a series of names, each one followed by a number and nationality. Antonio read them out loud: Janus, Caprella, Tasso, JB White. Ships, not people.

Partway down, he found a familiar one. A merchant ship sunk by a U-boat a couple of months ago. Its passengers had been rescued and brought to Lisbon. They were the lucky ones. Why Thomas had made this list was a mystery.

The next pages were in German, written hastily, as if Thomas's thoughts had raced ahead of his hand. Antonio flipped through them quickly. He'd see about deciphering them when he had more time. And better light.

Outside, Avó stopped singing. Antonio went to the window and poked his head out. In the dark square, the women were gathering up their chairs. The entertainment was over for tonight. They said their goodnights and disappeared inside. Frustrated, Antonio put the diary back in its hiding place. It hadn't told him anything. So far. Moments later, their door opened.

"What's for dinner?" Antonio asked.

Rita gave him a sour look. "Didn't you eat at the Chave d'Ouro?"

Antonio snorted. "Where'd you get that idea? And what about you? Don't you want to go home to eat?"

"I made it. I eat it," Rita said. She followed Avó into the kitchen.

"Eat. Never pay. That's your motto," Antonio grumbled under his breath. But at least when Rita came over, Avó didn't do all the work.

A few minutes later, Rita set steaming bowls on the table. Antonio leaned forward and inhaled appreciatively. Vegetable soup with a touch of coriander. The one nice thing about his cousin was that she was a decent cook. He lifted his spoon.

"Josephine Baker was in town Saturday night, singing at the *Coliseu*," Rita said.

Antonio and his grandmother looked at her blankly.

"Didn't you hear about the gala to raise money? For the victims of the cyclone a few months ago?"

"Of course," Avó said. "But who did you say was there?"

"Josephine Baker. The famous American singer." Rita looked disgusted at their ignorance. "And lots of other stars."

Antonio remembered the flyer mentioning Josephine Baker that he'd found in Thomas's room. "What about them?"

"I heard it was a spectacular evening." Rita leaned back into her chair with a sigh. "And I was this close to getting a ticket." She held up her thumb and a finger so they almost touched.

"How were you going to manage that?" Antonio asked. As far as he knew, tickets for galas weren't included in her budget.

"Vitor was going to get them. Through friends. But in the end, it didn't work out."

"Vitor?" Antonio asked. Beside him, his grandmother went still.

"Haven't I told you?" Rita ran her fingers through her hair. "I have a new beau."

"A beau," Antonio said flatly. "How wonderful. Who is it this time?"

"Don't mock me." Rita pinched her lips together.

"Mock? Me? Never." Well, not until about the fourth one. "Go on, tell all. We know you're dying to."

Rita tossed her head. "He's a keeper, this one. A policeman with a salary. And connections. He's already promised we'll go to the theater the next time an international act comes to town." She gazed contentedly into the air. "I've always dreamed of going to the theater."

Antonio finished his soup, wondering how far she'd fall this time.

"He's not married, is he?" Avó asked suddenly.

"Of course not." Rita tried to sound indignant, but she ended up sounding uncertain. "He says there's no other woman but me."

If Antonio remembered correctly, the married guy had said the same thing.

Rita took the soup bowls off the table and returned with a brick-colored dish holding duck with rice. Much more rice than duck these days, but who cared. It was still one of Antonio's favorites.

He shoveled in a mouthful, then asked, "When did you meet him?"

"He was at the hotel where I work, investigating something. With some of his men. I don't really know."

"His men, huh? He's the boss?"

Rita shifted uncomfortably. "He's part of a team, all right? I don't know who gives the orders."

"You don't know much about him at all, do you? Except that he's made you crazy promises you want to believe."

"Must you always go at each other?" Avó broke in wearily.

"Antonio, let your cousin have her happiness while she can. There's little enough of it around." She picked up her napkin, stifled a cough, and went back to eating.

Claire

Rossio Square was as animated at nine in the evening as it was during the day. A tram clanged its bell and rumbled away, the metal basket on its front looking like it would scoop up anyone in its path. Groups of people flitted in and out of the glow of the streetlights, chatting and greeting friends at the sidewalk cafés.

"Which way would you like to go?" Esther asked.

Claire shrugged. Even the brightly lit square didn't feel safe anymore. What if the men standing in the corner had killed Antonio's friend? Or the ones outside Gelo café were on the lookout for her uncle? She hooked her arm in Esther's and told herself to control her imagination.

"Have you been to the top of the Carmo elevator?"

Claire turned her attention back to Esther. "The what?"

Esther pointed toward one of Lisbon's hills. "The elevator that takes you up there, to Chiado. There's a beautiful view of Lisbon from the top."

"Really?" Claire was still thinking about her uncle. "Are you one of the people Uncle Vincent helped?"

"No. We met on a tram. Here in Lisbon." Esther started walking. "It stopped suddenly, and he wasn't holding on. He almost knocked me over."

"He didn't do it on purpose?"

Esther laughed. "Then he asked where I was from, and we started talking. I remember how normal the conversation felt, when the world around us was anything but."

"And then?"

"We crossed paths again at HICEM, some time later. He was..." She paused. "Well, you know what he was doing. When I saw him, he was surrounded by refugees, telling a wholly inappropriate joke that I won't repeat." Esther's eyes crinkled. "He had a group of very solemn men in stitches."

"Uncle Vincent, the entertainer? I've never seen that."

"Well, you should. It's something." Esther stopped. "Look. That's the elevator."

Claire leaned back, taking in the iron structure that towered above them. They waited while a cabin descended, the passengers' faces pressed against the glass. At the top, Esther led Claire to the guardrail. The streets and squares below them twinkled with light.

"That's the view I was talking about."

"It's lovely," Claire said. The castle on the hill drew her eye, then the black expanse of the river, broken by bright pinpoints from ships she couldn't see. Was the one her family was to take already there?

She turned to Esther. "Where is home, for you?"

"Antwerp, Belgium. The city of diamonds." Esther spoke wistfully. "It's lost its glitter now."

"Why do you call it that?"

"Antwerp has – or had – the biggest diamond industry in the world. I don't know now. A lot of the jewelers were Jewish."

"When did you come to Lisbon?"

"I left Belgium for Paris last May, the day after the Germans invaded." Esther tucked her hands under her arms and shivered in the light breeze. "When they attacked France, I came here."

"Alone?"

"Yes. Well, no. There were thousands of us, filling the roads with everything you can imagine. Carts and horses. Children wedged in wheelbarrows among the suitcases. Cars abandoned in the middle of everything. I had a bicycle, but it got stolen near Bordeaux." Esther's voice turned bleak. "Everything was horrible then, but losing my bicycle was especially awful."

Esther had biked from Antwerp to Bordeaux? Claire didn't know how far that was, but it was certainly hundreds of miles. She looked at Esther with new admiration. "What happened then?"

"I found other transport. Trains mostly. Sometimes they were so packed I couldn't sit down for hours. But I was glad to be away from the planes."

"What planes?"

"Herr Hitler sent the Luftwaffe after the refugees," Esther said bitterly. "They'd fly up and down the roads, shooting." She took a ragged breath. "I remember a car with mattresses tied to the roof. The first time the planes came, the people sat there, thinking they were safe. You can't imagine the carnage."

Claire shook her head. She could, but didn't want to.

"After that, as soon as we heard the motors, we'd all dive into ditches or run for shelter. Anything to get away from the road." Esther rubbed her temples tiredly. "I know we shouldn't forget — for the sake of those who have died, if nothing else — but remembering takes its own toll."

The breeze was picking up. It did nothing to blow the ugly images out of Claire's head. "Didn't you have any family?"

"I have a younger brother. Arthur." Esther spoke with unexpected force, as if saying it made it true. "He's in the Belgian army."

"But the Belgian army…"

"No longer exists. I know." Esther wrapped her hands tightly around the top of the guardrail. "He made me promise I'd leave Belgium if anything happened. I kept that promise, but some days I hate myself for it."

"You don't know where he is?"

"I had a neighbor whose son served with him. She sent word that her son had escaped to Britain, but that most of their regiment had been captured. I've written to everyone I can think of, but it's been one dead end after another."

"I'm so sorry." Feeling awkward, Claire put her arms around Esther and hugged. "You can't give up hope." The words were as much for herself as for Esther. Her parents had to arrive soon. They just had to.

A gust of wind hit them from the side, blowing her hair into her face. Claire turned her head, trying to brush it away, and jumped. A man was standing beside her against the railing, so close that their shoulders almost touched. Claire had been so focused on Esther's story that she hadn't even sensed him. The man brought a cigarette to his lips and gazed out over the river, seemingly oblivious to their presence. Claire wondered what he'd heard.

"Let's walk." Claire tucked her hand under Esther's elbow and gave her a nudge. As they crossed the elevated walkway into Chiado, Claire peeked over her shoulder. To her relief, the man hadn't moved. She shook her head. After two days in Lisbon, she was edgier than she'd ever been in Marseille.

The road from Chiado to Rossio was mostly downhill. Esther walked in silence, her well of stories seemingly emptied. Her hand was on the door of the boarding house when she stopped abruptly. "I'd promised you a coffee."

"That's all right. Another time." Claire wanted to be inside, away from prying eyes, imaginary or otherwise. She pulled the door shut behind her. "What are your plans now?" she asked as they climbed the stairs.

"What? Tonight?"

"No. I mean, are you coming to America with us?"

"I need to stay here and try to find Arthur. I promised myself I wouldn't leave Europe without him."

"But…"

"And I have work to do here. That's important too."

"But what about you and Uncle Vincent?"

"That's something we'll have to work out." She met Claire's questioning gaze. "I don't have a choice."

"Can't you write letters from anywhere?" Claire pressed as Esther fumbled with the key to their rooms. "You don't have to be in Lisbon."

"It's my decision, all right? And all the talk in the world won't change it." She opened the door and looked at the clock on the wall with a frown. "I hope Vincent comes home soon."

Antonio

"Thanks for dinner." Antonio pushed away from the table and pecked Avó and Rita on their cheeks. "I'm going out."

"Out? You work tonight?"

"I won't be late." Antonio ignored the reprimand in his grandmother's voice. She was always trying to keep him and Rita in the same room, hoping they'd start to get along. He grabbed his beret and took off down the stairs. There was nowhere he needed to be. But hanging around while they pulled their chairs close to the staticky radio and gossiped? No thanks.

The street was full of the noises of Lisbon. Pans clanged in the kitchen of a corner restaurant. On its terrace, men argued over soccer. Antonio climbed upward, passing a building where a baby cried. Further on, a woman scolded someone. Her husband or a naughty child, Antonio couldn't tell which.

He soon reached a place where the city butted up against the base of the massive wall surrounding São Jorge's castle. It was one of his favorite spots, where he could sit undisturbed. His gaze roved over the city, wondering where in the patches of dark and light Claire was. In a single afternoon, she'd gone from angry to sad to aloof to approachable to laughing. Refugees' moods reflected the instability of their lives, Thomas had told him once. That was certainly true for her.

She was different from any girl he'd known before, and he wanted more. Not just for the fun of the chase, although that was part of it. No point lying to himself. He'd like to touch her. But it was more than that. Each time he looked at her, there was a spark behind her tentative smile that pulled him in. If he had to explain it, he'd say it was courage and a charm she didn't seem to be aware of herself.

A car horn below drew his attention downtown. Thomas should be there now, massacring the Portuguese language over a beer in the Chave d'Ouro. Antonio shook himself impatiently. He should be thinking more about his friend, not about a girl who would be leaving in a few days. He thought back to Saturday evening. Mr. Silva didn't know anything more — or wouldn't talk. Antonio wasn't sure which, but there never seemed to be a good time to corner him. Mr. Thaler certainly had something to do with it, but what? Antonio slid off the wall. There were no answers up here.

Ten minutes later, he was in the tobacco shop on Rossio Square.

"Remember the other night, when that German refugee got kidnapped?" he asked the cashier as soon as the store was empty of customers. "Did you see what happened?"

"Less than you did, son."

"Have you heard anything though? People must be talking about it."

"Of course. But it's all wild stories and speculation." A bell jangled as a new customer walked in. "Excuse me," the man said, and went to help her.

Antonio stepped back onto the sidewalk. Rossio was filled with cafés and shops. Someone had to have seen or heard something he hadn't. He headed a few doors down to Café Gelo.

"You're on our turf, Antonio," one of the waiters lounging

outside the door called out mockingly. "Better watch out. Unless you're looking for a better job?"

From the bosses to the dishwashers, the Chave d'Ouro and Gelo were rivals. But tonight, Antonio bit back his sarcastic retort.

"What do you know about that refugee who got picked up the other night?"

"The dead one?"

"Yeah."

"Dunno. I heard he criticized the Nazis once too often, and too loudly," the waiter said.

"Nah. That wasn't it," another broke in. "Some guy was asking around to see if he came in here, and when I said yes, he asked if he'd ever done anything suspicious. Like he was a spy or something."

"What guy?"

"One of those fellows who sometimes works with Bruno."

"Bruno?"

"The PVDE guy. The one who trips everybody up."

Antonio knew who he meant. The man who'd been in the café with Mr. Thaler the other evening, who stuck his legs out into the aisles on purpose. A busy waiter's nightmare. "Did he ask anything else?"

"Just personal stuff. Did he have family, things I couldn't answer." The waiter shrugged. "He seemed pretty solitary. Why do you care?"

"Doesn't it bother you that someone can get picked up off the streets in Lisbon and killed?"

"I'd watch out if I were you," the waiter warned. "Snooping can be a dangerous business."

"What does that mean?"

"Just that you don't want to end up like him."

"I won't. Did you really get the impression he was snooping around?"

"I don't know. Try asking your boss. He was in here talking to mine, and they both seemed pretty worked up about it."

"I will." People who like to talk had no useful information. He should know that by now. Antonio walked away, wondering if someone had already been in the Chave d'Ouro, asking about Thomas. He shuddered. No one wanted to be questioned by Portugal's secret police.

He turned into the street that ran alongside the Dona Maria Theater. It was crammed. A show must have just gotten out. Antonio stared through the window of a fancy restaurant, the kind Rita dreamed of frequenting, then turned his attention to the well-dressed crowd on the street. Especially their feet. It was second nature now. Even when no stealing was involved.

A man reeking of alcohol bumped into him, then staggered forward into a woman. The woman's companion shoved the drunk off, and he lurched away. Beside the woman's sturdy heel, something glittered. Casually, Antonio knelt behind her and cupped his hand over the fallen earring.

An instant later, a hand grabbed his collar and jerked him upright. Its owner, a jowly, red-faced man, held him at arm's length. Keeping his fists closed, Antonio tried to shove him away. The man didn't let go. Beside him, a woman wearing a single golden earring trembled with indignation. Two couples with them glared. Six to one. Antonio tried to look innocent.

"What are you up to, cub?" The man shook him like a captured rat. "Check you have everything," he told his friends. The women drew their purses closer as the men patted their suit pockets.

"I'm not doing anything, sir," Antonio said, as politely as he could manage. He'd intended, for once, to return what he'd picked up to its owner. They'd changed his mind for him. "Just tying my shoe."

"Do it somewhere else." The man released him with a shove. All six of them radiated hostility. "You don't belong here."

"A good evening to you too," Antonio backed away, not caring if they caught the sarcasm. The gold earring was his, and he was out of there.

He pushed his way to where the crowd thinned, then turned into a narrow side street. In a recessed doorway that smelled of urine he stopped and felt in his pocket. The earring had to be worth more than a few *escudos*. Further down the alley, he heard two men arguing. Antonio peered out from the doorway. A gentleman in a tie who looked like he belonged to the theater crowd was nose-to-nose with a thickset man in workman's clothes.

"No, I won't," the well-dressed one said in French. "It's the stupidest thing I've ever heard."

"It's the best place. No one will poke around there."

"And I want to keep it that way. Rossio teems with people, night and day. Nothing goes upstairs without the concierge seeing it. Not to mention the risk if something goes wrong."

"Nothing will," the heavyset man said. "They're not even assembled. And there's lots of small stuff you could take. Timers. Wires. It's better not to keep it all in one place anyway."

Antonio backed farther into the recess. This conversation wasn't meant for him.

"Tell him to use the gallery. There's space there."

The heavyset man barked a laugh. "Talk about having too many people around. And a locked storehouse door won't stop anyone if they really want in. That's not a solution."

"I've got little enough room as it is, and other people living with me. Tell him I'm not taking it."

"This isn't the end of the conversation."

"It is for me. That's not the kind of help I promised." The well-dressed man turned and started up the alley. A few steps more and he'd see Antonio, and know he'd heard.

Merda.

Quickly, Antonio tried the door. It was locked. He pulled out his key and jingled it over the doorknob, his back to the street. Slowly, he straightened and turned, steadying himself against the wall. The well-dressed man was standing a couple of yards away, eying him warily.

"Whadayawant?" Antonio slurred in Portuguese. He took an unsteady step forward, then another.

Surprise flickered over the man's face. "Do you need assistance?" he asked. In English.

"*O que?*" Antonio wasn't falling into that trap. "Need a drink," he mumbled, still in Portuguese. He burped and wove away, humming tunelessly. At the far end of the street, he looked back. The man had disappeared into the crowd. He shook his shoulders, trying to ease their tension. Maybe he had more of the spy in him than he thought.

New attacks by the Royal Air Force on
Brest, Calais and Ostend

Diário de Notícias
April 8, 1941

CHAPTER 7 – TUESDAY, APRIL 8

A CHURCH BELL rang midnight. Claire twisted on the lumpy couch, unable to find a comfortable position. Sleep was impossible. Uncle Vincent still hadn't come home, and Esther paced and paced.

Claire sat up. "Do you want to read something?" If she had a rope, she'd seriously consider tying Esther down.

"No."

"Shall I turn on the radio?"

"No."

"Do you want to talk?"

"No."

Claire gave up. "I'm going for a walk."

Esther's eyes flew to the clock. "Not at this time of night, you aren't."

"I need some air." And time alone.

"No."

"You can't tell me what to do."

"Please, Claire. You can't." Esther's voice cracked. "It's not safe for your uncle, much less for a girl alone."

Claire knew she was right, but got to her feet anyway. "I'll stay inside the boarding house. I just can't lie here anymore."

Esther regarded her apprehensively. "Promise?"

"Promise."

Reluctantly, Esther nodded. Claire let herself out and started along the quiet hallway. None of the other inhabitants seemed to be stirring. Claire followed the corridor that ran from the front to the back of the building, passing the kitchen, toilets, and bathrooms that served everyone on their floor. A right turn led to a longer corridor with more rooms.

She hadn't met any of their neighbors yet. There were a couple of families, and a man from Poland whose heavy tread she recognized every time he passed their door. Thinking of him, she tried to step lightly on the threadbare carpet. The windowless hallways of the boarding house formed an angular horseshoe, and she'd already paced two-thirds of it.

Claire turned around at the end of the corridor and started back. What to do now? The other floors were equally airless, equally claustrophobic. As she passed the kitchen, a hint of freshness touched her skin and she heard a soft flapping sound. She looked inside. At this hour of the night, the cooking fire had died out, leaving the room dark and cool. She went inside, holding her hands out so she wouldn't bump into the rough stone sink. A faint light came from behind it.

The narrow glass door that Claire had noticed before was ajar. She stepped over its low sill into the rooftop patio. Laundry hung from lines strung head-high — sheets and towels, outerwear and undergarments. The breeze blew damp, clean-smelling fabric against her face. She pushed it out of her way and moved further in. At the center was a low platform. Claire tested it with a finger, then sat down. It was clean, probably used for folding and sorting. Fatigue washed through her, bringing with it troubling images of passports and airplanes and a blinding white beach.

She was glad she hadn't told Uncle Vincent and Esther about Estoril. They'd be horrified. And there was no way she could talk to them about the emotions that flooded her each time she thought about Antonio. She needed to find Eleanor, she thought sleepily. She ached for someone to confide in. Claire lay back and looked at the stars.

The next thing she knew, her back had gone stiff on the hard concrete. Her eyes popped open. What time was it? Claire scrambled to her feet.

Esther yanked the door open as soon as she knocked. "It's after one-thirty in the morning," she snapped. "Where have you been? I searched all over."

"I'm sorry. I was in the patio off the kitchen."

"You should have let me know." Esther sat down on a chair she'd pulled up to the window. Her foot tapped nervously.

"I dozed off," Claire admitted sheepishly. "Uncle Vincent isn't back yet?"

"No."

Claire resumed her place on the couch. "Why don't you go to bed, Esther? He'll be here before you know it."

"I can't. I just can't." There was an edge of panic in her voice.

"What's wrong?"

"Nothing. I just can't help worrying."

"He'll be home soon." Claire curled into a ball. There was something they hadn't told her.

At the window, Esther continued her silent vigil. Claire blinked and tried to stay awake. But sleep came, and with it a dream, Vincent winking into view and calling her, then disappearing into darkness.

Lisbon's eternal sunshine woke her in the morning, thrusting through the window like a solid, heavy weight. It was too cheerful. Claire rubbed her eyes, scowling, and pushed her blanket off her legs. The room was empty. No Esther, no Vincent. Anxiety clawed her. What if something had happened to him?

In stocking feet, Claire tiptoed to the bedroom door and listened. There was no sound. Carefully she turned the knob and peeked inside. Esther and Vincent were entwined on the bed, sleeping. Claire sagged against the wall. Her uncle was safe, and apparently no worse for the wear. The worries of the night before had been just that – worries, and nothing more.

Claire went out for bread and was at the table, serving herself still-warm slices with jam, when Esther and Vincent emerged a while later.

"You were out late, Uncle," Claire said.

"Not really, by Lisbon's standards. But I'm sorry if I made you two fret." He squeezed Esther's hand. "Do I smell coffee?"

"Was it worth it?" Claire asked.

"What?"

"Going out last night? Was it worth associating with people Esther can't bear to be around?"

"It's always useful." Vincent sat down. "Can you pass me the bread please?"

"Useful how?"

"Must you always ask so many questions?" he said as Esther brought over two coffee cups.

Claire stared at him and waited.

Vincent sighed. "All right. What did I learn? Let's see. The deputy Portuguese police chief isn't at all discreet about his new girlfriend. His wife looked like she wanted to skewer him all evening long. Mr. Thaler, a slippery fellow who wants people to believe he works at the German Legation but is really with the Gestapo, is horribly anxious about something, and I'd love to know what. But he's a close-mouthed bastard, even after a few drinks." Vincent looked thoughtful.

"Oh, and since rumors have it that Hitler is about to invade Portugal, the talk among refugees was all about plane tickets and departure schedules and U-boats attacking the shipping lanes. People are afraid to go, but even more afraid to stay." Vincent looked at Claire over the rim of his coffee cup. "Is that report satisfactory?"

Claire gave a curt nod. "You're sure no one knows what you are doing?" She knew from school that the gossiping hordes were always curious. "Who do people think you are?"

Vincent put down his cup. "I'm a small-town French businessman. Interesting but superficial. No one to think about twice."

"That works?"

"It has so far." He lifted his cup again, and stared at the newspaper it had been sitting on. "What's this?"

"Oh, nothing." Claire picked up the paper she'd scribbled on the night before. "Doodles."

Vincent took it from her. "Wait." He studied the signature she'd copied and started to laugh. "I think your strengths lie elsewhere."

"It's a first try," Claire protested.

"And a last, I hope. This is a signature few would dare to forge."

Claire looked at him questioningly.

"It's Salazar's. Portugal's prime minister." He was still smiling.

"Oh." Claire crossed her arms across her chest. "It was just something to do. While we waited."

"Don't be embarrassed. But I wouldn't advise doing it again."

Antonio

Avó had coughed through the night. In the morning, lying on his back on the thin mattress behind the couch, Antonio twirled the earring, imagining how much it might bring in.

"Do you want me to stay?" he asked at breakfast.

Avó shook her head. "I'm fine, and I know you have things to do." The circles around her eyes were darker than usual, but she waved him out the door with a smile. He slung the drawing tube over his back, tapped his pocket to make sure the earring was inside, and headed to the only shop he knew would buy just about anything.

The owner held the piece of jewelry to the light, squinted at it, then pulled out his magnifying glass and looked again. "It's not real gold."

"What?"

"Look at the scratch. It's gray below the gold. Looks expensive, but it's all for show."

Merda. "You'll still give me something for it, won't you?"

"Got the other one?"

"No."

"Don't know what I can do without the pair."

"It must be worth something." Anything, as long as he had enough to buy some cough medicine.

"A few *centavos.* That's the offer. I'm not a charity."

Antonio nodded grimly. He wanted to kick the counter. "Fine." Anywhere else, he'd get less. He pocketed the coins, picked up the smallest vial of cough medicine the pharmacy sold, and took it to Avó. He made her take it as he watched. Then he headed toward Alcântara, where the big ships docked.

It wasn't long before he found what he was looking for. An immense grey hull with *Serpa Pinto* painted in black letters on its side. It was the first passenger ship to leave this week, bound for New York. A long metal gangway linked the quay to the ship's upper deck. Beside the gate, hundreds of people waited among mounded suitcases. They were eerily quiet, considering how many they were. Uniformed policemen were posted around them at loose intervals.

To one side sat a low cart piled with bags and trunks, some of them held shut with lengths of rope. Antonio climbed onto it and looked over the crowd. Around him, children played hide and seek among the suitcases and parcels. A man who was anxiously watching the gate ordered them to be still. The children flopped down on the suitcases and sulked until he turned his back, then started playing again. Further in, sharp-eyed men with no luggage wove methodically back and forth through the crowd. Definitely not refugees. Antonio dropped down so he was lying flat. Did someone really want to sink this ship? With so many people on it?

"Get off, son. Gotta get this on board." A dock worker took the cart's handle. Antonio jumped down and pushed into the crowd. He smelled a baby's dirty bottom, a sweet pastry, sweat. Unwashed clothes. And fear.

He had no idea what he'd tell the parents of the little girls in white if he found them. That they shouldn't leave because of an alarming rumor? After all they'd gone through to get here? They'd never take him seriously.

The ship's whistle blew. The gate screeched open and ticket-takers stationed themselves beyond it, behind a long table. With a ripple of anticipation, the refugees around Antonio gathered up their luggage and pressed forward, carrying him with them.

"Boarding first class," one of the ticket-takers called, and from a small building to Antonio's right came a pack of elegantly dressed passengers. A small army of porters followed them. They swept past the refugees, caught in an ever-compacting mob. Someone's elbow jabbed Antonio in the ribs, and the sharp corner of a suitcase scraped his shin. There was nothing he could do here. He turned to leave and stepped on a woman's foot.

"Excuse me." He backed away and knocked over a little boy. "Sorry." He pulled the child to his feet, then escaped to the fringes of the crowd. Clumps of passengers were wiping away tears and offering last goodbye kisses.

Antonio leaned against an outbuilding, wondering if Gray could – or would – do anything if he knew. First class had finished boarding and now the refugees filed steadily up the gangway. Halfway up, a small child in white stopped and waved, its head barely visible above the guardrail. Antonio squinted, trying to see if he recognized anyone.

Near him, a family waved back, calling, "*Au revoir, petit Antoine. Bon voyage.*" It wasn't the little girl after all.

At the gate, the crowd shifted, and two familiar faces appeared. The two men from the train were there, scrutinizing every person who went through. Antonio put a tearful women and her husband between the men and himself. If they were here, their plan to sink the ship must be for real. And was probably already underway. Anger coursed through him. Who were they looking for now?

The last passengers filed through the gate and the ticket-takers pulled it closed. The men from the train left, scowling. He'd guess they hadn't found who they wanted. But neither had Antonio. Minutes later, dockworkers wheeled the gangway away from the ship. Another sharp whistle sounded, and a tugboat slowly pulled the ship away from its mooring. On the upper deck, passengers waved, or cried, or cheered. In their place, Antonio didn't know how he'd react. They'd escaped the war, but now were leaving behind everything that was familiar to travel across an ocean dotted with U-boats. He didn't think he'd handle it too well. Especially if he had the slightest suspicion that danger lurked not only outside his ship, but within.

Claire

"Here's our first stop." Vincent nodded at a corner shop on the hill ahead of them. Newspapers and magazines in various languages hung on a rack outside the door. Claire recognized a few of the French ones. A bell tinkled as Vincent opened the door, and a stooped old man with tufts of white hair above his ears appeared from a back room. He raised equally white eyebrows at Claire.

"*Bom dia,*" Vincent said. He opened his satchel and laid it on the counter. "Been busy?"

"The usual. Too many people who don't pay on time. You'll be wanting *The Times*?"

"Indeed."

The shopkeeper disappeared into a back room, and Claire let

her eyes wander around the shop. Pencils, paints, pens, a few books, and all kinds of art supplies lined heavy wooden shelves. Printed business cards and advertisements were displayed under the glass counter. Claire leaned over to peer at a collection of faded invitations with fancy lettering.

The shopkeeper reappeared with a folded newspaper, rang up the sale, and took Vincent's coin. The bell tinkled as another customer walked in.

"Thank you," Vincent said. He put the newspaper in his satchel. The two men shook hands, and Vincent ushered Claire out the door. "You need to pay more attention," he said mildly.

"Sorry?"

Vincent glanced over his shoulder, then continued. "There are minor things that can be done with the equipment I've got. Most need the capabilities of a full print shop. Understand?"

"So you said." She knew there was more to forging documents than stamps and photos and signatures. "He's your printer, isn't he?"

"Mine?" Vincent gave a short laugh. "He's the refugees' printer. But hopefully none of them will ever know it." Vincent walked in silence for a moment, then said, "So now you see how a pick-up can be made."

"Pick-up?" Claire gaped at him. Of course. The newspaper on the counter.

"That's why I said you need to pay attention." Her uncle's expression was serious. "Because even if you don't, others will, and they're the ones who will ask questions that could get us into trouble."

Claire nodded, amazed that her uncle was confiding in her. Especially after his reluctance to tell her about the forgeries in the first place. She pushed her apprehensions aside. "Was that only a pick-up? Or was it a drop-off too?"

Vincent smiled. "Not this time. But you're catching on." They climbed the Avenida da Liberdade until they reached the neighborhood where HICEM was located. Vincent stopped in front of a café. "Let's get a drink."

"I thought we were going to HICEM."

"You're in a hurry?"

"I promised to spend some time with those children. Serge and Alicia." Claire paused. "Can you imagine Frédéric in their situation? Here without us? He'd be terribly lost."

"Ah, yes. That's true. But work first. You can go to HICEM later."

Inside, the café was small and crowded. Paint flaked off the wooden tables. A couple of customers nursed their drinks, keeping to themselves. Vincent took a seat in a back corner. Claire brushed crumbs off a chair and sat beside him.

"Two coffees," he ordered, and started talking casually about the weather. His gaze, though, roamed the café, inside and out. Were they supposed to meet someone? Claire watched him, wondering if anything he said or did was a signal. If so, she wasn't seeing it.

"Relax," Vincent said under his breath. "We're having a nice morning outing, right? Act like it."

She sat back and forced a smile. "But it isn't just a nice morning, is it? It's something more."

"Patience. You'll see soon enough."

Bit by bit, the noise level rose as the café filled up. A couple slid into seats nearby and held hands across the table.

A man bumped into Claire's chair as he and another fellow settled in on their left. "Excuse me, miss," he said politely.

She scooted her seat closer to her uncle. Vincent had taken the newspaper out of his bag and was scribbling notes in the margins as he read. Moments later, a wafer-thin woman pushed open the café door and threaded her way through the tables toward them.

Vincent glanced up, then half-rose to greet her. "Hello Sara," he said. "Claire, you remember Sara, don't you?"

Vincent was nodding at her. Claire nodded back uncertainly.

"It's a pleasure to see you again, my dear." Sara kissed Claire lightly on both cheeks. The light scent of jasmine enveloped her. "You've certainly grown into a beautiful young woman."

"Um, thank you." She could play this game. "It's nice to see you too."

"Please, sit down," Vincent said, and they began talking about people Claire had never heard of, leaning into each other to be heard over the noise of the café. Was he suspicious of someone? Claire scanned the room as discreetly as she could. Vincent's body language didn't give her a single clue. If this was showing her the ropes, he wasn't doing a very good job of it. Assuming that's what he was doing. She really didn't know.

A few minutes later, after the two men had tossed back their tiny cups of coffee and left, Vincent straightened up in his chair.

Sara tapped the newspaper under his arm. "Are you done with this?"

Vincent slid it toward her. "You can have it."

"Thank you," Sara said, and glanced at the clock above the counter. "Oh my. I didn't realize what time it was."

"Not to worry. You've got at least two hours before the film begins."

"I know, but I have things to do." Without unfolding the paper, Sara put it in her purse and stood up. "I hope we'll see each other again soon, Claire." She gave them each a light kiss and was gone. Beside Claire, Vincent stayed on high alert. As far as Claire could tell, no one had followed Sara out.

"Could you do that?" Vincent asked.

Claire nodded. "I…I think so." If that was a drop-off, it didn't look that difficult.

Vincent raised an eyebrow. "Really?"

He tossed some coins on the table and pulled Claire up with him. They were far down the Avenida before he spoke again. "What do you think happened in there?"

"You gave Sara the documents you picked up at the shop," Claire answered confidently.

"No."

Sara had taken the newspaper. "What did you give her then?"

"The drop-off time and place."

"But…" She'd never had to think about it before. "Why didn't she take the documents now? Wasn't that the plan?"

"If you had that thought, so might others. Would you have handed them over?"

"Probably," Claire admitted.

Vincent shook his head. "It's not safe. Too many people around. The only thing I give her here is information."

"But weren't the people in the café refugees? Who you're helping?"

"There are spies even among the refugees. I told you before — caution everywhere."

"Was there someone you didn't like the look of?"

"A couple of people. But mostly a lot of unknowns. I'm not risking the documents — or myself."

"So you're going to meet her at the cinema in a couple of hours?"

"Close. Two hours is right. The location is in the newspaper."

"It must be urgent."

"This time it is."

"Do you know the people whose documents you work on?"

"Not usually. I avoid direct contact. They have no idea how to behave, what precautions to take." He stopped under one of the trees lining the avenue. "Listen, Claire, I need to run some errands right now. Why don't you go find Esther?"

"I'd rather go with you." With Uncle Vincent beside her, it wasn't hard to be brave. And she wanted to see the handover.

"Not this time."

"Why not? You brought me this far."

"It isn't convenient. Besides, didn't you want to go to HICEM?"

"I'll just watch. I won't do anything."

"Maybe another time. All right?"

He'd opened a door, then shut it in her face. She understood why. But she was smarter than he thought, and a fast learner. She just had to find a way to prove it.

Antonio

His drawing tube bumping against his back, Antonio jogged most of the way to the Praça do Comércio. He'd left the *Serpa Pinto* and the two men far behind, but not the voice in his head that kept telling him to do something. But what? He wasn't going near the police. And at the shipping company, they'd ask too many questions – and then maybe call in the police anyway.

Sun filled the square. Around him refugees strolled aimlessly, looking but buying little in the shops under the arcades, idling at a café, or lining up at the post office. Antonio sensed their frustration at being stuck in Lisbon, but at least they weren't on the *Serpa Pinto*. Staying neutral – it hadn't helped anyone Antonio knew. Not Thomas. Or the *Serpa Pinto* passengers. And his own prime minister was letting it happen.

He rubbed his temples. After his bad luck with the earring, now would be a good time to sell some portraits. Too bad he didn't feel like it. At the river's edge, he sat down, little waves slapping below his feet like reminders of everything that was wrong. Avó. *Slap.* Thomas. *Slap.* The *Serpa Pinto. Slap.*

Carefully, he slid paper out of the drawing tube and fingered his pencil, taking comfort in its slim solidity. He didn't know why, but drawing often slotted his thoughts into order without him even realizing it. Nothing else did that – or gave him the power to draw the world as he wanted it to be. He began to outline the looming stern of the *Serpa Pinto*, its passengers pressed against the rail, in the bottom left corner. The two angry plotters and a ticket-taker emerged at the top right. Across from them, an elderly woman cried a goodbye. Angling up from the bottom right to the center was the gangway, a child's hand waving above the rail.

Antonio finished and examined the drawing. It was as disjointed as he felt. He stared across the river. A transatlantic crossing took a week or so. Until then, he'd scour the papers, like Thomas had, and hope there'd be no news of the *Serpa Pinto*. Antonio turned back to the square, and saw Gray crossing it. The sabotage man. Could telling him make a difference? Or was it an unnecessary risk? Antonio followed the Englishman with his eyes, considering. When Gray noticed him, Antonio beckoned.

"Antonio." Gray squatted at his side. "I didn't know you drew. Have you had lessons?"

"Would you even know if I had? Are you really an art dealer?"

"I am."

Antonio shot him a skeptical look.

Gray studied the drawing again. "This is quite good. How did you learn?"

"When I was little, someone gave me a box of colored pencils, and I decorated all of our walls." He'd gotten a beating for it, but the memory of the first time he'd drawn with wild abandon was still a good one. That he was sharing it surprised him. "After that, my mother gave me every scrap of paper she could get her hands on. I never stopped sketching."

"Well, you've certainly developed a good eye for detail," Gray said thoughtfully. He studied the sketches again. "You watched the *Serpa* leave?"

Antonio nodded.

Gray pointed at the men flanking the gate. "Who's that?"

Antonio didn't answer for a long moment. Now or never. "If something happens to the ship, they're the ones responsible."

"What?"

"I overheard them in the train the other day. They said they'd hired someone to sink it."

Gray had gone still. "Do you know why?"

"Because it was carrying war materials, not just refugees."

"They didn't realize you were listening?"

"I'm not stupid."

"I wasn't suggesting that. But they didn't recognize you today, did they?"

"No. They were looking for someone. Whom I'm guessing they didn't find. They seemed pretty mad when the gate closed."

"Have you told anyone what you heard?"

"Who would believe me? Half the people in this town are plotting things that will never happen."

"Do you want to walk?" Gray stood up and offered Antonio a hand. "Moving targets are harder to hit."

"What does that mean?"

"It's just an expression. Shall we?"

Antonio checked the angle of the sun. "I work this afternoon."

"And you will." Gray took a path that led them under the arcades. "We could help each other, I think."

"In what way?" Antonio said warily. "I asked you for help once, and you said no."

"Perhaps I spoke too hastily." Gray paused and leaned against a column, weighing his words. "Mr. Schiller's death probably wasn't a random killing."

"Even I know that," Antonio said. "What else do you know? Who did it?"

"This isn't the time or the place to talk. But we could use your talents. And in return, I'll let you know what we discover about Mr. Schiller."

Antonio stared at him. If Gray was serious, the offer had just become much more interesting. "Talents?"

Gray jerked his chin in the direction of the river. "Your drawing, for starters. You can sketch the German ships that come up to Lisbon. And you're perceptive. What you saw today, for instance, can be more useful than you realize."

"Why are you so sure I'd want to help you?"

"I saw you the night Mr. Schiller was taken. If your sympathies lay elsewhere, you wouldn't have reacted as you did."

Merda. Everyone in the Chave d'Ouro had been shaken. His reaction hadn't been that unusual. "First things first. Do you have a way to warn the *Serpa Pinto?*"

"Maybe."

"What do you mean, maybe?"

Gray gave a brusque nod. "Are you with us or not?"

"Does my answer change whether you'll try to save the ship?"

"No, it doesn't," snapped Gray. "Stop playing games."

"I'm not," Antonio retorted. Joining Gray might help him find out why Thomas was killed. He needed to know. But a wrong step, and he'd have the PVDE all over him. It wasn't a game at all. "What you're asking isn't easy."

"I won't ask again."

The first time he had, Antonio hadn't known Thomas was dead. Now he did. And if he didn't like what was happening in his city, this was his chance to do something. As long as Gray kept his part of the deal too.

Antonio took a deep breath. "I'm in."

CHAPTER 8

CLAIRE LEFT HER uncle and retraced her steps toward HICEM. The café was still bustling when she passed. It didn't seem like a good place for a meeting between people who had something to hide. Uncle Vincent must have his reasons, but he hadn't shared them with her.

"Claire?" someone called, and she turned. Gina, the woman with red lipstick who worked with Esther at the aid agency, was coming up behind her. "Are you going to HICEM?"

Claire nodded.

"Good. So am I." They fell into step along the shaded avenue. "Do you live near here?"

"Just up there." Gina waved a hand toward a street on their left. "Second building, second floor, second window on the Praça da Alegria. Happiness Square. An ironic name, given the circumstances." Her painted lips turned down momentarily. "How are you finding Lisbon?"

"Unexpected," Claire said, then bit her tongue. So much for her uncle's warning not to invite conversation with someone she hardly knew.

"In what way?"

"Well, I saw a dead man being pulled out of the river the day after I got here. That was definitely unexpected."

"And unpleasant," Gina added.

"Very." Claire gave her a small smile. "And of course I thought I'd be here with my family. So that's unexpected too." She'd been in Lisbon for four days and there was still no word from them. Her chest tightened. She changed the subject. "Are you a refugee too?"

Gina nodded. "From the Netherlands."

"How long have you been here?"

"Longer than I'd like." Gina paused and seemed to steel herself, her gaze focused far into the distance. "My sister isn't well. No country will take in someone who's sick."

"I'm sorry."

"Everyone is sorry about something these days, it seems. Hopefully she'll be well enough to travel soon." They reached HICEM. Gina's drawn expression didn't change. "Meanwhile, there's always a lot of work to be done here."

They found Esther sitting at a table in a big, plain reception room on the second floor, sorting through a stack of correspondence. Three closed doors led off it.

"Claire, what are you doing here?" Esther looked from her to Gina. "I thought you," she hesitated, "were busy."

"Vincent had some errands to run, so I came to see if you can help me find Serge and Alicia."

"Who?"

"The children who came with us from the station the other day. Whose parents were taken off the train, remember?"

"Um…yes. I don't know where they are now though."

"Can you check? In your register?"

"Here it is." Gina had already pulled out the thick ledger where HICEM staff logged the names of the refugees as they arrived. Claire opened it and stared. There were hundreds of names, followed by nationalities, ID numbers, and addresses.

"Let me do it." Esther nudged Claire aside and flipped toward the back. "When did they arrive?"

"The day after I did. April 6."

Esther turned another page and ran her finger down the list of names. "I don't see them here." She paused. "Let me check with the director." She took the register and disappeared into one of the offices.

"You saw them, didn't you?" Claire asked Gina.

Gina sat down and continued Esther's sorting. "I wasn't with you then, remember? I'd taken another family directly to their boarding house. Lucky them — they're taking a ship to Brazil later this week. Almost no one leaves Lisbon that quickly."

The door to the side office opened and Esther reappeared without the ledger. "The children aren't registered here. They must have been moved elsewhere." She crossed her arms over her chest. "I'm sure they're in good hands. I wouldn't worry if I were you."

"I'm sure they are, but I promised to go see them. Can't you find out who took them?"

"We're busy here right now. Can we talk about it later?" Esther's usually calm voice was tight.

"But..."

Esther shifted so her back was to Gina, and gave Claire a hard stare. "Later, all right?" The words were almost inaudible.

"Later...is fine," Claire said reluctantly. Getting her family to Lisbon, wrapping her arms around her little brother – those things she couldn't control, and it made her crazy. But taking care of Serge and Alicia was something she could do. Something worthwhile and needed. She couldn't expect Esther to understand. But her attitude clearly said *stop pushing*. So Claire would, for now. "Is there anything I can help you with?"

"Now that Gina's here, I'll be off to visit a refugee who is having a hard time coping. You can come with me."

Claire hesitated. "I don't know anything about..."

The main office door opened with a bang, making all three of them startle. A big man in dark clothes entered. Behind her hand, Gina mouthed "secret police." The room suddenly felt much smaller.

"Can I help you?" Esther's face had become a pale, polite mask.

The man held a piece of paper out to Esther. "I need to know how many of these people are registered here."

Esther took the list and ran her eyes down it. "Certainly. If you could just wait a moment..." She went back into the director's office and shut the door.

Claire circled the table to sit beside Gina, keeping her head down. After spending the morning with Uncle Vincent and his forgeries, she didn't want to be on the receiving end of any questions about refugees.

A minute passed, then two. Gina kept going through the papers, passing each one to Claire with a muttered command: "To file. To answer." Claire smoothed them out, more than was necessary, and placed them in neat piles. The man stamped around, then stared pointedly at the clock on the wall. He gave an irritated grunt, paced back across the room, and grunted again. His face was turning red. Finally he banged on the office door.

Almost immediately, Esther emerged, closing it swiftly behind her. "Here you are, sir." She held the list out to him. "I'm sorry it took so long. The register is not alphabetical. I've put a cross beside the names I found."

His eyes bulged. He leaned over her. *"Idiota!"*

Esther flinched.

"I need to know where they're staying, woman!" he thundered into her face. "The addresses!"

"Oh dear." Esther's expression was remorseful. "Why didn't you say so? I'll go look them up." She made a move toward the director's office.

The man grabbed her arm. "No you don't. You're not disappearing again. Bring that register out here. I'll look at it myself."

"Of course."

Claire hoped she was the only one who caught the tremor in Esther's voice.

Esther shook off the man's hand and knocked on the director's door, then pushed it ajar. "Julien, could you please bring me the register?" She didn't go inside.

A boy came out with the book in his arms.

"Thank you." Esther took it. "You can go now."

The boy thumped down the stairs without a word.

"Give me that." The man reached for the book.

"Wait." Esther placed it on the desk and opened it to a page near the end. "Your names start about here, I think." She ran her finger down the page. "Yes. Look. Here's one of yours. She's at the Europa boarding house."

"I don't need you to tell me. I need their addresses written down, on this piece of paper. Clearly." He waved the list in her face. "Now, or I'll take the whole book with me."

"Of course," Esther said again. She pulled a chair over to sit between Claire and Gina. "Gina, your handwriting is better than mine. Claire and I will find the names, and you can write down the addresses."

"All right."

They set to work. The list was long, about forty names. Esther had made a cross beside about two-thirds of them. Claire studied the names, and froze. Alicia and Serge Lapéroux were on it. Esther had not marked them.

Her finger tapping each entry, Esther made her way down one page after another, saying the names. Claire checked to see if they were on the list. If so, Esther would read out the address for Gina. It was agonizingly slow. The man came to lean over them, his fists planted on both sides of the ledger.

Esther looked up at him primly. "It takes time to find names on these lists. I'm sure you don't want us to miss anyone." She bent over the register again. "Oh dear. Where was I? I've lost my place." She started over again at the top of the page. The man looked ready to tear the book out of her hands. Instead, he pushed himself upright with such force that the table moved and resumed pacing, his face redder than before.

Finally they were done, and Esther held up the list. The man snatched it from her. *"Idiota!"* he snarled again, and slammed the door behind him.

"All that work, and not even a thank you." Esther leaned back in her chair and stretched her shoulders. "I'm glad that's over."

"You did it on purpose, didn't you?" Claire stood up.

The corners of Esther's mouth turned up.

"A snail could've worked faster. You did it backwards."

"We have to cooperate with requests from the secret police. No one said we have to make it easy," Esther said.

"What's the list for, anyway?"

"The secret police want to talk to them for some reason. We never know why." Esther's eyes went from Claire to Gina, who had gone back to sorting the papers on the table. "They probably got the list from an informant. They sweep up a bunch of people and see if they've caught anyone of interest." She became businesslike. "Now, Claire, can you come with me? I have an errand for you to run."

"Sure." Claire followed her down the stairs.

As soon as they were outside, Esther took both of Claire's hands and leaned in close. "You know where the JOINT is, don't you?"

"Joint?"

"The American Jewish Joint Distribution Committee. They're in the Rua d'Ouro. Not far from Rossio."

"And?"

"I want you go to their offices. Timmy from USC should be there this afternoon, and you need to find him. You met him the day we went to the train station, remember?"

"I remember."

"Go as quickly as you can. You need to warn Timmy that the PVDE is looking for people who got off the train that day, including Serge and Alicia. Do you understand?"

Claire jerked back. "You do know where they are," she said accusingly.

Esther gave her a strained smile. "Now you know too. Go, and be discreet. We can't let them be found."

Antonio

Antonio was two hours into his shift when Mr. Thaler walked in and sat down at a table against the wall. His thin lips were pressed even more tightly than usual. He ordered a small coffee, downed it in one gulp, and ordered another, his eyes on the entrance. A few moments later, the Portuguese man Mr. Thaler had been with a few days before entered.

Another chance to eavesdrop. Good.

"Bruno," Mr. Thaler said.

"Hello, Hans," Bruno answered in English. He sat down and stretched his legs into the aisle.

"What do you have for me?"

"We're working on it." Bruno signaled for a drink. "The investigation…"

Antonio left to fill the order and missed the rest.

"It's taking too long," Mr. Thaler was saying as Antonio returned with the coffee.

"I'm sorry, sir," Antonio responded.

"I'm not talking to you, boy." Mr. Thaler frowned and waved him away with a hand. The two men waited until Antonio had stationed himself at the end of the bar, his back turned, before continuing. Antonio smiled grimly. As long as the Chave d'Ouro wasn't too noisy, he'd hear them.

"It's only been four days," Bruno said.

"Doesn't matter. People in Berlin are calling for my head. Too many people are escaping through Lisbon. These cannot slip through our grasp."

The front door opened and a man in dark clothes entered.

"Welcome to the Chave d'Ouro." José, the other waiter, pointed to an empty table. The man shook his head and went to talk to Mr. Silva.

"We're doing everything we can," Bruno said. He nodded at the newcomer. "Speaking of which."

From the cash register, Mr. Silva signaled to Antonio. "Table. Outside."

Antonio was only too happy to leave the PVDE agent to José. On the terrace, a family of refugees was settling into chairs. They chose their drinks carefully, with greedy anticipation. Inside, the agent was asking José questions. Antonio got his order and escaped outside again. Claire was coming his way, walking fast.

"Hello." He served the family, then went to meet her.

She gave him a nervous smile.

"Can you stop for a drink?"

"Maybe another time. I..." Claire hesitated. "I can't right now."

Normally, Antonio would've pushed, would've said, "My treat?" But not with the PVDE man inside. He shouldn't have suggested it in the first place. Claire started to step around him.

"What's the rush?"

She sighed and stopped. "Nothing. I'm delivering a message for someone who is very impatient."

"Oh. I thought it was important."

"It is."

The contours of Antonio's mouth turned up slightly.

"You're joking." Her laugh was shy, awkward. "Another time?"

"I sup-pose." He drew out the words, pushing away the worrying presence of the PVDE agent in the café behind him. She was fun to tease. "What are you doing tomorrow morning?"

"I really don't know."

"Then I'll take you to the castle." He pointed in the direction of the stone fortress that dominated the skyline. "You haven't been there yet, have you?"

"No, I haven't." She glanced over his shoulder, distracted.

"Are you all right?"

"I'm fine."

She didn't look it. She looked anxious and upset, very unlike the girl who'd argued with him in Estoril.

"Meet me here tomorrow then, at ten," Antonio said. She nodded, and on impulse Antonio leaned forward and kissed her on the cheek, just missing her mouth. "Take care of yourself." He watched her hurry away.

"Get in here." Mr. Silva was at the door. "There's someone who wants to speak with you."

The agent was sitting at a table, thumping his notebook with a pen and looking expectantly his way. Antonio's stomach clenched. He sat.

"You knew Thomas Schiller."

"He was a customer." Antonio wasn't giving him anything he didn't know.

"What was your relationship with him?"

"He was a customer," Antonio repeated. "I served him drinks."

"Is that all?"

"Yes."

"You had long conversations. What did you talk about?"

"Nothing important."

"I'll judge that." The agent puffed out his chest.

What would be common knowledge? "He talked about how he didn't like the war. Like everybody else, I guess."

The man scribbled something in his notebook. "What didn't he like about it?"

Antonio frowned. "What is there to like about war?"

The agent stared at Antonio silently. Challenging him was stupid.

"He said too many innocent people were dying," Antonio said. "I remember him repeating that a few times."

The man took more notes. "What else?"

"I don't know. He'd sometimes talk about what he saw in the newspapers." Antonio was suddenly glad he hadn't had time to read much of Thomas's diary.

"Did he have family? Friends?"

"He didn't talk about his personal life."

"I understood you were often seen joking together."

Under the table, Antonio fisted his hands in the fabric of his trousers. Their conversations in the Chave d'Ouro were never secretive, but apparently they made Antonio suspect. Hopefully no one had mentioned seeing them walking around the city together. From across the room, Mr. Thaler and Bruno were watching them. Antonio forced himself to relax.

"Oh, that. He was trying to learn Portuguese. But his accent was terrible. We all laughed at him." With him, really. Those were some of Antonio's favorite memories of Thomas. He tried to look indifferent. "He'd write the words down and practice them. That's all."

The agent looked up from his notebook. "Write them down? In what?"

Antonio wished he could rip his own tongue out. "I don't remember. On his newspaper?"

"Not in a little brown book? A diary, perhaps?"

Antonio forced every muscle into stillness and held the man's gaze. "Lots of customers come through here every day. I don't pay attention to things like that."

"So you don't know where the diary is?"

Antonio shook his head. "I can't help you."

The agent closed his notebook. "Do you know why I'm asking these questions?"

"You're investigating his murder."

"Murder." The man stood up. "Or it might have been an accident. We haven't determined which."

Antonio stood up too. He wanted to throw a chair at the agent's head. Instead he said evenly, "I hope you find out. May I go back to work?"

"Go ahead."

Antonio grabbed a tray and went to clear off tables outside. Gray was loitering off to one side, lighting a cigarette.

"This isn't a good time," Antonio said, his teeth clenched.

"I know. I've been watching. You all right?"

Antonio barely nodded.

"You'll come with us tonight. Look for me after work."

"What?"

But Gray was gone. Antonio braced his hands on a table full of glasses. Right now, he was shaking much too hard to pick them up.

Claire

There it was. The JOINT office. Claire walked down a long hallway, following voices to a room at the back. Timmy was there with three other people, sorting through mounds of clothes and shoes.

"Aha. Claire," Timmy said as she came in the door. "How nice to see you again. We could use an extra pair of hands."

"Not today, I'm afraid. Do you have a minute?"

Something in her voice made his smile dim. "Of course." He got up and joined her in the hallway. "What is it? Is Esther all right?"

Esther? Claire didn't have time now to figure out where that question came from. "She's fine. She wants to make sure Serge and Alicia Lapéroux are safe."

Timmy took a step back. "What?"

"The secret police are looking for them, and for a lot of other refugees. A man came by HICEM this morning, and Esther had to give him the addresses of people they had registered. She said you should expect a visit too."

"Damn them to…" Timmy stopped, looking uncomfortable. "Apologies for my language, Claire. It's just that…" He hesitated again.

"The children aren't listed in your ledger, are they?"

"That's not it," Timmy said. "Come with me." He stuck his head into the room with the clothes. "Mind if I use your telephone?" A woman's voice said yes. Timmy led Claire up a flight of stairs to a simply furnished office.

He dialed a number and waited, his tapping foot the only sound. "Hello? Yes, hello. All well?" He paused. "Good. Yes. Keep the dogs quiet today, all right? The neighbors are complaining." Another pause. "Right. We'll talk later. Goodbye." He hung up the phone.

"Really?" Claire said. "Dogs?"

"It works. That's all that counts." Timmy squeezed her shoulder. "Tell Esther the children are fine. No one will find them through us."

"But why are they looking for them?"

"That's a question I don't ask," Timmy said. "They needed

protection. That's all I know." With a hand on her elbow, he guided Claire back to the landing at the top of the stairs. "You'd better go now. It's best you're not seen here."

"Can you tell me where they are, at least? I'd like to see them."

"You'll have to talk to Esther about that." Timmy held her gaze, not giving in.

"But…who is taking care of them? They must be frightened."

"You need to go now."

On the floor below, the front door creaked open.

"Stay here. I'll see who it is." Timmy hurried down the steps. "Good afternoon, sir. Can I help you?"

There was a murmured answer.

"Yes, I understand. The register. If you'll follow me, I'll take you to the people in charge."

His voice faded to the back of the hallway, and there was silence. Claire crept to the bottom of the stairs and peeked around the wall. The hallway was deserted. As quietly as she could, Claire ran to the front door and let herself out. If it was the same man, and if he saw her here… Now she really needed to get out of sight. Claire headed back to the boarding house, hoping Vincent would be home. She had so many questions.

All of the tables outside the Chave d'Ouro were occupied as she hurried by, but Antonio wasn't serving them. Claire glanced through the window and glimpsed him leaning against the bar. His kiss had grazed the corner of her mouth. She put a hand to her lips. Had he done it on purpose? A glow of pleasure spread to her chest. She let herself enjoy it a moment, then damped the memory down with a heavy dose of guilt. She should be thinking about her family and Serge and Alicia. The glow faded but didn't disappear altogether. She climbed the boarding house stairs, hugging it inside.

No one answered the door. Claire leaned against it and closed her eyes. Everyone she knew in Lisbon had a purpose except her. She might as well just curl up on the couch until her family came. If she could persuade the concierge to give her the key so she could get inside, that is.

She sighed and started downstairs just as familiar voices floated up the stairwell. Claire looked over the banister. Vincent and Esther were at the third floor and climbing. Their timing couldn't have been better. Vincent pulled her into a hug as soon as he reached the top.

"You heard what happened?" Claire asked.

"I did." Vincent unlocked the door to their rooms, and they went inside. "Esther said you handled it very well."

"What about Serge and Alicia? Why are the secret police looking for them?"

Esther and Vincent exchanged glances. Esther sat down on the couch and motioned to Claire to join her. "It's another big secret to keep. Are you sure you want it?"

After a brief pause, Claire nodded. If she wanted them to treat her as an adult, she had to act like one.

"Their parents were taken off the train at the Portuguese border – you're the one who learned that. When I asked around afterwards, one of the refugees told me he thought they'd been running a few steps ahead of the Gestapo. He didn't know why, just that it had something to do with a German plane that crashed in France a couple of weeks ago."

"They made a plane crash?"

"A German plane did go down in France at the beginning of the month," Vincent said. "We don't know much more than that."

"But if the Gestapo have the parents, why do they want the children? They're too small to know anything."

Vincent and Esther exchanged glances again.

"Would you stop that?" Claire blurted, exasperated. "Just tell me."

"I imagine the Gestapo think the parents will be more cooperative if they know their children are being held," Vincent said.

"They'd hurt Alicia and Serge?" Claire had trouble getting the words out.

"We don't know. And we don't want to find out," Vincent said.

"Let me stay with them," Claire said impulsively. "They know me. I can take care of them."

"Absolutely not," Vincent said. "They're being protected by people who know what they're doing. That's enough."

Esther put a restraining hand on his arm. "Don't worry, Claire," she said gently. "They're in a safe place. And right now we don't want any unusual movement that could draw attention to them. You understand, don't you?"

"Of course," Claire snapped. "I wouldn't go today. But they

must be scared. I want to help."

"You already did," Esther said. "Between you and young Julien, we were able to warn a lot of people today. They might have had time to disappear, or at the least get their documents in order. You might've helped save a life today."

She'd never know though, would she?

"I can't help my own family. I can help Serge and Alicia," Claire said stubbornly. "I need to do something. You must understand that. And I promised I'd visit them."

"Out of the question," Vincent said firmly. "End of conversation."

Hundreds of German planes attacked
Britain and Northern Ireland last night

Diário de Notícias
April 9, 1941

CHAPTER 9 – WEDNESDAY, APRIL 9

NTONIO LEFT THE Chave d'Ouro well after midnight, when the final customer finally staggered out the door. The muscles in his legs throbbed from running in and out, and up the stairs to the gallery. Mr. Silva was never one to waste a good business opportunity by closing early. Now Antonio needed to find out if Gray had had the patience to wait for him.

After the smoke-filled, crowded café, the night air was refreshingly cool. There was no sign of the Englishman. In the middle of Rossio, someone was singing. Antonio crossed the street to see if Gray was part of the surrounding crowd. He wasn't.

Then, near a corner of the square, a match flared, illuminating Gray's face. As Antonio walked toward him, Gray turned and went in the opposite direction. Antonio kept to the same pace, following him at a distance. A moment later, Gray turned a corner. Antonio sped up until the man was in view again. He wasn't losing him now. Gray took another turn. This time he waited for Antonio.

"Where are we going?"

"You'll see soon enough."

A few minutes later, they reached the road that ran along the river. A battered car pulled up beside them almost immediately. Two men were in the front seat.

"Get in." Gray opened the back door and gestured to Antonio to slide to the other side. Gray climbed in behind him and they drove off. The driver kept to the same speed as the other cars, but to Antonio it felt fast. He could count on one hand the times he'd ridden in a car.

"Pick an animal," Gray said.

"What?"

"This is Locust." Gray indicated the driver, then the other passenger. "And this is Flea."

Antonio choked back a laugh. Flea wasn't as bulky as Thomas, but almost. "You're joking."

"It's better if we don't use real names. You can be a horse's trough for all I care. Just choose something."

Antonio thought for a minute. "Ferret," he said. "I'll be Ferret."

"How'd you come up with that?"

Antonio shrugged. Probably from a book he'd read as a child. He'd never seen a live one, but imagined a small, agile creature with sharp claws that was good at getting out of tight spots.

"It'll do," Gray said.

They drove on in silence, the river on their left. Antonio rolled down the window and stuck his hand outside. The wind pushed against it, cool and insistent.

"Where are we going?" he asked again.

"We want to have a look around the power plant."

"In Belém?"

Gray nodded.

"Why?"

"Hitler's been talking to General Franco. We need to have things in place if Franco decides to let the German army cross Spain."

"What exactly do you want to do?"

"Make it difficult for them. It's hard to move an army if the rail lines and bridges are cut, and there's no electricity."

Antonio glanced around the car. "I think we'll be a little outnumbered."

"You'd be surprised what small, well-prepared groups can accomplish," Gray said. "Even against an army. Besides, you haven't met everyone. And you won't."

Locust turned into an alley and parked. There was no one in sight. He extinguished the headlights. "Bus stops here," he said.

"Quiet now," Gray warned. All four of them got out. Antonio watched as they silently clicked the car doors shut, then followed them to the end of the alley. Across the road was a big red brick building with tall smokestacks jutting into the sky. Beyond it flowed the river, dark and quiet. Despite the late hour, the air hummed, clanked and thumped as coal was moved and burned. The whole area was enclosed by a wall that was taller than Antonio. Gray flicked his hand at Flea and Locust. Without a sound, they crossed the street and circled the wall.

"Rule number one," Gray said. "Don't get caught. None of us want to be shipped off to Tarrafal."

"Tarrafal? The prison in Cape Verde?"

"It's where your government sends people it wants to get rid of," Gray said. "Forever. The doctor there brags that his job is to sign death certificates. And I assure you, your prime minister would not appreciate what we're doing here."

That Antonio knew. He didn't like to think he was siding against his own government. But he wasn't, really. He was defending his country. "What are we doing here? Where did the others go?"

"That doesn't concern you. Tell me, if we asked you to get inside, how would you do it?"

"Sorry?"

"Where's the entrance?"

There was none in sight.

"Let's find it," Gray said. They circled the compound until they got to a long, flat track that ran between the river and wall of the power plant. A short concrete dock protruded into the river and they walked out onto it. Parallel to the dock, several big tubes ran from below the water's surface into the plant. On the other side of the wall rose hills of black coal, higher than a house. Grandiose buildings built for Portugal's World Expo the year before formed the backdrop.

"How would you draw this plant?" Gray asked quietly.

"To scale. As accurately as possible."

"I know that. But think. What would you focus on? What would we need to know about a place like this?"

Antonio studied it again. What he might normally draw and what Gray wanted were obviously not the same thing. "Where the doors are. Windows. Places where you can get inside," Antonio said, thinking aloud.

"Right." Gray nodded. "What else?"

"The fence, the gate. The river." Far away, a dog barked. "Security. Lights. Dogs." Pulling the pieces together was easy. "And guards."

"Exactly." Gray sounded pleased. "And the weakest points?"

A number of long wooden planks lay along the base of the wall. Put them on top of each other, and it wouldn't be hard to scale. Or they could break the gate down. Antonio brought his gaze back to the water. "Those tubes. What are they for?"

"Cooling system. They bring water into the plant."

"Then that's the weakest spot, isn't it? Destroy the tubes, and they'll have to turn off the machinery so it doesn't overheat."

"I think you're right," Gray said. "Good." They lapsed into silence. Flea and Locust were nowhere in sight.

"Does anyone know you're doing this?" Antonio turned to watch the river.

"What do you mean?"

"You're not just a bunch of people who came up with this crazy plan on your own, are you?"

Even in the dark, Antonio could sense Gray's smile. "Be assured, this is bigger than the four of us. Much bigger."

"Bigger in what way? The British government? Aren't they busy enough elsewhere?"

"The less you know, the safer it is for all of us. But it's in Britain's interests to encourage resistance efforts wherever we can. And right now Hitler is busy with Yugoslavia and Greece. That gives us more time to prepare."

"How much time do you need?"

"It's hard to say. We should be ready to take out oil installations, power plants like this one, strategic bridges. The weapons factory upriver. Can you imagine if the Germans got their hands on that? Or if they took control of the mines? They'd have all the wolfram they need to harden their tanks. And you can be sure they'd deny it to everyone else."

"But people here need the power plants and bridges. If you succeed, it'll make our lives awfully difficult."

"More difficult than being occupied by the Nazis?" Gray gave a quiet, harsh laugh. "I don't think so."

Something clanged behind the wall. Gray signaled for silence. They waited but heard no other sound, saw no movement. Gray let his hand drop.

"And you really think it'll do some good? Us against tanks and warplanes?"

"None of us would be here if we didn't."

One of the plant's doors opened and a guard began his rounds, his light glinting off the coal as he swung it from one side to another. Gray and Antonio ducked down and sprinted around the wall. Flea and Locust were already there.

"Time's up," Flea whispered. "Let's go."

Claire

"I'm going to see the castle this morning." Claire set the table with precision, giving the cutlery more attention than it warranted. Lies of omission didn't count, did they? A thrill of anticipation ran up her back. Even in Marseille, she'd never dared sneak off with a boy without permission.

"São Jorge?" Vincent asked. "It's a ruin. Why are you going there?"

"It does have the best view in Lisbon," Esther said.

"Exactly." Esther had unknowingly given her a good excuse. Claire felt a little guilty.

"Well, I'm glad to see you're getting out," Vincent said doubtfully. "But Esther and I are busy. You don't mind going alone?"

"How many times have I told you...?"

"That you don't need a babysitter." Vincent finished her sentence. Claire gave him a mock frown. The last thing she wanted was for him to think she needed a watcher.

"I meant female company. I wish you weren't on your own so much." He paused, thinking. "Didn't you say you'd run into a friend from Marseille?"

"Yes. Eleanor. But I don't know how to find her."

"Maybe Esther can help."

"I can try," Esther said.

"I'd appreciate that." Claire paused. Although what she wanted most was for her parents to show up. "Uncle Vincent, have our neighbors answered the telegram you sent?"

"Not yet. I'll check at the post office again today."

"I'll do it." Claire stood up and started clearing off the breakfast table. "I was going by there anyway."

Vincent nodded. "All right."

A church bell was ringing 9:30 a.m. when she reached the arcade outside the post office. This was a place of dashed expectations, and she knew it. She went inside and took her place in line. The clerk was polite but brief. "Sorry miss, there's nothing for Lemoine today."

Claire nodded and left. What could it mean if even their neighbors weren't responding to Uncle Vincent's telegrams? Not knowing was a constant wrench.

A clock on a building said 9:45. Claire set off on a zigzag route back to Rossio, pausing as she went to peer into the front windows of cafés, bakeries, shipping companies, and shops. It was still shocking to see their windows bursting with merchandise. People jostled each other at the entrance to a shipping company, hoping for a lucky break. Thank heavens her family already had their tickets.

Further on, Claire stopped to admire a dressmaker's display. Big bows decorated the mannequins' throats; slim waists gave way to pleated, knee-length skirts. A year ago, those fashionable clothes would probably have come straight from Paris. Claire doubted they did now. But maybe some of the Lisbon dressmakers had studied in France. Or were refugees like herself. She rubbed her thumb across the tips of her fingers. Her skin was losing the calluses that came from constant needlework. She sighed and made her way to the Chave d'Ouro, keeping a wary eye out for Vincent and Esther.

Antonio was already there, chatting with another waiter, his drawing tube slung over his back. "Ready?" he asked as she approached.

She nodded, aware of the other waiter's eyes on them.

"Let's go then."

They caught a tram a few blocks away and rattled upwards through narrow, winding streets. Antonio stared out the window, lines between his eyebrows. He was unusually quiet.

"Are you all right?" Claire finally asked.

"What? Yes, of course," he said. "I should ask you that. Did you get that errand done? The one you were so worried about?"

"Yes, thanks."

There was another pause. "Claire, when does your boat leave?"

"On the thirteenth."

"Have you heard from your family?"

Claire shook her head.

"So you still don't know if they'll be here in time?"

"No."

"And if they aren't? Will you leave anyway?"

"I don't know." She propped her elbow on the edge of the window and rested her chin on her palm. "We still have four days. They have to get here." She yearned to have only a daughter's responsibilities again. Although she was sure her relationship with her parents would never be the same.

The tram jerked to a stop and Claire swayed, off-balance. Antonio steadied her with a hand against her back. She didn't move, enjoying the firm pressure of his fingers through her blouse. The bell clanged, and they were off again.

"Could you stay if you wanted to?" Antonio broke into her thoughts.

"In Lisbon? Alone? What would I do?"

"You couldn't work?"

"I was studying to be a dressmaker. Before the war began. But refugees aren't allowed to work, are they?"

"I bet you could find a way. Women always need new clothes."

"Perhaps." She had no idea how she'd go about it. "At this point, staying without my uncle and leaving without my parents are both horrible options." She could only imagine Uncle Vincent's reaction if she said she didn't want to go. And it would be even worse if she told him she was considering going back to Marseille to look for them. He'd argue the idea was unrealistic, and she knew it was. If Esther couldn't locate her brother after all her efforts, what made Claire think she could manage better? But she couldn't help thinking she owed it to her family to try.

"Maybe," Antonio said doubtfully. "But you need to think about it."

"Can we talk about something else?" Claire asked a little desperately. "The castle, maybe?"

"Sure." He craned his neck, looking for the huge stone edifice, but the houses on the street their tram was climbing hid it from view. "It was built by the Moors. They occupied most of the land that is now Portugal for hundreds of years, until the Crusades liberated it in the twelfth century."

"Go on." In school, she'd always enjoyed history. It sounded like he did too. She liked watching him talk.

"According to a legend, during the siege of Lisbon, a knight named Martim Moniz saw an open gate and threw himself into it. He died, of course. But his body kept the gate open."

Claire winced. "That sounds awful."

"The crusaders got inside, conquered the castle, and then all of Lisbon. Dom Afonso Henriques, their leader, became our first king." The tram slowed and Antonio stood up. "We get off here."

Claire followed him. They crossed a square, climbed a gentle hill, and passed through the castle entrance. Her uncle had been right – inside, it was a roofless ruin. Walls had tumbled and blocks of stone littered the ground. Weeds and flowers grew in the cracks between them. Antonio led her through what had once been a grand hall to an open expanse bordered by a low stone wall. Seagulls flew below them, dark silhouettes against the sparkling river and roofs of Lisbon.

"Oh my." Claire didn't know what else to say. "I see why they chose this spot to build." With a foot, she tested the solidity of the wall, then sat down. The stone was hot against her legs. At least there was a breeze. Lisbon was peaceful now, but even these stones had seen their share of conflict.

"It's such a waste, isn't it?"

Antonio sat beside her. Distractingly close. Claire didn't move away.

"What do you mean?" he asked.

"The wars. The fighting. You should see Marseille now. It's full of people who were uprooted from their homes. For what?"

"Territory. Power. Control," Antonio said. "That's what Hitler wants."

"And ordinary people and families don't matter at all, do they?" Claire said bitterly. "You might be a brilliant scientist or the kindest person in the world. But if you fall into a category the Nazis don't like, you're a target." She thought about Mrs. Deauville and her husband, a respected doctor – and a Jew. "Why do they get to decide who's left in peace and who isn't?"

"You can't do anything about the war. None of us can." Antonio hooked a strand of hair off her face with a finger. "You have to accept that."

Claire thought about Serge's and Alicia's small hands in hers. "How? When you think of all the lives being destroyed?" She pressed her palms into her eyes.

Antonio ran a comforting hand across her back. "Then we do the little things that might make someone's life better, I guess."

Claire lowered her hands. His face was unexpectedly close, as if he were trying to read something deep inside her eyes. She held still, hardly breathing.

But he pulled back and changed the subject. "What will you do when you get to New York? I mean, what do you want to do?"

"Take up my dressmaking studies again, if I can."

"You said you have family there?"

"Yes. But I've never met that uncle." She gave a rueful laugh. "I hope he doesn't regret it when Mother arrives on his doorstep with a bunch of complete strangers."

"He's family. They stick together, right?"

"I hope so. What about you? Tell me about yours."

Antonio dug the toe of his shoe into the grass. "Not much to tell. My dad was a shoemaker. He died when I was young. I remember his hands were rougher than the leather. My mother got sick two years ago. I moved in with my grandmother after she died."

"I'm sorry."

"It's okay. We keep each other company."

Claire smiled. "What do you dream of doing?"

"I want my art to hang on the walls of one of those fancy galleries someday."

"Really?"

He grinned. "You asked, and I told you." He became serious again. "Even if it'll never be more than a dream, probably."

"Why do you say that? Can't you take lessons or something?"

Antonio made a dismissive sound.

"I just thought…"

"That I had a secret patron who'll pay for me to study?" he scoffed. "I wish. But I don't care. I'll get better on my own."

"Do you have any of your art with you?" Claire touched the drawing tube on his back.

"No. Not really. I'd like to do your portrait though. Would you mind?"

"Draw me? Why?" Claire was taken aback. And flattered.

Antonio acted as if he hadn't heard. "Wind blowing your hair, the city behind you. It would be good."

"Have you done this before?" she blurted out. He seemed so sure of what he wanted. "Brought other girls up here?" Drawn their portrait – and then what?

"Nope," Antonio replied cheerfully. He pulled the tube off his back. "You're the first. So, may I?"

"What will you do with it?"

"Nothing. Keep it with the others, unless you want it." He smiled suddenly, his expression pure joy. "Come on. You'll be helping me. I'll only get better if I practice."

Why not? If she hated it, she'd be polite. But now she was curious. And – if she was honest with herself – she liked his eyes on her. "All right. What do I do?"

"Stay there on the wall, like you are now, and look at me." He placed the paper on a rectangular stone and pulled out a pencil.

Claire sat up straighter. She tried clasping her hands in her lap, then rested them on the wall, then moved them back onto her legs. He'd better not portray her looking as stiff and unnatural as she felt.

Antonio studied her face for a long moment, then began drawing, his eyes flicking between her and the paper. Claire watched him right back. He curved his body around his hand when he was drawing, as if every bit of concentration was being poured into his pencil.

Their gazes locked. Claire blushed. She'd been studying him as intently as he'd been regarding her, imagining what it would be like to run a finger along his warm, tanned skin. She tried not to squirm. They were yards apart. Her first kisses, given in hurried secrecy to a boy in Marseille, hadn't felt nearly as intimate. She needed to think about something else.

"What do you draw, besides people?"

"Oh, anything." His hand continued to sweep over the paper. "City scenes. Whatever people ask for. Have you heard of Picasso?"

"Yes."

"I'd like to paint like that. But no one would buy it."

"They will when you're famous."

"Thanks for your confidence," Antonio said wryly. "I'll let you know when that happens. Now hold still." A few minutes later, he lifted his pencil from the paper. "Do you want to see it?"

"I don't know. Do I?" What if he'd drawn her in cubes and odd lines?

"Scaredy cat. Yes, you do."

Pushing aside a twinge of envy, she went to look over his shoulder. He was so certain his drawing would please. Even after formal training, she didn't have that kind of confidence in her dressmaking skills.

Antonio held the paper at arms' length. Claire's mouth dropped open. The resemblance was there, but the girl in his picture was poised and serene. Independent. Unafraid.

"Do you always do that?"

"Do what?"

"Draw people the way they want to be seen."

"Is that what I do?" His lips twitched. "I draw what I see."

Claire shook her head.

"Maybe I see something under a person's skin. Something they wouldn't see themselves," he offered. "Do you like it?"

She nodded. "It's…fascinating. I'm just not sure it's me."

"Do you want to keep it?" Antonio held the drawing out to her.

"I do. But I can't pay for it today."

"It's a gift." Gently, he turned her hands palms up and placed the portrait in them.

"I can't…"

Antonio made an impatient noise in his throat.

"Thank you," Claire amended. "It's lovely. But can you keep it until I leave?"

Antonio raised his eyebrows, giving himself wrinkle lines.

"My uncle would wonder where it came from."

"And that's a problem because…?"

"He doesn't know we've met."

The wrinkle lines got deeper.

"Don't make this so hard," Claire said in exasperation. "He doesn't know you."

"He wouldn't approve. Is that it?" Antonio's expression was unreadable. "Because I work in a café? Don't come from an important family?"

For those reasons, and so many more. "He wouldn't approve of me seeing anyone on my own."

"We're seeing each other? That sounds serious."

Claire rolled her eyes. "Don't say such silly things. I don't want my uncle forbidding me to go out alone, that's all."

Antonio relented. "All right. I'll keep the picture as long as you want." He rolled it up and slid it into the drawing tube.

"Thank you."

"You're welcome." Antonio stood up. "You wanted to see art, right? I'll show you some."

"Where?"

"In Chiado. There are a couple of galleries there." He pointed to the hill on the other side of the city. "Shall we go?"

Claire followed him. Yes, she wanted to see more art. His.

On the tram, they found seats near the back. It bumped down the hill, more people getting on at each stop. An elderly woman with two big bags climbed aboard, and Antonio stood to give her his place. She sat down and massaged her lower arms. Then, on a steep slope, the brakes screeched and the tram came to a sudden halt. The woman beside Claire let out an irritated sigh.

"This isn't a regular stop," Antonio said.

The driver opened the front door to talk to the policeman who had waved them down. The passengers fell silent.

"Ticket check," the driver announced grumpily in Portuguese, French, and German. "Hurry up. Show your tickets so we can get going."

A slightly built man sitting in front of Claire slid down in his seat, making himself even smaller as the policeman swung aboard.

"Tickets." The policeman took each one, examined both sides carefully, then handed it back and moved on to the next passenger. The elderly woman said something Claire couldn't understand.

"She says this happens almost every day now, and it's getting tiresome," Antonio translated.

"Ticket," the policeman said loudly to the little man in front of Claire.

The man shook his head. "No ticket," he said. "Sorry. I pay now?" He held up his money purse.

"No ticket?" the policeman asked. "Show me your papers."

Claire stiffened. Her passport. It was still with her uncle.

The man tapped his pockets frantically. "I'm sorry. Papers in boarding house."

"Off the tram." The policeman pulled the refugee out of his

seat.

"I pay for ticket now. Here. Money." The refugee held out two coins.

"You pay before you get caught, not after." The policeman shoved him down the steps. "Get off."

"Antonio," Claire whispered. "I don't have my passport."

"What?"

"My uncle has it. For safekeeping."

"What's safe about not having your passport?"

"I'd forgotten about it. What do we do?"

Antonio handed her one of the two tickets he was holding. "Maybe he won't ask for more than this."

Claire folded her hands in her lap, making sure the ticket was clearly visible beneath her thumbs. Outside, the refugee was arguing with the policeman, his arms gesticulating wildly.

The driver leaned out the door. "Can I go? I've got two trams stacked up behind me."

"Move on." The policeman waved his hand and the tram rumbled into motion.

Claire breathed out, a long sigh of relief, and unclasped her hands. They were trembling. She'd have to get her passport back from Uncle Vincent. He, of all people, wouldn't appreciate the irony if she got caught without her documents.

Antonio

"Do you still want to go to the art gallery?" Antonio looked down at Claire. Her face was tense and pale. *Merda.* More scares like that, and she wouldn't go out with him at all anymore.

She nodded. "But can we walk from here? I don't want to ride the tram anymore."

"Sure. We needed to get off soon anyway."

They descended at the next stop, strolled across the downtown, keeping to the shade, and were soon climbing the hill into Chiado.

"Don't you work today?" Claire asked as they reached a square with benches and trees, their leaves drooping in the heat. A plaque on the wall of a building said *Largo do Carmo*.

"I've got some time. Look, we're here."

Across the square was the *Edgeway Galeria de Arte*. Gray's gallery. Through its large front windows, he could see framed paintings lining the walls. Displayed on low shelves and tables was a mishmash of other items – a silver tea service, a porcelain jewelry box, an elaborately carved trunk, and more.

She hung back. "You want to go inside?"

"I've been here before. It's free entrance. No one's going to ask for your papers." Gray would surely act like an art dealer if Claire was around. And Antonio wanted to know if he had any news about Thomas.

Claire managed a small smile. "They'll know we're not going to buy anything."

"Most people don't. Come on. Let's go closer." He took her hand and pulled her across the square. They peered in the window. A door at the back was open, but the exhibition space was empty.

"Are you sure you don't want to go in?" he asked.

"Of course you do," said a voice behind them.

They both jumped.

"My young friend from the café. How nice to see you here," Gray said, and clasped Antonio's hand in a firm handshake. "And with a lovely companion." He smiled at Claire, then regarded her more carefully. "Haven't we met before? In the Negresco? Vincent Lemoine's niece? Catherine?"

"Uh…Claire," she responded nervously.

"What an unexpected pleasure to see you again. Please, come in and look around."

Gray knew who she was? And he knew her uncle? Antonio grimaced. It was too late to leave now.

Gray ushered them inside and went to sit at a small desk against the back wall, leaving them alone to wander among the paintings. Antonio hung back, letting Claire take the lead. She stopped in front of a detailed still life, then moved on to a dark French cityscape. She stayed there only a second, then halted before a colorful, impressionistic scene of water and flowers. There she stayed, hands clasped behind her back, tilting her head up and down, side to side.

Antonio grinned. For this, at least, they had similar tastes. The painting, clearly the gallery's current masterpiece, had jumped out at him the moment he saw it. If he had oil paints and a proper canvas, he'd like to try this style too.

"Not bad, is it?" Antonio asked.

Claire didn't turn her head. "I don't know anything about art. But this painting" – she searched for words – "makes me feel hopeful." She pressed a palm against her chest. "Can a painting give off warmth, like a living creature?" She laughed at herself. "That's a strange thing to say, isn't it?"

"No. It means you know more about art than you think you do. It doesn't matter what other people say. Or how much it's worth. Not really. What counts is what it does when you look at it. Or when you make it."

"I hadn't thought about that. What do you…?"

"This is a beauty, isn't it?" Gray had come up behind them again.

His timing was rotten. Antonio turned and glowered at an innocent painting on the other side of the room.

"It's a lovely gallery," Claire said politely. "Are you the owner?"

"No. But I found many of the pieces you see here today."

"Where do they come from?" Claire asked. "The artists aren't all Portuguese, are they?"

"On the contrary. These are the riches of wartime, unfortunately."

"They're stolen?"

"Of course not," Gray said crossly. "Why would you say such a thing?"

Claire bit her lip and looked away. Antonio glared at him.

Trying to hide a smile, Gray mouthed "sorry." He softened his tone. "Many refugees arrive with paintings, family heirlooms, and the like," he said. "Some get stranded here for longer than they expected and have to sell some of their belongings. That's how we get them."

Claire bristled. "They brought them all the way here because those things mean something. Buying them is like stealing their history."

"You're determined to think the worst of me, aren't you?" Gray chuckled ruefully. "We have the fairest prices in the city. People can't eat a painting, or sleep on a sculpture."

Claire moved on to the next picture without answering.

"New girlfriend?" Gray asked.

"You could be politer. And it's none of your business."

"Depending on what you're saying to her, it might be."

"I know when to keep my mouth shut. Do you have anything on Thomas?"

"No. Sorry."

Antonio gave an exasperated snort and turned away.

Claire was on the opposite side of the room, her nose almost touching a painting hardly bigger than Antonio's hand. She drew back as he approached. In it, a woman and a girl were reading by firelight in a dim room. The lace and velvet of their clothes were so finely rendered that Antonio pushed his hands into his trouser pockets to keep from touching it.

"Found another favorite?" he asked.

"I don't know how the painter was able to squeeze so many details into such a small space."

"He used a very thin brush."

"Ha. That's not what I meant."

Antonio was glad to see Claire relaxed again. "I know. I'm sorry, but I have to go to work. We can come back another time if you want."

Claire nodded. "Thank you for bringing me. These paintings..." She glanced around the gallery again. "They remind me that people are also capable of doing spectacularly beautiful things. I don't want to forget that."

"Then don't." Antonio hoped he'd be able to follow his own advice.

Gray had stepped into the room at the back of the gallery. Antonio called out a goodbye from the door, and they left without waiting for an answer. The man knew where to find him if he wanted to.

War materials for Yugoslavia are being loaded
in the United States

Diário de Notícias

CHAPTER 10

FROM THE LARGO do Carmo, Antonio went one way, after giving her another tantalizing kiss on the cheek. Claire headed in the other, toward HICEM. She desperately wanted to talk to Eleanor. Twice today, if he'd tried, she'd have allowed him a proper kiss. But he hadn't. He was more of a gentleman than she was a lady, apparently. Eleanor would understand her disarray. Her friend would also share her shock at seeing remnants of refugees' lives up for sale. But for fate, the flowered dishes in the gallery could have been Mother's pink and white wedding china, passed down from her great-grandmother. Claire couldn't shake a mental image of parents weighing their heirlooms against the empty stomachs of their children.

When she reached the Avenida da Liberdade, she sped up. Even if Esther wouldn't tell her where Serge and Alicia were, she certainly wouldn't refuse to help Claire locate an old school friend. At HICEM, Claire knocked lightly and opened the door. Gina was there, sorting shoes.

"Good day, Claire. You're just in time. Can you give me a hand matching these up?"

"Actually, I'm looking for Esther. Is she around?"

"She should be back soon. Can I help you?"

"Maybe. I want to find a friend from Marseille. She arrived in Lisbon a few days ago, but I don't know what agency she went with."

"Well, if she's not with HICEM…"

"She's not. Her family didn't come with us."

"Then you'll have to try JOINT or the USC. And the Quakers. I'm sure they'll check for you. Do you need the addresses?"

"I know where JOINT is. But I'd appreciate the others."

Gina copied the addresses onto a piece of paper and pointed out their locations on a wall map.

"Thank you." Claire took the paper.

"A bosom buddy?"

"Kind of. With two other girls. They called us *les inseparables.*" They'd worked hard but had such fun, slipping outrageous designs onto the teacher's desk, then putting on the most innocent of faces.

Gina smiled, a little wistfully. "It must have been nice."

"How is your sister?"

"She's…stable." Gina didn't seem to want to say more.

Heels clicked on the stairs, and Esther appeared. "Why, Claire, I didn't expect to see you here. How was the castle?"

"It was fine." No details requested, none offered. "I asked Gina to help me find my friend."

Esther tensed. "Oh?"

"Eleanor. My girlfriend from Marseille," Claire said defensively. "Remember? We talked about her this morning."

"Ah. And have you found her?"

"I thought you said you'd help," Claire said pointedly.

"I'm sorry. I haven't had time."

"Well, Gina suggested I ask at the other aid agencies. I was leaving now."

"I'll walk you downstairs."

In the entry hall, Esther paused before opening the door. "You're being careful what you say to people, aren't you?"

"Of course. Whom would I talk to anyway?" She thought of Antonio and pushed a twinge of guilt away. She hadn't told him any secrets.

"You're an attractive young lady walking around on her own. Anyone could approach you."

"You do it all the time."

"You can too. When you're my age. Just pay attention to your surroundings, all right?"

"I will." Claire changed the subject. "How are Serge and Alicia? Do you have any news?"

"Not of their parents, unfortunately. But the children are fine."

"What exactly do you mean by 'fine'?"

"They're not at the Ritz. But they're fed and clothed and have a safe place to stay. They have everything they need."

"What will happen to them?"

"There are places for orphans here in Portugal, and the refugee agencies are helping some go abroad. But each case is different, and Serge and Alicia are very special children. They might need new identities altogether."

Yet another family ripped apart. "I'm good at taking care of children, you know."

"I'm sure you are."

"Really. When the boys and girls on our street came to play with Frédéric, I always made up games for them and kept them busy. You have to let me help with Serge and Alicia."

"The best way to help is to leave them alone."

Claire stared at her. An uprooted, insecure child could become a severely distressed one. Surely Esther realized that. With Claire, Serge and Alicia had laughed.

But Esther just kissed her on the cheek, dismissing her. "Go find your friend. I'll see you at dinnertime."

Claire bit her lips together and nodded. Another battle lost. When Esther was gone, she followed Gina's sketch to the USC. Timmy was in an office off a narrow hallway, sifting through unopened mail. She shut the door behind her.

"Back again?" His greeting was less enthusiastic than before. "Not with news of another unwelcome visit, I hope."

"Not this time. I'm trying to find a friend who arrived on April 6. May I look at your register?"

Timmy unlocked a cabinet behind his desk and lifted the ledger out. "You can sit over there." He indicated a table near a window. "They're listed in order of arrival."

Claire opened the book and began searching. The handwriting was cramped and smeared. Probably on purpose. Her finger slid down the list slowly. Bucher, Kotowski. Was the next one Lefevre or Lehavre? She imagined illegibility was an effective tactic when the secret police came calling. She kept looking, but couldn't find Eleanor Bonner anywhere.

The phone rang.

"USC," Timmy said. He listened, tapping his pencil

rhythmically on the desk. "So they're better?"

Claire kept her eyes on the register.

"What do you mean, you're out of medicine?" A pause. "No. Can't you come get it?" Another pause. "I'm sorry. They'll just have to wait. Maybe tomorrow." He sighed and replaced the receiver on its cradle.

Claire checked over her shoulder. The door was still shut. "Was that about Serge and Alicia? Are they sick?"

Timmy started. "What?"

"Are the children ill?" Esther had said they were fine.

"Nothing too serious, we think. But they need a few supplies." Timmy nodded at a small package in the corner of the office.

"You can't take it?"

"Not today."

Claire hesitated. She might be powerless when it came to her own family, but she could still help someone else's. "I can." She held her breath and waited for his answer. If he'd talked to Vincent or Esther, he'd say no. Going against their wishes – Claire would have preferred not to. But Esther had lied. And they needed medicine. And she'd promised to visit them. Three reasons right there, and they weren't the only ones.

"Are you sure?"

Claire tried to keep her voice even. "Just tell me where to go."

"You have to be very careful."

"I will."

"Do you know where Belém is?"

Claire nodded again. Antonio had pointed it out on the train to Estoril.

Timmy pulled a map from a desk drawer and unfolded it. "I'll show you on the map. You'll have to memorize it." He pointed to a street. "The Travessa do Páteo das Vacas. Can you remember that?"

Vacas were *vaches* in French. Cows. So this was Cow Patio Lane. A strange name. "I'll remember." Claire felt the deep thud of her heart in her chest and wiped her hands on her skirt. She was doing the right thing. "What's the best way to get there?"

"The tram. You'll get off here. At Jerónimos. A huge monastery. You can't miss it. There's a street to its right, all uphill. Follow that, and the Travessa will be on your right." He stopped and looked at her, suddenly anxious. "If you attract attention in any way, it'll be much worse than if you don't go at all."

Claire reached for the package. "I can do it."

Antonio

The Chave d'Ouro was dead – and stifling – that afternoon. Even Rossio was quieter than usual. A couple of regulars appeared, but they didn't stick around. Outside, heat pulsed at him from the sidewalk. He didn't blame people for staying indoors.

After clearing off a table, Antonio tucked a left-behind newspaper under his arm and escaped to the relative coolness of the café. Inside, he spread the newspaper on the counter and scanned the headlines. One article reported that hundreds of German warplanes had launched an attack on Britain and Northern Ireland. Another said America was preparing to help Yugoslavia with some kind of war materials. He snorted. Even Portuguese newspapers were careful to stay neutral, splitting their coverage between the warring countries.

Then he saw it, on page two, and for a split second the world narrowed to one five-word headline. "Explosion Aboard the *Serpa Pinto*." *Merda.* He raced through the short paragraph.

On April 8, soon after leaving Lisbon, an explosion occurred in the boiler room of the Serpa Pinto, *a Portuguese ship carrying refugees to America. There was minor damage to equipment, but the ship was able to continue its voyage to New York. There were no injuries. The cause of the explosion is under investigation.*

Relief washed through him, then a hot slash of anger. The plot had failed, and the *Serpa Pinto* was still afloat. But Gray hadn't kept his part of the bargain.

Claire

Timmy had been right. The road from Jerónimos monastery to the Travessa do Páteo das Vacas was long and all uphill. To her right was a tall wall. Two-story houses lined the street on her left.

Claire shifted the package from one hand to the other and wiped her palm on her skirt for the umpteenth time. Her nerves were playing havoc with her stomach, and it was just so hot.

Halfway up the incline, where bright pink bougainvillea cascaded over the wall, Claire stopped and put her hand to her waist, catching her breath. From here she had a clear view up and down the street. As far as she could tell, no one had paid any attention to her during the trip. She trudged the rest of the way up the hill, found the street and the house, and rang the bell. Moments later, a stern-faced woman cracked the door open.

"I'm Claire. You're expecting me?" She repeated herself in French.

The woman's eyes traveled to the package in Claire's hand, then flitted left and right along the street. Claire followed her gaze. No one was nearby. With strong, chilly fingers, the woman grasped Claire's arm and pulled her inside.

They were in a small, dark entry hall. All of the doors off it were closed and heavy curtains on the one window blocked most of the light. Claire sniffed. The air was cool and slightly musty. A truck rumbled by on the street, but otherwise it was completely silent. Serge and Alicia were kept here?

The woman held out her hand. "Give it to me," she said in French.

Claire handed her the package, and the woman moved to open the door again.

"Wait." Claire held it shut. "I want to see the children."

"Children?"

"Alicia and Serge."

The woman gave her a wary look and didn't budge. "Why did they send you?"

"You needed the medicines, didn't you?"

"Yes. But you shouldn't be the one bringing them."

"No one else could. Besides, I found the children when they got to Lisbon. They know me."

"No."

"I won't stay long. But I'm not leaving without seeing them."

The woman hesitated. "Five minutes," she finally said. "Then you must go." She led Claire up the stairs, her dress darker than the surrounding gloom, and pushed open a door. Muted daylight spilled into the hallway.

Inside, Serge lay on the wooden floor, fitting pieces into a puzzle cut out of paper. Alicia sat listlessly beside him, her puzzle untouched. They both had runny noses but otherwise looked clean and unharmed.

"*Bonjour,*" Claire said.

At the sound of her voice, Serge bolted to a sitting position and hugged his sister. She clung to him. They both watched with worried frowns as Claire knelt in front of them.

"Do you remember me?" she asked. "We met after you got off the train."

Alicia's lip wobbled.

Claire sat down on the floor. "I said I'd come see you, and here I am." Without thinking, her voice took on the tone and cadence she used when Frédéric was distressed.

Alicia dropped her eyes to a worn stuffed bunny in her lap. Neither of the children answered.

"Are you all right? Are you getting enough to eat?"

Behind her, the woman made an impatient noise.

Claire swung around. "What's wrong with them?" she asked. "Don't they talk?"

"To each other. In whispers. Not much otherwise."

"They talked when I found them."

"We've instructed them not to make noise. They understand."

Claire doubted they understood much of anything, except that their parents had disappeared.

"You've done your duty, miss. I'll see you out."

Claire held up a hand. "Not yet." She shifted around the puzzle pieces in front of Alicia. "I bet you can do this. Look. Don't these two fit together?" She moved them into place. Alicia's gaze followed her hands, then darted to Claire's face. "Why don't you try?" Claire held another piece out to her. "Where does this one go?"

In one swift movement, Alicia flung herself onto Claire's lap. She huddled against her, her hands clutching Claire's blouse.

Claire wrapped her arms gently around the little girl. "You're all warm and cuddly," she said after a moment, when she was sure her voice wouldn't shake. Alicia pushed her small body even closer. Serge leaned his head against her, and Claire pulled him into the hug. She wanted to say, "It'll be all right," but the words wouldn't come. "Would you like to play patty cake again?" she asked.

Below, the front door opened and shut with a bang. All three of them jumped. A moment later, a man with the muscles of a boxer stalked into the room.

"What were you thinking, coming here?" he hissed.

Claire gaped at him.

"You've got no experience. Anyone could have followed you. I did, easily. Did you even notice?"

The man wore a dark jacket, trousers, and shoes, like so many others in Lisbon. She didn't remember seeing him on the tram coming here, or on the street with the bougainvillea.

"The children needed the medicine. And I'm sure I didn't do anything to draw attention to myself."

"That's not the point. If someone was already watching you, you'd have led them straight here. Can you imagine the consequences?"

Claire pressed her lips against Alicia's hair and breathed in her soapy little girl smell. Her small frame was no larger than Frédéric's. She'd been watchful. And her visit was unplanned. No one would've known she was coming.

"You need to go," the man said. "Now. You shouldn't have stayed in the first place."

Claire sighed and stood, Alicia clinging to her neck. Claire pried the little girl's fingers apart and lowered her gently to the floor.

"I'll come back," she told her. "And next time I'll bring a book. Would you like that?" She took Serge and Alicia's hands, laced them together, and backed away. The children wrapped their arms around each other and began to sob.

Antonio

Business at the Chave d'Ouro picked up in the late afternoon, sporadically, and would-be plotters were back in force. Two men, talking about blowing up the wolfram mines so no one could use it to harden steel. Were these plans or dreams? Antonio memorized their faces and filed the conversation away. Something to tell Gray later. Or maybe not, if Gray couldn't give him a good reason for not warning the *Serpa Pinto*.

Nearby, two younger men in round, scholarly spectacles were hoping for a communist revolution in Germany. "We'll sweep everything away," Antonio heard one say as he served a couple fretting about an elderly father left behind in Italy. Like the furniture, Antonio received little attention. Maybe they thought he couldn't understand them, or simply didn't care.

"Remember Archduke Franz Ferdinand?" one of the young men was asking when Antonio brought them drinks and small pastries.

"The heir to the Austro-Hungarian Empire? What does he have to do with this?

"Think about it. How did he die?"

"Driving through Sarajevo like an idiot, in an open car."

"Exactly. Hitler travels too, doesn't he? In vehicles. That's when he's vulnerable. One shot could change the world, like in 1914."

"Hitler wouldn't be stupid enough to ride in an open car."

"Are you being thick on purpose? Bullets shatter glass. My point is…"

Antonio moved to another table and didn't hear more. He was taking an order for drinks when Gray walked in.

"I'll be with you immediately," Antonio said, loudly enough so that the other waiters could hear. Gray was his. Antonio was at his side as soon as he sat down. "Why didn't you warn the *Serpa Pinto?*" he asked in a low voice.

"Hello, Antonio," Gray said pleasantly. "And how are you this evening?"

"I'm fine, you're fine." Small talk was a waste. "The *Serpa Pinto* almost wasn't. Why didn't you warn them a bomb was on the boat?"

"What makes you think I didn't?"

"Because there was an explosion. I saw it in the paper."

Gray's lips twitched. "You believe everything you read?"

"What game are you playing?" Antonio couldn't hide his frustration.

"Antonio!" Mr. Silva's voice cracked across the room. "You've got more than one customer."

The people he had just waited on were throwing him impatient looks. He took their order to the bar and headed back toward Gray's table.

Mr. Silva intercepted him. "If you need to have a heart-to-heart conversation," he said sarcastically, "you take time off and go outside. I'm paying you to work."

"I am working." Antonio shot back. He could feel anger coiled in his chest. "What may I serve you?" he asked Gray in his most formal waiter's voice.

"Tea please."

"Certainly."

Antonio loaded both orders onto a tray at the bar, along with the newspaper with the *Serpa Pinto* article. He deposited it on Gray's table beside his tea. "Your order, sir," he said, and waited.

"I'd expect you to know by now when and where this kind of conversation is acceptable," Gray said tightly. "It's not in the middle of a busy café."

"I want you to answer a simple question."

"To which there is no simple answer," Gray responded. "Will 'they already knew' suffice?"

"I don't understand."

"Exactly. But I'm not going to explain it here." Gray stood up, his tea untouched. "We'll talk later. If you've calmed down."

"Antonio!" Mr. Silva barked. "To work!"

Claire

When the man said the street was clear, Claire slipped out of the house and headed toward the tram. He'd ordered her to watch for anyone following her. The children's sobs echoed in her head, making it hard to concentrate. They weren't fine. And there was nothing for them in that bare room.

Claire stopped and took off her shoe, shaking it to get rid of an imaginary pebble. As she straightened up, she looked carefully up and down the street. The man from the house was at the top, watching her. Briefly, she stared back. He wouldn't reproach her again for not being alert. But now everyone looked suspicious. The woman watering flowers on a balcony – Claire had seen her when she arrived but had no way to tell if she was monitoring passers-by. In front of the monastery, a man was sweeping the street. What if someone was paying him to watch, and to report? Claire kept going, avoiding eye contact. She had to prove she could do this, or they'd never let her come back.

Claire got back to the boarding house an hour later. Vincent and Esther were waiting for her.

"Explain." Vincent's voice crackled with anger.

"Explain what?"

"This afternoon. Going to the safe house," Vincent said.

"And the boy," Esther added.

Claire felt the blood drain from her cheeks. They'd found out about Antonio. It had to be the man in the gallery. Mr. Gray.

"Sit down," Vincent snapped.

Claire dropped down on the couch.

"What the hell are you doing?"

What would they find easiest to accept? "When I was at USC, Timmy got a phone call saying Alicia and Serge needed medicine," Claire said. "There was no one else who could go, so I took it."

"We explicitly told you not to try to see the children," Vincent said.

"You – explicitly – said they were fine," Claire shot back. "They aren't."

"And you think you can make it right? By showing up at a safe house? In broad daylight, when anyone could follow you?"

"It would've been better if I'd shown up in the middle of the night?"

Vincent glared at her.

"Uncle, I look like every other foreigner walking around Lisbon."

"Don't be ridiculous," Vincent said. "You're not trained for this."

"And you're giving me mixed messages. Just yesterday you were showing me how to make drop-offs and pick-ups. Now you're telling me not to put it to use?"

"You did what?" Esther turned white. "You're both crazy."

Vincent gave Claire a hard stare. She felt a stab of satisfaction. She wouldn't be the only one in trouble.

"Those children are scared and unhappy. If my brother were in this situation, I'd want someone to comfort him. There must be other people who come and go without raising suspicion. I can too."

"Why?" Esther asked quietly. "So they can get attached to you? And then in a few days you'll disappear?"

"That's not the point at all!" Vincent exploded. He jumped to his feet and strode across the room. "If she blows the hiding place, there will be no children to take care of. You'll have handed the Gestapo a gift!"

Claire pinched her lips together.

"Do you understand the consequences?" he went on. "Do you understand 'no'?"

"Uncle, I can't talk to you when you're yelling. There must…"

"We'll talk all right, but not about that." He switched the subject abruptly. "Who was the boy you were with today?"

There was no point playing the innocent. "His name is Antonio. He works in a café on Rossio. Almost next door. He offered to show me around Lisbon."

"You went by yourself?" Esther began.

"Well, yes…"

"When did this start?" Vincent talked over them both. "Have you been out with him before?"

Claire hesitated. What was the likelihood they'd been recognized in Estoril? "He took me for a walk along the water the other day. He doesn't mean any harm."

"How would you know?" Vincent sputtered.

"I'm not ten years old."

"Your parents…" Vincent shook his head. "You have no idea what this boy's intentions are. Where did you go?"

"His name is Antonio. We went to the castle." She could see it out the window, and wished she were still there. "Then to Mr. Gray's gallery," she said pointedly.

"You were at the castle with him?" Esther repeated. "It's so isolated. What if something happened?"

Then Antonio would help her, not hurt her. There were a lot of menacing things in Lisbon, but Antonio definitely was not one of them. "If it would make you feel better, I can introduce you."

"I don't want to meet him," Vincent spat. "And you're not to see him either."

"What?"

"From now on, you will cross the street to avoid him if you

have to. Is that clear?"

"You're not my father!"

"I am responsible for your safety, and that's my decision. From now on, you'll spend your days with Esther. You will not leave her side for an instant. Understand?"

"You're being unfair." Claire looked at Esther for support, but Esther shook her head.

"Am I? After what you did today? You sneak around, you lose our trust. Accept it."

Antonio

Meu Deus. The last customer was out the door, finally. Antonio wiped tables and mopped the floor in double-time. He wasn't waiting for Gray to look him up.

"What's up?" José snickered. "Hot date?"

"A better-looking one than you'll ever have," Antonio retorted, and kept working. Five minutes later he was out the door and searching for Gray's angular frame.

The night had retained the day's heat, and Rossio was still full of movement. A car honked, a seagull cried, a woman laughed. A typical Lisbon evening, worlds away from the explosion he couldn't get off his mind. Where was Gray? Antonio circled Rossio twice, then followed the route they'd taken to meet the car. No sign of him. Maybe he'd been out of line at the café, but even so, Antonio couldn't believe Gray would leave him hanging.

Retracing his steps, he circled Rossio again. He paused to greet the shoeshine boy, then headed up the hill toward the Largo do Carmo. The art gallery was dark, but a thin line of light shone from the office at the back. Antonio pushed on the front door. It was locked. He rapped on the glass. The sliver of light disappeared. Instants later, Gray emerged from the darkness and unlocked the door.

"You weren't looking for me very hard," Antonio said.

"Patience, boy." Gray led him to the office and shut the door, plunging everything into blackness. Then he clicked on the light, revealing a small room with shelves of books and binders lining the walls. Paintings, several deep, were stacked to one side, beside a wooden desk with a stained top.

Gray cleared off a chair and motioned to Antonio to sit down. "How old are you?"

"Seventeen. Why?"

"Impatience won't serve you at all in this business. You have a lot to learn." Gray leaned against a bookshelf and crossed his arms.

Antonio crossed his arms too, and waited. They'd see who could wait the longest.

Gray finally broke the silence. "About the *Serpa Pinto*. You overheard the men on the train talking about hiring a dockworker to sink the ship, correct?"

"Yes."

"It so happens that this dockworker had approached the Germans some time before, and told them he wanted to work for them. He said he was angry about Portugal's refusal to take sides, and wanted to help the German cause."

Gray knew about this, and hadn't stopped him?

"The dockworker was in a good place to carry out this particular task," Gray continued, "because his job was loading ships, and specifically loading coal. This gave him access and knowledge coveted by the Nazis. It wasn't long before they said yes, and he started spying for them."

Antonio opened his mouth to interrupt, then clamped it shut. He'd show Gray he could be patient all right.

"One day he told them that war supplies were being loaded onto the *Serpa Pinto*. His handlers decided that the best solution would be to sink the boat so these supplies would never reach America. The dockworker would plant a bomb, then get off the ship."

"When did you learn this?" Antonio burst out. "Why didn't you arrest him?"

"It would have been counterproductive."

"Counterproductive? How?"

"Because the dockworker is one of our agents."

Antonio blinked. "A British agent working for the Nazis was going to blow up a neutral Portuguese ship full of refugees?" He spoke slowly, trying to get his head around what Gray had said. "Do I have it right? And you didn't stop him…why?" Anger coiled again in his gut.

"You have it wrong. The agent had learned that the Nazis had developed a new kind of explosive. Devastatingly powerful, but so small it could be placed in a hollowed-out lump of coal. We needed to get our hands on it."

"But you didn't. It went off."

"Not really. The dockworker delivered the coal directly to the captain – as planned – who locked it away in his safe. Then the captain went down to inspect the boiler room. We'd given him something that would pop, very loudly. When no one was looking, he tossed it into the boiler. Everyone scattered, of course, and news quickly got out that there had been an explosion on board the *Serpa Pinto*."

"But the Nazis expected the ship to sink. Don't they suspect anything?"

"As far as we can tell, they think the bomb malfunctioned. They don't seem to be blaming the dockworker."

"Lucky for him." If he were the dockworker, Antonio wouldn't feel reassured.

"He's careful."

"So now what?"

"Nothing. I doubt they'll try something that risky again. None of the belligerents attack refugee ships on purpose. I suspect they made the exception because they thought significant war supplies were aboard."

"Weren't there?"

"No."

"Your man played a risky game with a lot of lives."

"He won't do it again. It would be too much of a coincidence if he planted two bombs that didn't go off. Now, what do you have for me? Have you been drawing?"

"Some." Not enough. "I did pick up some interesting information though. Do you have any paper?"

Gray handed him a sheet and Antonio quickly sketched the faces of two men. "They were in the Chave d'Ouro tonight. Talking about blowing up Portuguese wolfram mines."

Gray studied the drawing. "They're not ours. Fortunately. I'd have their hides for talking about that in such a public place."

Antonio snorted. "Then you might want to know I overheard two men in an alley a couple of nights ago, arguing about whether bomb-making equipment should be stored in a gallery or not."

Gray stiffened.

"I'm right in thinking they were talking about this gallery, aren't I?"

"Damn it." Gray spat the words. "Can no one keep their mouths shut? What did they look like?"

"I only saw one of them, and not for long. It was dark." Antonio started drawing again. "And I was busy playing the drunk."

"You were?"

Antonio grinned. "Yup."

"Another hidden talent," Gray said approvingly. Then he glanced down at the portrait and frowned.

"You do know him."

"Can't be. He's more careful than that."

"Not careful enough, it seems. Who is he?"

"It's safer not to know. I've told you that."

"Right." Did the man trust him or not? Antonio stood up abruptly. "I need to go. I'll see you around."

"Wait." Gray shut off the light before opening the door. "We're going out tomorrow night. You'll be at the Chave d'Ouro?"

"Yeah." It wasn't worth wasting his breath to ask where they were going.

"See you at closing time."

"Sure." Antonio shoved his hands into his pockets and left, not sure what to think. What he'd provided on the bomb had been worthless, but the ship was safe, and apparently the information about the conversation in the alley was valuable. Most important of all, Gray had asked Antonio to go out with them again. He'd been accepted.

Halfway home, Antonio realized he hadn't asked about Thomas. *Merda.* His diary was still hidden in his grandmother's cabinet, waiting to be read. When he got home, Antonio tiptoed into their living room. Avó's door was shut. Good. He got the diary, turned on a lamp, and lay down on his mattress behind the couch. There had to be a clue in it somewhere – if he could read it.

The words on the first page were cramped and densely packed, and all in German. The entry was dated December 1940. Almost five months ago, around the time Thomas had first shown up in the Chave d'Ouro. Christmas time, in a year that few celebrated.

Antonio flipped to the last page. Cheese, bread, wine, butter. On the day he was killed, Thomas had written out a grocery list. In Portuguese. Antonio rubbed his thumb over it, then studied a passage in English on the preceding page.

The river
a rod of silver
hard on the eyes

To look away
is to ignore
not acceptable

To observe, to understand
death on the inside, death underneath

To stop, to warn
~~impossible~~

Thomas had been thoughtful, funny, angry. He loved to read. But a poet? Even the handwriting here was looser, more flowing, except for the hard black line where he'd crossed out the last word. Antonio didn't know this side of him. He shook his head and turned more pages.

Baby to V.

Antonio frowned. That was cryptic. Thomas had never talked about a baby. Except… Antonio reread the telegram he'd seen the other day. A newborn in France, a baby mentioned here. If there was a connection, he wasn't seeing it.

Drawn on another leaf was what looked like a child's drawing of a hexagon. Lines, some labeled with numbers, crisscrossed the shape. Little x's dotted the paper in no apparent pattern. No text, no explanation. Whatever secret the drawing held, Thomas had taken it with him.

The bed in his grandmother's room creaked. Antonio switched off the lamp and lay with eyes closed, the journal tucked out of sight.

Her door opened. "Antonio?" she said softly.

He stayed still and evened out his breathing. Some evenings she'd wake up and they'd talk, but tonight he needed the solitude.

She padded across the living room and peered at him over the couch, then went to the bathroom. He followed the sound of her footsteps back to her room. The door closed, the bed creaked, and all was silent again.

Antonio turned on the lamp and reopened the diary. With a start, he came across another sketch, this time of something he recognized. A diamond-shaped radio transmitter behind a three-story building, like the one he'd seen behind the store the night he followed Mr. Thaler. Antonio bet Gray would give a lot to see the contents of this little book. But not yet. Antonio yawned and opened another page at random. The entries were so disjointed it didn't seem to matter what order they were read in.

Going to visit Madam Jolly. What gifts will she shower me with tonight?

Antonio ran his finger along the words. A baby, and now a woman? As much as they'd talked, Thomas had never hinted at a girlfriend. Was the baby hers? His? He'd found pleasure in her company, at least.

Then it clicked. Pleasure. Madam. Thomas meant the Jolly Roger. It was one of the most popular brothels in the city, located in a row of whorehouses down by the docks. Some catered more to Germans, and others to the English, but seamen from every ship that came to Lisbon spent their energy and money at the Jolly Roger.

Antonio slid the book under his mattress and turned off the light, wondering why he was surprised that Thomas would pay for sex. Then again, maybe he didn't, if he knew the Madam. Tomorrow, he'd pay his own visit to the Jolly Roger.

German columns operating in southern Yugoslavia
are 50 km from the Albanian border

Diário de Notícias
April 10, 1941

CHAPTER 11 – THURSDAY, APRIL 10

AT BREAKFAST, CLAIRE kept her head down and concentrated on her hands, her knife, the bread. Anything to avoid Vincent's and Esther's glaring disapproval. She wasn't apologizing for trying to help.

"We'll run by HICEM first," Esther said finally. She stood and took her dishes to the sink. "Then we have a train to meet."

Claire took a bite and didn't respond. Vincent was doing riskier things than she had. By far.

"Did you hear me?" Esther's voice was uncharacteristically sharp. "We leave in ten minutes. Please be ready." She disappeared into the bedroom.

Claire turned to her uncle. "Can't I keep looking for Eleanor instead? I didn't have a chance to visit the other refugee agencies. It'll keep me busy, if that's what you're worried about." It was hard to keep the sarcasm out of her voice.

"Don't keep Esther waiting." Vincent deposited his dishes in the sink with a clatter and put on his jacket. "I'm going out." He paused with his hand on the doorknob. "You're not to give Esther any reason to worry. Do you understand?"

How could she, if they were to be chained together for the entire day? Claire nodded, and Vincent opened the door.

"Uncle, wait. Did you make the drop-off?"

Vincent shot her an exasperated look and checked the hallway. "Tell the world, why don't you?" he said, and left.

Claire stared at the closed door for a moment, then went to

wash the dishes. She hadn't spoken that loudly. A glass slipped out of her hand and shattered in the sink, slicing a red line in the meaty part of her thumb. She staunched the blood with a dishtowel and threw the broken pieces into the trash. Apparently she couldn't do anything right today.

"Ready to go?" Esther reappeared, slinging her purse over her shoulder. Claire folded her fingers over the cut and nodded.

They walked to HICEM, the silence between them still awkward. That suited Claire fine. Esther would probably say no to anything she suggested anyway. How she regretted not finding Eleanor the day before. She'd never imagined feeling so alone in a city full of people.

At HICEM, Esther directed her to a seat in the reception area. "I need to talk to the director. We'll leave for the station," she consulted the wall clock, "in fifteen minutes."

Claire sat down. If all she was allowed to do was to twiddle her thumbs for the next three days — and fret about her family, and avoid seeing Antonio and the children — she'd go mad. She looked at the clock. How many more minutes? Fourteen? She closed her eyes and slumped down in her chair.

"Don't we look lovely?" Gina's playful voice came from the doorway, and Claire opened her eyes. "Don't you have anything better to do?"

"I'm waiting for Esther," Claire said grumpily. "We're meeting a train."

"I know. I'm going too. But why so miserable?" Gina sat down beside her.

"It's nothing."

"Maybe so, but lots of nothings become something if they're not taken care of."

"I don't understand why my parents haven't been able to get a message to us."

"It's wartime. Everything is disrupted." Gina gave Claire's shoulder a squeeze. "Did you find your friend?"

"No. Not yet."

"You should. A girl needs company, and I don't mean old folks like us."

Claire managed a small smile. Gina was probably only a few years older than she was, but she seemed decades worldlier. At least she was easy to talk to. And willing to listen. "The problem is that Uncle Vincent and Esther don't want me to go looking for her anymore."

"Why ever not?"

What could she say? Certainly nothing about Serge and Alicia. "They're not comfortable with me walking around Lisbon alone."

Gina looked alarmed. "Did someone threaten you?"

"Nothing like that. I think they're just worried I'll attract unwanted attention."

"From whom?"

Claire shrugged. "All of the dangerous people roaming the city, I guess. Police, spies, murderers. Boys with bad intentions."

Gina's eyebrows arched. "You have boy problems?"

The door to the director's office was still closed.

"No," Claire said. "I have uncle problems." Gina looked at her, her expression open and concerned, and Claire's words tumbled out. "But they do involve someone I met."

"Really?" Gina leaned forward to listen. Just like Eleanor would have. "Tell me."

Claire found a loose hem on her skirt and picked at it. "His name is Antonio. He's been showing me around the city, a little. He wants to be an artist."

"Do tell."

Claire glanced up, afraid she was being mocked. But Gina smiled, and Claire went on. "Uncle Vincent found out and told me not to see him. They won't even meet him."

"Give it time." Even Gina didn't sound convinced.

"I don't have time. Not if I leave." Claire gouged a line in the wood of the table with a fingernail. It was more than that. She wasn't even sure she was willing to go. Not without some news of her parents. But talking to Uncle Vincent about a change in plans – or anything else – right now was impossible. "It's unbearable having no control over my life."

"You're not the only one."

Claire looked up. Gina's voice was unexpectedly hard.

"Think about the people who know those they love won't ever arrive, or have no prospects of getting out of Portugal. I know that doesn't help, but many people are in the same situation you are. Or worse."

"You sound like you're speaking from experience." Except for the sick sister, Claire realized that she didn't know anything about

Gina's family. "Have you lost...?"

"I don't want to talk about it." The words must have come out more harshly than Gina intended, because she added, "if you don't mind."

"It's okay." Claire changed the subject. "Gina, when we warned people about the secret police the other day, what did they do? There's nowhere to run from here, except into the ocean."

"It depends. Some people do have their papers in order, and hopefully have nothing to worry about. The ones who don't – well, it's better if they're not home when the banging on the door starts." Her eyes were dark and bleak, and Claire wondered again what Gina wasn't telling her. "Sometimes the secret police won't come back a second time. Or the people move to another boarding house and gain some time. Of course, if they're on a Gestapo watch list, the pursuit can be relentless."

Claire suppressed a shiver. Father was on one of those. Maybe Antonio's friend Thomas had been too.

"I know it's upsetting. But people can be resilient. And resourceful. Some will get papers with a new name, a new nationality, and they'll get away. Trafficking in forged documents is a flourishing industry."

"I know," Claire said. "A precarious one, though." She wondered if the convoluted way her uncle conducted the drop-offs would keep him safe.

"Woo-oo, Claire." Gina waved a hand in front of her face. "Where did you go just then?"

"Oh, sorry. I was thinking."

"About what? All of your experience with forgeries?"

"What? Of course not."

"Don't look so flustered. I'm teasing," Gina said, although her expression was thoughtful. "Tell me more about your boyfriend." She laughed then, so clearly not expecting a serious answer that Claire laughed with her. It started out as a chuckle. Then Claire, trying to stop, snorted instead. Gina stared, then giggled, and instants later they were both gasping with laughter. Claire didn't know why, but it didn't matter. All that mattered was that it eased the tension between her shoulders, and that for one fleeting moment everything felt normal.

The director's door opened, and Esther regarded them searchingly. "Ah, Gina, I should have guessed you were here.

What in the world set you two off?"

"Nothing," Claire said.

"Is that so?" Esther looked from Claire to Gina.

Claire almost started giggling again. Even Esther's displeasure was somehow funny. She looked down at her hands and tried to compose herself.

"Well, it's time to go," Esther snapped. "Gina, I take it you're coming too?"

Without waiting for an answer, she handed Claire the sign that said HICEM, and the three of them set off in silence. Claire's euphoria evaporated, leaving her feeling more contrary than before. It didn't help that a cluster of young boys followed them into the station. Street kids, with dirty faces and clothes no mother had seen to in a while. She was about to shoo them away when they stopped by the columns at the end of the platform. Claire, Esther, and Gina joined the other refugee aid workers by the tracks.

Timmy was already there. Claire tried to catch his eye, but he turned away. She sighed. He must have gotten reprimanded too, for letting her visit the children. All around her, conversations buzzed. She was alone, isolated in a sea of useful, well-meaning people. Again.

Gina laid a light hand on her arm. "We have a couple of minutes before the train arrives. You can ask the others about Eleanor."

"No, she can't." Esther had overheard. "Claire needs to focus on the task at hand, and that's helping us here. Her personal plans can wait."

Claire swallowed. Gina rolled her eyes, but let the subject drop. Minutes later, the train chugged into the station. The latest contingent of bedraggled, desperate passengers had arrived in Lisbon.

"Hold up the sign, Claire," Esther ordered as they began to disembark.

Claire held it in front of her chest.

"Higher."

Claire hoisted the sign above her head and saw faces turn her way. If only, if only her family would finally be among them. But everyone she saw was a stranger. Besides, her parents wouldn't look for her under a HICEM sign. They'd go straight to Vincent's, as she had.

A group of refugees gathered around her, bringing with them the sweaty sourness of clothes that had been worn for too many days. A woman with stooped shoulders deposited her suitcase on the platform and ordered her two boys to sit on it. The older one flopped across it on his stomach and started rocking back and forth. The younger child wailed and fell off.

Their mother lifted a hand in warning, then turned to Claire. "Miss, is it far to our lodging? My boys must eat."

Esther would know. "I..." Claire began, when a man interrupted her.

"I'm looking for the Unitarians. Do you know where I can find them?"

Claire pointed him Timmy's way and turned back to the stooped lady.

A girl about her own age touched her arm. "I need to go to the Europa boarding house. Can you tell me how to get there?"

Claire was giving her directions when the stooped young mother tugged on her sleeve. There were too many demands, too many people closing in around her. She couldn't breathe. Claire closed her eyes and let the station noises flow over her – a shrill whistle, an anxious mother calling, squeaky wheels on a porter's cart. What these people were asking wasn't unreasonable. She could do this.

"We'll get you some food," she told the woman with the little boys, and finished giving directions to the boarding house. The girl thanked her and left, and someone else took her place. Claire was amazed she could answer most of their questions. It felt good.

Over a man's shoulder, she saw an odd movement. A jacket draped over a stack of large suitcases was slipping out of sight. Then the small, crouched figure of a boy emerged from behind the suitcases. He made for the exit, the jacket clutched to his chest.

Without thinking, Claire charged after him. "No, you don't!" she yelled, and brought her sign down across his shoulders. The boy dropped the jacket with a cry and dashed away. When he reached the columns, the other kids turned and fled with him. Claire watched until they were out of sight, her blood pounding. The refugees who had been crowding her stared and kept their distance. Maybe she'd overreacted. She'd certainly surprised herself. She returned the jacket to its place on the suitcases and held the sign up again.

"What a Fury you are." Gina had come up behind her. "And here I thought you wanted to help little children, not scare them to death."

"Not if they're stealing," Claire protested.

Gina grinned. "I know. I approve. Just watch out for Esther. She probably wouldn't like knowing that you're using her sign to beat people up."

"I'll be careful," Claire said, relaxing. Gina's easy banter was a relief after her uncle's lectures. If only he could blunt his stern edges and try to be understanding. Just a little.

"Whew. I'm glad to see you with something other than a frown on your face," Gina said. "You're too young to have wrinkles, and face cream is so hard to find. You want to look lovely when you see Antonio."

"If I see him," Claire said. "I don't..."

"Gina, Claire, would you come over here and help?" Esther didn't hide her exasperation.

Discreetly, Gina squeezed Claire's hand. "We'll talk later," she said. "We'll figure something out."

Antonio

The Jolly Roger was located near the docks, the largest brothel in a long row of seedy-looking three-story buildings. Girls his grandmother would tut-tut about clustered around the doors with red-lipped pouts and their hips thrust out. They beckoned to him, but Antonio brushed them off and kept walking. He didn't need to find his pleasure here. Besides, next to Claire, they all looked...well, he couldn't think of a word, but it wasn't good.

Despite the early hour, uniforms from a half-dozen countries were already filing inside, the war temporarily put on hold. Other men, in suits, arrived in cars. At each entrance, the girls jostled over who would escort them inside.

Close up, the girl working the front door of the Jolly Roger had badly hidden wrinkles at the edges of her eyes and loose skin at her throat. She waved Antonio in with a languid swoop of her cigarette and turned back to the street. He didn't know whether to laugh or be offended.

Inside was a large, dim room decorated in deep red and gold, its air heavy with perfume and smoke. Tables in front of low couches brimmed with bottles and half-filled glasses. Thomas had come here? Antonio had a hard time imagining it.

As his eyes adjusted to the lamplight, a girl approached.

"Welcome to the Jolly Roger." She placed a finger on his throat and slid it lightly down his chest. "What are we drinking today?"

"Nothing." Her lipstick was too bright, the makeup around her eyes too thick. "I came to see Madam." Hopefully without making an ass of himself. He stood his drawing tube upright on the floor, where it was less noticeable.

"Madam?" the girl scoffed. "Not your first time. You have to work your way up to Madam." She stepped closer, flattening her hands against his chest. He could feel their warmth through the fabric of his shirt. She pressed into him, and he caught a whiff of roses. "Why don't you start with me? We'll see if you're good enough for Madam."

"You don't need to worry about that." Antonio pushed her hands away. "Go find her. We need to talk."

"She's busy."

"I'll wait." Antonio looked around for a place to sit. Somewhere away from the half-reclining couples on the couches.

"What do you want to talk about?"

"It's personal."

The girl smirked. "Everything here is personal."

"It's about a mutual friend."

The girl crossed her arms and regarded him suspiciously. "You're just saying that."

Antonio forced himself to remain polite. "Could you please find her?"

"I'm prettier than she is."

Antonio didn't bother to answer. He found a stool at the bar and inserted himself between a portly gentleman and a girl draped over a tipsy British seaman not much older than Antonio.

The girl signaled for a beer and raised it to the seaman's lips. "One more, my love, and then it's upstairs for you."

He gulped and giggled.

"Now what were you saying? That your ship leaves tomorrow? What a pity." She batted her eyelashes, little girl-like. "Where are you going?"

"We're accompanying a convoy of merchant ships to Ecuador." The seaman tried to puff out his chest importantly, but instead slipped off his barstool. The girl propped him up. "Can't let U-boats get them, you know."

"Of course not," the girl purred. "Will you stop in the Canaries on the way? I've always wanted to go there."

Antonio watched them from the corner of his eye. For a whore, she had a surprisingly good grasp of geography.

"Yes." The seaman downed the rest of his beer. "Can we go upstairs now?"

"Of course, my love." She held up five fingers for the bartender and led the boy upstairs. The bartender scribbled something on a piece of paper, then turned to Antonio and the stocky gentleman.

"What can I serve you?"

"A glass of port," the other man said. "And Jacqueline."

"I've already sent for her," the bartender said smoothly. He poured a ruby liquid into a small stemmed glass. "And you?"

Antonio shook his head. "I'm waiting for Madam."

"Are you now?" The bartender took in his well-worn clothes with a barely disguised sneer.

Antonio turned and surveyed the room. Three new customers were engrossed in conversation with their escorts on the couches, their hands hidden in the curves of the women's bodies, heads close together, whispering secrets. Secrets. Maybe that's the reason Thomas had been coming here. Or at least one of them.

"What can I do for you, young man?" A woman wearing clinking colored bangles and a maroon skirt that fell to her ankles loomed over him. Antonio leaned back to get a better look. She was at least six feet tall, with a cool, professional expression.

"It's about Thomas."

"I've got hundreds of men coming in here. We don't ask for names."

The portly gentleman's back was to them, but he was still too close.

"Can we go somewhere quieter?"

"I don't see the point. I can't help you."

Antonio stood up. His mouth barely reached her ear. "Thomas Schiller," he murmured. "He definitely knew you."

Her face didn't change, but she clicked a long, ruby-red

fingernail on the bar. The bartender snapped to attention. "I'll be in the office. Don't disturb me."

"Yes, Madam."

She turned sharply, her long skirt twisting gracefully after her, and led Antonio toward a door in the back. Her charmless office was a stark contrast to the reception area.

Madam pointed him to an armchair, and settled casually on the edge of the desk. "What's this about?"

"You knew Thomas Schiller." Antonio waited for a response but got none. "He kept a diary. You're in it."

Her lips turned up slightly. "I'm flattered that some of our guests enjoy their experience enough to write about it in their journals." She held out a hand. "May I see this diary?"

She'd make a good poker player. "I don't have it with me." He could feel its weight in the pocket of his jacket.

She sighed with exaggerated patience. "If you made the effort to come here, I hope you're at least planning to tell me what it said."

"He wrote that he was expecting gifts from you," Antonio said. "The evening he was killed."

Madam drew herself to her full height, then leaned forward and placed her hands, very deliberately, on Antonio's armrests, penning him in. "You wouldn't be suggesting that I had something to do with his death, would you?"

"No. Of course not." The lace of her neckline tickled his face. He tried to pull back, but had nowhere to go.

"So what did you think?"

"I thought you might remember what the gifts were."

Her warm breath held a touch of red wine. She stayed still a moment, then pushed herself upright with a mocking smile. "Aren't we the nosy boy? What gifts would you expect a man to receive in an establishment like mine?"

Antonio let out a breath. This wasn't going anywhere.

"Did he write anything else?" Madam asked.

"He mentioned a baby. A newborn." A child, a brothel – they could be linked. Unless Thomas was using some kind of code, and meant something else entirely.

Madam shook her head. The earrings that matched her bracelets clinked. "None of my girls has had a baby. Your friend must have been going elsewhere. Now, may I see you out?"

"Wait." Antonio jumped up and blocked the door with his foot. "Thomas was killed for a reason, and whoever did it is looking for something they think he had, or something he was working on. I want – I have to find out what it was."

"Why?"

"He was a friend."

She shrugged, unimpressed.

"Whatever it was, it was important to him. And you were involved somehow. If I found you, they might too."

"Is that a threat?"

Antonio shook his head. He was going about this all wrong.

"Then I'd advise you to destroy that diary before someone else reads into it what they shouldn't."

"Won't you help? Please."

With a wave of her hand, Madam motioned him away from the door. Disappointment lodged in his stomach like a stone. She wasn't going to give him anything.

"I'm sorry I can't assist you." She put her hand on the doorknob but didn't turn it. Antonio brought his eyes back to hers. "Perhaps you should search in another direction."

"Such as?"

"Perhaps this 'baby' your friend wrote about was something else. A reference to something he'd consider just as precious as a child."

"You do know something," Antonio said. "Tell me."

"I have nothing to tell. Now if you'll excuse me." She opened the door and ushered Antonio into the main room, appraising it with a quick glance and a nod. She turned to Antonio. "Do you need the services of one of my girls?"

Best be polite, or he'd never be allowed back in with more questions. "Not today, thank you." Antonio didn't blame her for not trusting him. He was angrier at himself than at her. He hadn't been convincing enough.

"I'll leave you then. Be careful." Madam gave him her fingers to shake and left to greet a new customer.

The girl who had approached him earlier was on one of the couches, sitting in a man's lap. She threw him a flirty smile. Her client grabbed her chin, pulling her face down, and her smile wavered. She forced it back and played with the buttons on the man's shirt. Antonio grimaced and pushed through the girls in the doorway. Madam had confirmed one thing. Thomas was writing in code. It wasn't a baby. Something else precious. But what?

Outside, the sun blazed down. Antonio squinted, repositioned the drawing tube on his back, and headed toward the river. Halfway down an alley between two warehouses, a big seaman was pressing a girl against the wall. His mouth pecked at hers, seeking a kiss.

She pushed him away. "Enough," she said. "You don't have anything to tell me that can't be said inside."

The seaman swayed like an upside-down pendulum, then steadied himself. "Stay with me, lovely lady," he slurred. "I need you."

"But you don't want to pay for my company, is that it?" She shoved him again. He fell back and she darted away toward the brothels, weaving around Antonio as fast as her sharp heels would allow.

"Lady, wait!" The seaman staggered after her.

Without thinking, Antonio blocked his path.

"Get out of my way." The seaman tried to sidestep him as the girl disappeared around a corner. Antonio didn't budge.

The seaman groaned. "Asshole! I've lost her!"

He swung a fist and the side of Antonio's face exploded. He reeled backwards. The seaman stumbled after the girl, moving fast for someone who was so drunk. Antonio leaped onto his back. The seaman went down, yelling. Antonio hit the ground and rolled, right over his drawing tube. He came up in a crouch. The seaman lumbered to his feet and Antonio rammed his shoulder into the man's chest. The seaman's breath left him with a loud groan. He crashed backwards into a warehouse, his head slamming against the wall. Slowly he slid to a sitting position, eyes unfocused.

"She wasn't yours to lose," Antonio said. "Nothing here is yours." He kicked the bottom of the seaman's boot. "Get up."

The seaman moaned, then leaned to one side and vomited. Antonio stepped back, clamping his nostrils together, and waited.

The man got to his hands and knees, then slowly climbed to his feet, spitting and honking his nose. He glanced down at his spattered uniform and his shoulders slumped. "Shit."

"Get out of here," Antonio said. "Go back to your ship."

The seaman raised a fist. Antonio tensed. But then he turned and staggered toward the waterfront, bracing a hand against the wall for support.

Antonio trailed the man at a distance, his fingers gently probing his left eye. Not much blood, but too much damage to hide from Avó. She'd fuss. Idiot seamen. What made foreigners think they owned the place? But no, that wasn't fair. He knew better than to put them all in the same box. Stupid seaman. Stupid girl. What had she been thinking, going off where her Madam couldn't protect her?

Antonio left the warehouses behind and found a pile of crates near the water. High up was a niche where he could sit. The perch gave him a good view of the long expanse of the dock. Tied along it were ships of all sizes, flying flags from Britain, Italy, Portugal, Brazil, and others he couldn't make out.

In the distance the seaman, trying to walk straight, finally reached three of his crewmates waiting at the gangplank of a hulking gray warship. He turned toward the warehouses and mimed a fight. One of his comrades took off in the direction of the brothels, only to get yelled at. He turned back.

Antonio slid down. They'd never notice him among the crates. Not much had come from his trip to the Jolly Roger. He'd go back to the diary tonight and try to figure out what might have been precious enough to kill for. And decide whether he was ready yet to show it to Gray.

On the river, a boat with an Italian flag steamed by, followed by a merchant ship. Antonio reached over his shoulder for his drawing tube, hoping it hadn't been damaged in the fight.

"Get down off those crates, boy."

Antonio froze. Two harbor policemen were standing below him, their legs apart, fists planted on their hips. Despite their severe expressions, Antonio had to bite his cheek to keep from grinning. One was tall and lanky, his legs thin as a bird's. The other looked like a soccer ball with a head on it.

"You've got no business here," the skinny one said. "What are you doing?"

"Taking a break." Antonio began to climb down, keeping the crates between them. They might look ridiculous, but it was still two to one. "Is there a problem with that?"

"A break from what?" The stocky policeman regarded him more closely. "A fight? What trouble are you in?"

I've been defending the honor of Portuguese women, Antonio almost said, but didn't. "There's no harm in watching the water, is there?"

The tall policeman must have caught the sarcasm Antonio was trying to keep in check. He circled the crates, following him.

Antonio tilted his wrist, looking at a watch he didn't have. "If you'll excuse me," he said in his politest Chave d'Ouro voice.

"Wait. Where do you think you're going?"

"Work. Can't be late." He struck off for the far end of the dockyard, ready to run if they did.

Instead, they split up. The spindly one followed him at a leisurely pace and fell steadily behind. The soccer ball headed toward the gray warship, where the seamen still clustered. Antonio started jogging. He wanted to be long gone before the policeman heard about the fight.

Capital of the Reich bombed for 3 hours
by the Royal Air Force

Diário de Notícias
April 11, 1941

CHAPTER 12 – FRIDAY, APRIL 11

CLAIRE'S MORNING STARTED just like the day before. "You'll go with Esther to HICEM," Vincent said, first thing.

"But uncle, I need to…"

"You need to help Esther."

"But…"

"No."

Claire set the breakfast dishes down so hard they rattled. She couldn't tell which he was angrier about – her visit to the kids, or Antonio. Or if it was something else, he was certainly too upset to confide in her now. Sharing drop-offs and pick-ups was a thing of the past. She sawed off a chunk of bread, still favoring her thumb. Their ship was leaving in two days. Two days to decide – if her parents didn't arrive – whether she'd go or stay. And no matter what, she wasn't disappearing without saying goodbye to Antonio.

"What are we doing today?" Claire asked Esther as they left the boarding house. A normal conversation might get her more than silence would. "Do you have another train coming in?"

"No. We got new medical supplies. We need to put them away, and see what's still running low."

"Oh." Claire didn't see how she could be of much help with that. Maybe she could convince Esther to let her go out with Gina instead. Although if she thought about it, that might not be the best strategy. "You don't like Gina much, do you?"

Esther gave her a sideways glance. "Why do you say that?'

"When we're with her, you seem…tense."

"It's not that I don't like her. She asks a lot – too many – questions. It's uncomfortable."

"She's always been nice to me."

"Oh, she's perfectly nice. But I'm suspicious of everyone these days. As you should be."

Claire just nodded, unwilling to start the argument up again. She'd said nothing to Antonio about her uncle or the children. And Gina? She was the only person in Lisbon who seemed sympathetic to Claire's predicament. Besides, they weren't talking about anything secret. Just about Antonio.

At HICEM, Esther showed Claire a storeroom and put her to work sorting bandages. Gina poked her head in the door an hour later to say she'd arrived. Claire willed her to come inside, but Gina shot her a preoccupied frown and disappeared. Esther set Claire to work counting aspirin tablets and a multitude of remedies Claire didn't recognize. Finally she escaped to the toilet, and found Gina alone in the main room, opening the mail.

"Help me get out of here, will you?" Claire begged in a whisper.

Gina looked up. "What?"

"Please. You know why. Make up a delivery I can help you with. Anything."

"You're asking for trouble."

Claire shook her head. "I'm being treated like a prisoner. It's ridiculous."

"You wouldn't be planning to take off on my watch, would you?" Gina asked. "You'll get me into trouble too."

"You can tell them you didn't know what I was planning, or that I just disappeared. Please."

"Let me think about it."

Claire nodded and went to the toilet. On the way back, she stopped by Gina's table again. "Well?"

"Still thinking." Gina didn't glance up.

Claire let out a loud sigh and returned to the storeroom. The interminable sorting continued.

Finally, Gina appeared in the doorway. "Esther, I have some errands to run. Remember, I told you?"

"You did?"

"Yes. Yesterday afternoon. I can't pick up the food coupons for you."

"Oh dear. I guess I forgot." Esther let her hands fall in her lap. "I'll never finish if I have to go out now."

"What if I borrow Claire? She can bring them back to you."

"I'd rather Claire stayed with me. Are you sure you can't do it?"

"Not if you want them today. She'll be quick. Come on, Claire, let's get going."

Claire set down the list she was holding and got to her feet.

"Claire." Esther's voice caught her before she reached the door. "No foolishness, do you understand? I want you back here as soon as you've got them."

"All right." Claire ran outside after Gina. "Thanks," she said after the door had closed behind them. "Do you really have errands to run?"

"I do, and so do you. Even if you're, uhum, delayed, you still have to take the coupons back to Esther."

"Can't we find Antonio first?"

Gina lifted an eyebrow. "Do you know where he is right now?"

"Well…no. I'll ask at the café."

"But we get the coupons first. You can't go back to Esther empty-handed."

"Fine."

"It's not far." Gina gripped her arm and they set off quickly. They were in and out of the office in fifteen minutes. Gina handed Claire the small package she'd been given. "Now to the café."

Claire shot her a surprised look. "You're coming with me? I thought you had something to do."

"I do. Later. But do you think I'd miss the chance to get a glimpse of your Antonio?"

Claire wasn't sure this was a good thing. Then again, if they ran into Vincent, having Gina at her side could be useful. "All right."

They made their way to the café, taking a wide detour around Rossio so they wouldn't pass in front of number 59.

Antonio wasn't there. "He comes in later," said the waiter who greeted them at the door. "Do you want me to give him a message?"

His smile was a little too friendly, a little too sly. Claire hesitated.

"No, thank you," she said.

"What next?" Gina asked.

Claire knew some of the spots he frequented — the art gallery, the dock, the castle. But going all over the city was out of the question. "First we get away from Rossio," she said. "My uncle could come down anytime."

"You don't think I could deflect him?"

Not if Vincent caught her with Antonio, Claire thought, but she didn't say it. She was too grateful for Gina's help.

"Miss." It was the sly waiter again. "There he is." He pointed at the center of the square. Antonio, his drawing tube slung across his back, was chatting with a shoeshine boy by one of the fountains.

"I can't go out there," Claire said. Antonio stood in the direct line of sight from her uncle's windows. "You get him. I'll meet you," she searched for a landmark, "at the Carmo elevator."

"Wait," Gina protested. "He doesn't even know me."

"I'll introduce you afterwards." Claire turned her back and took off, walking fast. The further she got from the boarding house, the better. The shoeshine boy saw Gina coming first, and started his patter. Over her shoulder, Claire saw Gina ignore him and address Antonio. He whirled around. They caught up with her in less than a minute.

"Antonio, meet my friend Gina. Gina, Antonio," Claire said. She peered at him more closely. "What happened to your face?"

He touched the corner of his eye. "Nothing. Me being clumsy."

"Is that so?" She'd watched him move – every chance she got – and he was anything but. Claire gave herself a shake. Now wasn't the time to be thinking about that.

"You were looking for me?"

"Do you have time to talk?"

"I have to work later." His voice held a question. "But I'm free now."

"Good," Claire said. "Gina, you'll excuse us?"

"Sure. But don't forget about the package for Esther."

"I won't." In silence, they watched Gina leave. "Is there somewhere nearby where we can talk?"

"I know a little café in Chiado. Is something wrong?"

"It's just…I don't have much time."

A few minutes later they passed through a big square teeming with people and turned into a narrow side street. Partway up was a small café with five tables inside and two outside against the windows. It was empty.

"How's this?"

They chose an outside table and sat down side-by-side, their chairs facing the street. The sun had warmed the spot and Antonio took off his jacket. He put it and his drawing tube on the seat of a chair, beside Claire's package. "What's up?"

"My uncle found out about you. He told me not to see you again." She folded her hands on the table and concentrated on them. Would Antonio even care?

"You're not very good at obeying, are you?"

She looked up. His mocking smile was back, but it was gentle. Claire was tempted to reach out and trace his lips, but didn't dare. "It's not funny. He was furious. I've hardly been let out of Esther's sight. I thought I might not see you again before..." Her voice trailed off as Antonio unclasped her hands and held them between his. If he noticed she was trembling, he didn't say anything.

"How did you get out now?"

"I'm making a delivery." She nodded at the package.

"How did your uncle find out?"

"I think it was that man we met at the gallery. He must have told him."

"They know each other that well?"

"Uncle Vincent seems to know a lot of people."

"What does he do?"

"He's a businessman." She had no intention of telling him what kind of business. "I'm pretty sure he knew your German friend too." She stopped speaking as the waiter came to take their order.

"Thomas?"

She nodded.

Antonio leaned even closer, speaking more quietly now. "What makes you think that?"

"I saw him leaving my uncle's boarding house the day I arrived. Then that evening, when Thomas was kidnapped, Uncle Vincent reacted really strangely."

Antonio went still. "Strange? In what way? He wasn't expecting it, was he?"

Claire shook her head. "Not at all. He pulled our curtains shut in a hurry."

"Did he know why Thomas was killed?"

"I don't know. But he said it would complicate things."

The waiter arrived with two cups of coffee, and they paused

again.

"Nothing more?"

"No, and I never found out what he meant. Maybe they were working on some kind of project together?"

Antonio didn't respond for a moment. A couple paused beside the other outdoor table, then moved on. "V and a baby," Antonio said under his breath. "So V is Vincent. But where is the baby?"

"What?"

Antonio looked her full in the face. "I need to trust you. Can I?"

Claire nodded slowly, glad he was willing to, but hoping she wouldn't regret it. Revelations in Lisbon never seemed to bring good news.

"Nobody seems to care why Thomas died," Antonio said, then paused. "Maybe I should say our secret police cares, but for the wrong reasons."

"What do you mean?"

"When they started questioning people, they made it sound like Thomas was the one who had done something wrong. They're not really investigating. I'm wondering if it was because the Gestapo was involved."

Despite the sun, Claire shivered.

"But why?" Antonio continued. "That's what I need to find out. What did he know? What was he doing? What did he have that someone could want?" Antonio halted abruptly, as if seeking a connection. "Claire, was Thomas carrying anything when you saw him at the boarding house?"

Claire thought back. He'd held the door open for her courteously and gestured her inside. "No. His hands were empty."

Antonio blew out a loud breath. "Thomas got a package from someone on your train," he said slowly. "When he came to the café a few minutes later, he didn't have it. What if the package is the baby?"

"What are you talking about?"

Antonio looked up and down the street. Claire followed his gaze. It was empty except for three men who had just turned onto the street. They were too far away to hear anything.

"After he was killed, I went to Thomas's room and found his diary. I think the secret police might be looking for it too."

Claire blinked. Worse and worse.

"Lots of what's in the diary doesn't make sense, at least to me." Antonio's voice cracked with frustration. "But he wrote about giving a baby to V. I think he gave the package to your uncle."

"Even if he did, what does it mean? What was in it?"

"You'll have to ask your uncle. Will you? It's important."

"It's not a good time. He won't tell me anything now."

"Because of me?"

"Partly. And…" Claire broke off suddenly as the three men she'd noticed earlier formed a dark wall around their table. She froze as one of them jerked Antonio to his feet. A second man thumped his cane on the ground, its sharp metal tip grating against the sidewalk. He barked something in Portuguese.

"*O que?*" Antonio yanked away, but couldn't free his arm. In the rapid-fire back-and-forth that followed, Claire didn't catch a single word. Two of the men positioned themselves on either side of Antonio and started marching him down the street. He tried to turn around, but a rough hand on his back pushed him forward. He stumbled and kept going.

"My apologies for interrupting your conversation," the man with the cane said in English. He touched his hat to her mockingly and left. He didn't limp.

Antonio

"Interrogation." It was the only word the men holding Antonio would say. People passing them made their faces neutral and scurried away. He knew that reaction. He'd done it too, trying to make himself invisible to someone who was likely a member of the PVDE. But never before had he been the one no one dared help.

Two long blocks later, they arrived at the unmarked entrance of a massive building. In a featureless room at the end of a corridor, the men patted him down, then pushed him onto a stool beside a table and left him. Antonio rested his head on his fists, avoiding the tender spot beside his left eye. It was throbbing. If this was about stealing, they'd have arrested him on the spot. Going to a brothel wasn't a crime, or hanging out at the docks. Claire. He didn't think they'd taken her. He fervently hoped not.

Which left Thomas and Gray. He had no desire to talk about either of them. What he and Claire had figured out was too fresh in his mind. The room was airless and sweat soaked his shirt. It would be easy to slip up. And if they had his jacket and drawing tube…

The door rattled. Antonio tensed, but no one came in. He prayed Claire had been left alone and had had the wit – and courage – to take his things with her. Thomas's diary would be better off with her than in the hands of the PVDE. Except that it would put her in more danger. The shock on her face as they dragged him away…

Merda.

Under the table, his knee jiggled. He forced it into stillness. What were they waiting for? A steel box around his memories – that's what he needed. Thomas, Gray – they were only customers he'd met at the Chave d'Ouro. He knew nothing about their personal lives or activities. Antonio wiped his hands on his trousers and tried not to think how little effort it would take to catch him in a lie.

The door banged open and Antonio jolted to his feet. The man with the cane entered, followed by one of the fellows who'd gripped his arms so tightly they had started to go numb. Going up against him would be like colliding with a tank in street clothes.

"Sit," said the man with the cane.

Antonio sat. His leg twitched again. "Who are you? What do you want?"

The man with the cane glanced down at his dark suit. "Call me Mr. Black," he said humorlessly. He leaned across the table until his face was inches from Antonio's. His eyes were as expressionless as a snake's. He looked familiar, but Antonio couldn't say why.

"Where did you get that black eye?"

"In an argument with a drunken seaman."

"A troublemaker, eh?"

"No, sir."

"Yet you knew Thomas Schiller."

"The German refugee?" Antonio was acutely aware of the second man moving around behind him.

"So you know who we're talking about."

That wasn't worth denying. "He was a customer at the Chave

165

d'Ouro."

"What did he tell you?"

"One of your agents already talked to me. I told him everything I know."

"Did you tell him you'd paid a visit – or several – to Mr. Schiller's room?"

"What?" Antonio swallowed. That's where he'd seen this man. Coming up the stairs with Thomas's landlady. He hadn't carried the wicked-looking cane then. "I'm sorry. I don't follow you."

"I think you do." Mr. Black's breath, a sour mix of cigarettes and bad teeth, washed across the table. The second man moved up, directly behind Antonio. "You were in Mr. Schiller's room."

"Really, I…" He'd barely gotten the words out when a hand slammed his head forward onto the table. Jagged blocks of color danced in front of Antonio's eyes. He groaned.

"I saw you there. Admit it."

"I don't know where he lived," Antonio said shakily.

The hand ground his cheek and the swollen flesh around his eye into the surface of the table, twisting his neck at an unnatural angle.

"I saw you at the Astoria boarding house on April 6," Mr. Black said. "You deny that?"

"The Astoria?" Antonio stalled. "I, uh, have friends who live there. But I haven't seen them in a while."

"Is that so? You were there, but didn't see them?"

"No one was home."

"Are you sure?"

The man behind him grabbed Antonio by his hair and pulled his head up, then let go and backed off. Where his face had been, the table was smeared with blood.

"You and Mr. Schiller talked a lot."

Antonio didn't answer.

"Why don't you tell me what you talked about?"

"I told your agent everything."

Two hands settled heavily on his shoulders.

Antonio hunched down on the stool. "Wait. He talked about the war, about what he read in the papers. Ships going down. That kind of thing."

"Planes shot down, perhaps?"

"Uh, no. What planes?"

"You saw him the night he disappeared, did you not?"

"The night he was kidnapped, you mean."

There was a sudden pressure on the sides of his neck and everything went dark.

Dimly, Antonio heard, "We're not done yet." The hands released his neck, and slowly his vision returned.

"I repeat: Did you see him that evening?"

"Yes." Antonio swayed on the stool. "He was in the café." They knew this.

"What did he give you?"

"Sorry?"

"He gave you something. What was it?"

Aside from some good laughs and urgently needed loans, Thomas had never given him anything. "Nothing." The hands tightened on his neck again. "But he left his glasses and keys," Antonio added.

"Keys? Do you have them?"

Merda. "Mr. Silva put them somewhere for safekeeping, until Thomas came back. I don't know where."

Antonio's questioner regarded him thoughtfully. "So it's Thomas now, is it?"

Antonio didn't answer. So many mistakes.

"You're not very good at hiding things." Mr. Black laid his cane across the table, positioning its sharp end near Antonio's chest. "I want to know – now – where the documents are."

"I told you. I don't know about any documents."

The second man pulled Antonio's left hand behind his back, then yanked it upwards, pitching him forwards. The end of the cane was even closer now.

"I don't know," he moaned. "I don't."

Mr. Black regarded Antonio impassibly, then nodded. There was a quick movement behind him. Antonio felt a bone crack, and screamed. The man twisted his broken hand, forcing Antonio off the stool and flat onto the floor. Still holding Antonio's arm behind him, the man dug a knee sharply into his back. He was going to dislocate Antonio's shoulder. Antonio groaned.

"What an unfortunate accident," Mr. Black said from above him. "You're sure you have nothing more to tell us?"

"Nothing." Antonio closed his eyes and waited for the next blow.

Claire

As soon as Antonio and the men turned the corner, Claire bolted from her chair.

Behind her, the waiter called, "Miss. Miss. Wait!"

She turned and saw him holding the package for Esther and Antonio's drawing tube. She ran back. The waiter lifted them out of her reach.

"You owe me for two coffees."

Claire fumbled in the pouch around her neck, keeping one eye on the street. What if the men came back?

"Here." Claire shoved two coins at the waiter. She grabbed Antonio's jacket and the package and drawings and ran, feeling something in his pocket bumping against her hip. Where could she go?

She turned two corners at random, then slowed to a walk and tried to get her bearings. The street was unfamiliar, but the city sloped down to the river at her back. She knew which way she was going. Claire angled to the right, where any downhill street would lead toward the center of town. A few minutes later, she recognized the São Pedro de Alcântara garden. She approached it cautiously, momentarily wondering if the skinny old man who called her Catarina had ever gotten his envelope back.

The garden was empty except for a few people staring out over the city. No one seemed to be following her. Claire sat down on a bench, looked around once more, then turned to the items in her lap. Again, she felt the bulk in the jacket pocket. She lifted the flap, just a fraction. Inside was an old brown book. Antonio had brought Thomas's diary and its dangerous secrets with him. She pressed the pocket shut with trembling hands. She didn't know what was happening to him or where to go for help. And what to do with the diary? She wrapped her arms around the jacket and tube. Keep Antonio's possessions safe. If nothing else, she could do that.

But the boarding house was out. If her uncle was there, he'd be angry, then he'd pry, and if she told the truth he'd be furious. Gina? That would involve going to HICEM. Esther would have a fit if she showed up with Antonio's things. Besides, Gina was out running errands somewhere. And after what she'd seen of the other waiters, leaving Antonio's things at the Chave d'Ouro was out of the question.

She ran through a list of the other people she'd met. Mr. Gray. No. Timmy. No. Antonio's grandmother? She didn't even know how to find her. And she hadn't located Eleanor. She looked at the jacket and saw one of the cuffs was frayed. She ran her finger along it. That would be easy to mend before she saw him again. If she saw him again. She shuddered. Antonio had to be all right.

Claire shook her head, trying to stop her mind from butting up against the same questions. What to do? Who could help? Each time, her thoughts returned to Vincent. If the diary was as important as Antonio thought, her uncle needed to see it. The secret police were questioning people Thomas knew. If someone had seen them together, her uncle might be under suspicion too. She and Antonio had figured it out. So could someone else.

But would Vincent even listen? Claire felt suddenly resentful. Why weren't her parents here, so she didn't have to go through this alone? She pushed the thought away. It certainly wasn't their fault they hadn't made it to Lisbon yet. She couldn't – wouldn't – stop hoping. Claire draped Antonio's jacket over the drawing tube and made her way out of the park.

Glancing back, she saw a man rise from another bench. Claire sped up. She felt transparent, as if anyone who looked at her would understand what she was carrying. Behind her, the man took the same path. She'd never be able to hold her own against someone like that. As quickly as she could, Claire walked downhill, trying not to look as if she was running away. At the corner of Rossio Square she stopped, pretending to look in a shop window. In its reflection, she saw the man pass behind her and continue on his way.

Antonio

The blow Antonio expected didn't come. Instead, the man behind him yanked him to his feet. Antonio cradled his broken hand against his body.

"You know something," Mr. Black said. "And I can assure you

we'll find out what it is. But I'm done with you – for the moment."
His eyes bored into Antonio's. "What a pity you tripped."

The message was clear. Antonio nodded. The men left. Behind
them, the door closed with a decisive click.

Claire

"What are you doing here?" Vincent's anger filled the doorway.
He wouldn't let her pass. "Where's Esther?"

"Still at HICEM, I think. Please let me in." Claire's legs weren't
going to hold her up much longer.

Grudgingly, Vincent stood aside. "What are you carrying?" His
voice sharpened. "What have you done?"

Claire sank down on the couch, her arms still wrapped around
Antonio's things. "Don't yell," she whispered. "Please."

"Why not? You've disobeyed again. Don't you understand how
dangerous it is?"

"I'm not dangerous," Claire said defensively. "But your friend
Thomas was."

"What are you talking about?" Vincent went still.

"I think the Portuguese secret police killed Thomas. If they
know you were friends, they might come after you too."

"Where did you get that idea?" Vincent asked through gritted
teeth.

Claire steeled herself. "I saw Antonio today."

"Damn it. We told you not to."

"Uncle, listen. Antonio thinks Thomas was killed because he
had something the secret police wanted."

"And how did Antonio come to that conclusion?"

"He found Thomas's diary."

"Where?"

Claire shifted uncomfortably. "In Thomas's room. After he
died."

"This is who you spend time with behind my back?" Vincent
exploded. "Someone who steals from a dead man?"

"Stop it. They were friends. Antonio is trying to find out why
Thomas got killed. And he thinks you're involved."

"Me?" Uncle Vincent tried to hide it, but the quick flash of fear was unmistakable.

"Whatever Thomas had, whatever the secret police are trying to find – Antonio thinks Thomas gave it to you. We don't know what it is." Claire saw Vincent's eyebrows rise at her "we," but she plowed on. "In his diary, Thomas called it a 'baby'."

"Baby? That's ridiculous," Vincent snapped.

"I know that. So what did he really give you?"

Vincent went to the window and looked out. He didn't answer.

"Uncle, you have to tell me." Claire's voice shook. "I think the secret police have Antonio. Or someone does. Three men took him away this afternoon when we were talking at a café. I'm afraid it's because of Thomas."

"*Mon Dieu.*" Vincent rasped his fingernails through the stubble on his cheeks. "You have no idea what you've gotten into."

"Then tell me."

"Thomas was crazy to keep a diary. Completely crazy. Do you know where it is now?"

Claire slid it out of the jacket pocket. "Here."

Vincent's eyes bulged. "You must be kidding." He grabbed the diary and leafed through it hurriedly. "Where does he mention me?"

"I don't know. I haven't looked at it."

"Does anyone know you have it?"

"Besides Antonio? I don't think so."

"Were you questioned? Did they ask your name?"

Claire shook her head.

"You're sure you weren't followed?"

Mentioning the man in the park – who in the end had paid her no attention – would only worry him. "Pretty sure."

"Let's hope not." Vincent cleared a space at the table and began going through the diary page by page. Claire sat beside him, her hands wedged under her legs, dreading what he might find. Two people who'd known what was in the diary had run into trouble with the secret police. And now she'd brought the danger home to her uncle.

"I don't see any names in here," Vincent said after a while. "At least Thomas was careful about that. What makes Antonio think he mentioned me?"

"Somewhere in the diary, Thomas writes about giving a baby to someone called V. Antonio thinks baby is a code for something else."

"Why?"

"The day I arrived, Antonio was at the station, and he saw Thomas receive a package from someone on the train. Soon afterwards, I saw him leaving your building without the package. We put the two together, and figured he'd given it to you."

Vincent scrubbed the stubble on his cheeks again. "Will Antonio talk?"

"I don't know." Claire swallowed, trying to keep her voice from shaking. "Is there anything you can do to help him?"

"Me?" Vincent gave a short laugh. "I pull no strings in this city. My involvement would only lead to very uncomfortable questions. But if he tells them what you've told me…" He rose abruptly and flicked the curtain aside to peer down at the square, then returned to the diary.

"So we were right? Thomas did give you something?"

After a long silence, Vincent nodded. "I've been meaning to tell you, just in case. But it never seemed to be the right time."

"In case what?"

Ignoring her question, Vincent checked the lock on the door, then opened one of the cabinet's bottom doors. It was filled with old newspapers. Vincent pulled them unceremoniously onto the floor until only a plain brown envelope was left. He placed it on the table beside the diary.

"What's that?" Claire laced her fingers together, remembering the day she'd regretted asking about the forgeries. From the expression on Vincent's face, what he had now was probably worse.

Carefully, Vincent opened the envelope and drew out another one with a stamped-on swastika and words in German scribbled across it. Inside were several folded sheets of paper. Maps. Her uncle spread them on the table. The one on top showed what looked like shipping routes across the North Atlantic. Claire shifted it aside. The next was a detailed drawing of the eastern United States. Red dots marked some of the biggest cities and ports – Boston, New York, Philadelphia, Washington, Newport News.

"These," Vincent said, "are German plans to attack America's east coast if the United States enters the war. This is what they're after."

Claire took a deep breath, then exhaled slowly. "This is what Thomas gave you?"

Vincent nodded.

"Where did they come from?"

"Remember we told you about the plane that crashed in France? The plans were on it, and they fell into the hands of people who decided it was worth risking everything to get this information to the Americans."

"Wait. Didn't you say Serge's and Alicia's parents had something to do with that plane? Isn't that why you've got the children in hiding?"

"After the crash, the Lapéroux made it to the scene first. They took everything they could carry. Even a lockbox that had been nailed to the floor. It contained these plans."

"And then?"

"They went underground with the children until they managed to get out of France. During the voyage, they gave the plans to someone else – I don't know who – who gave them to Thomas. But from what I've heard, they made an awful mistake." He paused.

The room was silent, as if the whole world had stopped to listen.

"What kind of mistake?"

"They thought the pilot was dying. They didn't have much time, and left him. Given what's happened since, I'd say he lived long enough to tell the Gestapo what he'd seen."

Claire swallowed. "And they followed the trail to Thomas."

Vincent nodded. "So now it's up to me – us – to keep the plans safe. At least until we dock in New York."

"Isn't forging documents enough? Why you?"

"Come on, Claire. You know where my sympathies lie. We all do what we can." His shoulders slumped. "But if Antonio tells them what you've told me..."

Claire steadied herself against the table. A stone seemed to be blocking her airway. "Yet you're still set on keeping the plans here. In our rooms." This was so much worse than the diary.

"What do you expect me to do? Take them out for a stroll?"

"I don't know. Why don't you give them to the American Legation? Anything to get them out of here."

"The Americans apparently don't have time to meet with a

Frenchman. Or they don't want to. I can't even get an appointment."

"Even when you tell them what you have?" Claire couldn't believe it.

"Why should they trust me? Besides, I can't tell just anyone. This is for the ambassador's eyes only, and I can't get near him."

"What makes you think it'll be easier in New York?"

"Here they have hundreds of desperate people lining up to see them. And they're very suspicious of foreigners from occupied countries. It won't be like that in America." They sat for a moment in silence.

Someone started pounding on the door.

CHAPTER 13

GINGERLY, ANTONIO EXAMINED his left hand. It was so swollen the skin looked ready to split. He held it against his chest and waited. The men didn't come back. After a few minutes, without much hope, he tried the doorknob. Locked. He moved to the other side of the room and leaned against the wall, trying to stop his shaking. He'd be far away from that stool, and standing, when they returned. At this point, that was all the defiance he could muster.

Finally the door banged open and a man Antonio hadn't seen before beckoned him out. "Time to go."

Antonio didn't move. "Go where?" If they were taking him to the PVDE prison, he wanted to know ahead of time. Too many people went in there and never came out again.

The guard waited by the open door, his lips stretched in a smirk that said *don't try me*. Dread lodging in his stomach, Antonio followed him into a long hallway with walls that looked like they'd been beaten too. Halfway down, the man pushed him through an unmarked door into a bathroom.

"Clean up," he ordered.

A broken mirror above the sink reflected Antonio's bruised face and red-spotted shirt. He'd been kidding himself, thinking he could investigate Thomas's death with no consequences. As well as he could with one hand, he rinsed off the blood.

"Enough," the guard said.

Antonio was nowhere near done. He dried his face and they resumed their march through the long, bare hallways. After a couple of turns, the corridor widened. The entry hall was straight ahead.

The guard nodded toward it. "That's the way out."

"I can leave?"

"You want to stay?"

Antonio was outside almost before the man finished speaking, running downhill toward Rossio. He had to find Claire, make sure she was okay. Find Claire. Get the diary. Get the drawings. The words ran through his mind like a mantra, timed to the throbbing of his hand. Halfway there, he slowed, then stopped and checked behind him. They probably wouldn't send people he could identify, but someone might follow him. He couldn't lead them straight to her.

Nearby, a church bell clanged three times. *Merda.* He should've been at the Chave d'Ouro an hour ago. He'd have to get through his shift as best he could. He held up his hand, not daring to bend it. It was twice its normal size, the skin stretched so tight it was shiny. The pain went all the way up to his shoulder. He'd never manage a tray.

The café was full of mid-afternoon customers. From behind the cash register, Mr. Silva took in Antonio's shirt and the odd way he carried his arm, and headed him off as soon as he got in the door.

"Get out of here." His voice was tight with barely controlled fury.

"I'm very sorry I'm late, sir," Antonio said quickly. "I can explain."

"Have you looked at yourself? How dare you?" Mr. Silva hissed. He took Antonio's left arm in a strong grip and turned him toward the exit.

Antonio's eyes watered. "Let go. Please."

Mr. Silva released him. The café had gone silent. "The door."

"Wait. Once I clean up, it'll be fine. Really."

"Fine?" Mr. Silva gave him another appraising look. "The black eye too? You should have listened when I warned you to stay out of trouble. I don't want you in the Chave d'Ouro."

"It won't happen again. I promise."

"Out." Mr. Silva pointed at the door.

"Yes, sir." Antonio bowed his head and left. Arguing would only make it worse.

Claire

The pounding on the door stopped as suddenly as it had begun, and Claire heard Esther's panicked voice.

"Vincent, are you there? Claire's disappeared." A key turned in the lock, and a second later Esther was inside. Her face crumpled, then flushed red. "You're here?" She grabbed Claire's shoulders and shook her. "Why? Why did you run off?" Esther dropped her hands and took a step back. "You had no right to put me through that."

"I'm sorry. I was going to bring the package, truly I was. But something happened." Claire faltered.

"Gina said you gave her the slip. You did it deliberately."

Vincent interrupted her. "We have a more serious problem now." He pulled out a chair and ran through the afternoon's events. Esther's face went pale.

"None of this can stay here," she said. With one finger, she pushed the uppermost plan away from her. "Not this, not the diary. You have to give them to someone else for safekeeping. At least until you sail."

"It's probably more dangerous to move them around the city than keep them here," Vincent said. "Besides, it seems the secret police – and whomever they're working with – will do their nasty business whether you have the plans in your possession or not. Suspicion is enough." He slid the plans back into the envelope and returned it to the cabinet. "We need to stay low, and hope they don't trace the plans to me."

"You really think you're the only one in Lisbon who can be trusted with them, don't you?" The edge was back in Esther's voice. Claire was sure they'd had this discussion before.

Vincent shrugged. "It's two more days."

"Uncle, what about Antonio?"

"I told you there's nothing we can do for him."

A heavy weight settled in Claire's chest. She couldn't bear to leave Lisbon, not knowing what had happened to him – or where her family was. If the Gestapo had arrested them, they might already be in a concentration camp. Or worse. She put her hand on Vincent's sleeve. They had to have this conversation now. "Uncle, if my parents don't arrive, I can't leave."

Vincent gave her a long look. "Do you honestly think we could stay? Knowing what you know? The longer we're in Portugal, the riskier it becomes."

"You don't have to. But you can't tell me to desert them." Or to abandon Antonio. No matter which way she looked, none of her choices were good ones. She wouldn't forgive herself if she left. But remaining in Lisbon alone, or attempting to get back to Marseille? She wasn't sure she had the courage.

"You can't. Changing our tickets is impossible. The shipping companies aren't even taking reservations right now. You'd be stranded. And I'm not leaving you."

"Do you even care that something might have happened to them?" Claire hated her voice for wavering.

"Of course I do. We've tried to locate them. We'll keep trying. But wherever they are, I know they'd blame me forever if I didn't get you safely out of Europe when I had the chance."

Claire dug her nails into her palms and didn't answer. Leaving would be running away. She couldn't do it.

Antonio

Antonio circled Rossio Square twice, nodding at Scrappy but keeping his distance. No one seemed to be following him. Casually, he let his gaze wander to the fifth floor of the boarding house. No movement showed behind the windows Claire had said were her uncle's. What if she hadn't made it home safely? He had to know. He wandered aimlessly for a few minutes more, still surveying the surrounding area, then stepped up to number 59 and yanked the bell pull. The door creaked open. On the first-floor landing, an old man with spindly legs barred access to the boarding house.

"What do you want?"

"I'm here to see a friend."

The concierge looked him up and down. "Who might that be?"

"Vincent."

"Vincent who?"

Antonio didn't know. "The Frenchman who lives on the top floor. With his niece Claire."

"No."

"What do you mean, no? I need to see them." To reassure himself that Claire was safe. To get the diary and his drawings.

"If they were expecting visitors, they'd have left word. You're only allowed upstairs if you're expected." The concierge crossed his arms. "And if you are, at a minimum, presentable."

"Go up with me now then." The pain was getting worse. Antonio started to cradle his hand again, then changed his mind and slid it behind his back. "You'll see I'm telling the truth."

The old man shook his head.

"Can you tell me if they're home?"

"That's their business, not yours."

Antonio took an angry step upward. Even in his current condition, it wouldn't take much to muscle past a scrawny old man. The concierge regarded him fiercely, not backing off. Antonio paused. His arm throbbed fiercely and he looked like a bloodied tramp. If he got upstairs and Claire wasn't there, her uncle might throw him out too, before he even started talking. Or worse, call the police. Antonio couldn't stomach the thought of a second run-in with police today, secret or not.

He held up his good hand in a gesture of surrender. "Can you give them a message?"

The old man hesitated, then nodded. "What is it?"

No. Bad idea. "Never mind. I'll come back later."

"I wouldn't bother. This is a respectable establishment."

Antonio swallowed a curse and retreated to a street that led away from Rossio. He stood for a moment in a quiet spot, watching for anyone watching him. Out here, he was too visible. He could go home, where his grandmother would bind his hand. And ask questions.

Bracing his arm against his chest, Antonio headed the other way, in the direction of Gray's gallery. He definitely had something to tell him now. The narrow streets all ran uphill and Antonio's pace slowed. If anyone wanted him, he'd be an easy catch. He detoured once, then a second time. No one was behind him.

Except for two birds fighting over a chunk of bread, the Largo do Carmo was quiet when he arrived. Almost too quiet. In his imagination, PVDE agents lurked behind every corner, ready to erupt from the side streets. Gray was nowhere in sight. Antonio chose a bench on the far side of the square, opened an abandoned newspaper and pretended to read, hiding his spotty shirt behind it. The side of his hand was purple. He placed it gingerly on his lap and looked over the newspaper at the gallery.

Inside, a woman was turning a gleaming silver teapot in her hands. A stout man Antonio didn't recognize hovered, showing her one piece after another. The woman shook her head, put down the teapot and left. The man retreated into the back office.

Antonio checked out the square again. Still empty. What if the art dealer wasn't there today? A couple walked by, arm-in-arm. As they left the square, a tall, familiar figure crossed their path.

Antonio eyed him but didn't move. Gray noticed him seconds later. With a quick movement of his hand, he signaled *wait* and disappeared into the gallery. The stout man soon left with a small package in his arms. As soon as he was out of sight, Gray scanned the square, then beckoned Antonio inside. He locked the door and drew Antonio into the office, out of sight of the window.

"What the devil happened?"

"The PVDE took me in for questioning."

"Damn it. About what?"

"Thomas."

"Not about us?"

"No," Antonio snapped. "But it was bad enough without that." He held up his swollen hand.

"Broken?"

Antonio nodded. "Hurts like hell."

Gray rummaged in a box under the desk and emerged with a roll of bandages and some tape. "I can't do much, but at least we can get it bound. Go wash your hand."

Antonio did. The cold water sent shockwaves up his arm. This was what happened when the PVDE went easy on someone. He started to pat his hand dry, flinched, and left it damp. He fervently hoped there wouldn't be a next time, when they might decide to get serious.

"Sit down. This'll hurt," Gray warned when Antonio came back to the office. "Don't yell."

He probed Antonio's hand with the tip of a finger. Antonio

braced himself. Suddenly Gray pulled. Bone grated against bone, shooting fire through Antonio's hand. He jerked away. Gray held on, maintaining the pressure.

"What are you doing?" Antonio gritted out, his jaw still clenched. "Breaking it again?"

"Putting your bones back into place." Cautiously, Gray ran his fingers down Antonio's hand again, and nodded. "Better. But you need to see a doctor."

That wasn't going to happen. For a lot of reasons. He'd bear it and hope it would heal – quickly. His heart still pounding, Antonio sat still as Gray wrapped the bandage around two fingers, four fingers, and finally his whole hand. He could feel his heartbeat in every fingertip. The bandage was anything but discreet.

"And here I was thinking we'd have a lock-picking lesson soon." Gray knotted the end of the bandage. "Bit difficult now." He put the supplies away and faced Antonio. "What were you doing? Why did they pick you up?"

"I wasn't doing anything. Claire and I were having coffee. Three guys showed up and dragged me away."

Gray looked alarmed. "Vincent's niece? They took her too?"

"I don't think so. I've been trying to find out. She's got the diary…"

"What diary?"

Gray couldn't ask all the questions. "You said you'd try to find out who killed Thomas," Antonio said. "Have you?"

"For god's sake, don't change the subject," Gray snapped. "You weren't keeping a diary, were you?"

"No. Thomas was."

Gray stared at him, unblinking. "You can't be serious."

Antonio didn't answer.

"And you had it?"

"Yes."

"What's in it?"

"All kinds of stuff. Shopping lists. Notes about ships sunk by U-boats. Something about a valuable baby." Antonio watched Gray carefully, but the man's expression didn't change. "And sketches."

"Of what?"

"One night, I followed that German who comes into the Chave d'Ouro. Mr. Thaler."

Gray nodded.

"I heard him talking with a PVDE agent about something they were looking for, and saw him with the driver of the car that took Thomas." Antonio hesitated. "So one night after work, I followed him to Chiado. Behind the building he went into was some kind of radio transmitter. A big diamond-shaped one. In his diary, Thomas drew the same one. Same building, same setting, everything."

"He found it then," Gray said under his breath.

"Found what?"

"The Germans have been transmitting information on our ship convoys – and more – from somewhere in Lisbon. We knew there had to be a transmitter somewhere, but couldn't locate it. Maybe you and Thomas have. Where was it exactly?"

Antonio gave him the details.

"And Claire has the diary now?"

"I hope so. Unless she left it at the café. With my drawings." Without them, he felt naked. Knowing that strangers might be pawing through his sketches made it even worse.

"The *Serpa Pinto* one?"

"Yeah. And a portrait of Thomas."

"Very recognizable faces." Gray grimaced. "Not the transmitter, I hope?"

Antonio shook his head, and regretted it. The throbbing in his arm was making him nauseous. "Not that." But there was more than enough to get him in trouble. "You said 'we' were trying to find the transmitter. Was Thomas part of your network?"

"No. But we were both interested in knowing what the Nazis in Lisbon are up to. He had his sources of information. I had mine. Sometimes we compared notes."

"Do you think that's why he got picked up? Because they knew he was spying?"

Gray shrugged. "The important thing now is to track down Claire and find out where the diary and drawings are."

"I already went to their boarding house. The concierge wouldn't let me in."

"Damn. Did you think he would, given your appearance?"

"I was worried about her. And I want my things."

Gray rolled his eyes. "Now the concierge will remember you, and that's unfortunate. This isn't the time to make a scene."

"I controlled myself." Barely.

"That's not the point. You can't go back there now. And if you'd been thinking straight, you wouldn't have gone there at all. Not right after a run-in with the PVDE."

Antonio didn't reply. The criticism was deserved. "You can go."

"Not a chance." Gray changed the subject. "You're not going to the Chave d'Ouro today, I take it?"

"No. Mr. Silva kicked me out earlier this afternoon."

"You went there too?" Gray didn't try to hide his irritation.

"I was late for work."

"I see you have a clear sense of your priorities," Gray said shortly. "What you should have done was get out of sight. You should know that."

"No one's followed me so far. And I'll go home now." Antonio managed a small smile. "Avó will think I've been brawling." And would yell at him. Even so, he'd be glad of the chance to lie down with his hand in the air. "But we need to find out about Claire. You know her uncle. Send him a message."

"I'll think about it. But don't come back here."

"Why not?"

"Damn it, boy. Don't you see? You could be leading the PVDE to every contact you have. If they didn't follow you today, they might tomorrow. Or the next day, or the next. It's too dangerous."

"You said we were going out tonight."

Gray gave a slight shake of his head.

"You're cutting me off?" Just after he'd handed Gray valuable information? After showing he wouldn't break under pressure? Antonio heaved himself out of the chair. "That's what you're saying? I'm on my own?" He sounded like a petulant child and hated himself for it.

"Once you're back at the Chave d'Ouro, I'll pass by as usual. You can let me know there if you have anything to report."

"You still expect me to eavesdrop for you? Why would I do that?"

"This is for your safety, as well as everyone else's."

Antonio glared at him.

Gray stared back, unperturbed. "You should go now." He walked to the front window and gazed out, then unlocked the door. "You need…" he started to say.

Antonio threw him a defiant look. "I don't need anything from you."

"Listen to me." Gray grabbed Antonio's arm.

Antonio shook it off and slipped outside.

"Antonio, wait."

"What?" He'd heard more than he wanted already.

"You got out of their grasp today, but they'll be watching. Be careful. The game has changed."

CHAPTER 14 – SATURDAY, APRIL 12

"UNCLE, YOU'VE GOT to let me out." Claire tucked her pouch under her blouse and stood up. The night had been full of horrible imaginings. She needed air – and time alone to think.

Vincent shook his head. "It's better to stay inside. We can't draw attention to ourselves."

"If the secret police thought I knew anything, they'd have taken me yesterday, wouldn't they?" She had to know if Antonio had been released.

"We don't know what Antonio's told them." Vincent glanced at the shelf over the sink. He'd hidden the diary there the night before, among a pile of neatly folded dishtowels. "We leave tomorrow. This isn't the time to go around asking questions."

"I'll walk by the Chave d'Ouro and see if he's at work. Besides, didn't you want to talk to him?"

"Claire, don't get your hopes up. The secret police…"

"I know." Claire didn't let him finish the sentence.

Vincent sighed. "If you see him, come and let me know. You are not to go near him. Is that understood?"

Claire nodded.

"Stay alert. And come back soon. We have to pack."

"All right." Claire let herself out the door. Packing to leave, when her family still hadn't arrived. She didn't think she could.

At the first-floor landing, the concierge waved her to a stop. "Good day, miss," he said formally. Claire stopped, surprised. He

185

usually ignored her.

"I had an unusual visit yesterday afternoon," he continued. "A young, uh, man, asking for you and your uncle."

Claire's stomach lurched, but she kept her expression neutral. "Yes?"

"He asked to go upstairs, to your rooms. Of course I refused." The concierge gave Claire a self-satisfied smirk.

The old man expected a thank you. She wanted to shake him. But at least he'd told her that Antonio was alive, and free.

"You turned him away? Why?"

"Monsieur Lemoine does not appreciate unexpected visitors. And this lad…" He clicked his tongue disdainfully. "He was in no condition to be presented to you and your uncle."

The night's visions flooded back. "Was he hur…?" The words spilled out before she could stop herself. Claire bit her lips shut. The concierge could be working for anyone.

He looked at her inquiringly. "You believe you know him?"

"Possibly. What condition was he in?"

"He was…unkempt. Not at all someone Monsieur Lemoine's niece should be associating with." He clicked his tongue again.

As if it were any of his business. Claire forced a smile. "Did he leave a message? Or say where he could be found?"

"No, miss." His voice was leaden with disapproval. Claire nodded her thanks and made quick work of the remaining stairs. Antonio might be hurt, but he was walking. Outside the Chave d'Ouro, she found the sly waiter.

"Is Antonio here?" she asked.

"He works this afternoon." He gave a short laugh. "That is, if he's cleaned up enough to make the boss happy."

"Pardon?"

"You don't know? I assumed he'd gotten into a fight over you." He winked, making Claire think of a weasel.

"Oh." She wasn't going to enlighten him. Or ask more questions. "Well, thank you." She'd come back later.

"My pleasure," he said smoothly as she turned away. Too smoothly. No way was she leaving a message with him.

Messages. The post office. Claire stood in line once more, only to hear the attendant say again, "I'm sorry, Miss Lemoine. There's nothing for you." She fled outside and to the riverfront. Even there, she felt like she couldn't get enough air.

Near the docks, a crowd was gathering below a massive warship that had just arrived. Dockworkers secured thick mooring lines, then winched a long gangway into place. Claire stopped. Around her, all eyes were lifted to a group of passengers on the high deck, waiting to disembark.

"Manny!" yelled a man near Claire. He started to climb over a wooden barrier separating them from the wharf.

One of the dockworkers intercepted him. "*Para*," he ordered. He pushed the man back. "Stop."

"It's my brother. I feared he was dead."

"You must wait."

The man tried to argue, but the dockworker allowed no one to pass. A low chatter, in English and Portuguese, rose around Claire.

"I heard a U-boat sank their ship and then left them in the middle of the ocean," said a quiet voice behind Claire. She turned around. A group of people had circled in close around the woman who was speaking. "They say only about half the crew made it onto the lifeboats." The woman fell silent as the sunken ship's crew started down the gangplank. One man limped down on crutches.

"None of the sea lanes are safe anymore," the woman started again.

Claire had had enough. *Not safe. Not safe.* She left the crowd, the words reverberating in her head. At Cais do Sodré, she stopped and sat down on the base of the statue. Not far away, ripples slopped against the riverbank. On the open ocean, the waves would be so much bigger. Claire gripped her perch as if it could anchor her to the shore. There were so many reasons not to leave on the ship tomorrow. She'd be okay. She could help at HICEM. Find work as a seamstress. Take care of Serge and Alicia. Esther and Gina would help. So would Antonio, surely.

Antonio. Who saw the person she'd like to be, and put it into a portrait. Whose touch gave her heart an uncertain new rhythm. Common sense said she had no future with someone like him. And maybe in normal times they didn't. In wartime, though, what was possible took on a whole different meaning.

Her pouch lay against her chest, sticky with sweat. Cautiously, she pulled out her boat ticket, holding it close in cupped hands, and searched for the departure time. "*Excalibur:* Boarding at nine a.m." Less than twenty-four hours from now. Uncle Vincent would be furious. The choppy water drew her eyes again. She stared at it, wishing it could give her some answers.

A young boy appeared at her side. "Money, miss," he said, holding out a hand. "A coin?"

Claire shook her head. "I'm sorry," she began. "I don't…" From behind her, on the other side, something jerked her hand. She looked down. Her boat ticket was gone. The boy who had sneaked up behind her was already halfway across the square, sprinting away.

"No! Stop!" Claire jumped to her feet. The boy who had distracted her was running hard in the opposite direction. She chased after her ticket. "Come back! Come back!"

On an uneven patch of cobblestones, she stumbled, her ankle twinging in protest. She righted herself and raced on. Far ahead, the boy turned a corner and disappeared. Claire reached the corner moments later. The street was empty, except for a bent old lady carrying flowers wrapped in newspaper. Claire leaned against the wall, panting. The boy was gone. And so was her ticket.

She felt dizzy. Minutes before, she'd been planning how she could stay. Now she couldn't leave if she wanted to. Claire bent over, pressing her arms against her stomach, afraid she was going to be sick. She stayed there for a moment, trying to breathe, then pushed herself upright and started walking. Up the hill, anywhere, as long as it was away from this cursed square.

She followed her feet in a daze, the surroundings a blur. Her uncle was going to kill her. Her mind couldn't leap beyond that. If she'd had a chance earlier to convince him that remaining in Lisbon was for the best, he might've considered it. But if he thought he was abandoning her, he wouldn't go. Even if he felt he had to. He'd made such careful plans for their departure, and her carelessness had ruined them.

Claire stumbled on. When she finally looked up and paid attention, she saw she was crossing the square where Gina lived. Claire found her building and rang the bell. She desperately needed a hug, and someone to tell her it would all work out.

No one answered. Claire sagged against the door. Gina was probably at HICEM, but so was Esther. Claire couldn't face Esther, or Uncle Vincent. Maybe Timmy could make a call for her. Walking fast, she took off for the USC. Once there, she tucked her blouse in neatly and patted her hair into place before knocking.

There wasn't much she could do about her splotchy face.

Timmy greeted her with an unhappy twist of his lips. "Bringing more trouble?"

"Not at all." Her pretend smile hadn't fooled him. "Could you please call Gina at HICEM for me?"

"Can't you go over there?"

"We'd planned to meet, but I'm going to be late. I need to catch her before she leaves."

Timmy looked skeptical.

"It's a surprise. Esther can't know. Could you see if Gina's still there? Please?"

Timmy's suspicious expression didn't change, but he picked up the receiver and dialed. "Good morning. May I speak to Gina?" Timmy held the phone out to Claire. "She'll be on in a minute."

Relieved, Claire took it and turned her back to him, pressing the receiver against her ear so her hand wouldn't shake. If Esther came on, she'd hang up.

"Hello?" It was Gina.

"It's me, Claire. I know we were supposed to meet this morning, but I'm running late." Gina started to say something, but Claire talked over her. "Can you meet me at the park at the top of the Avenida da Liberdade?" It was quiet, and nearby.

"Wha...? What are you doing there?"

"I'm at USC."

"Claire, are you all right?"

"Not really." Claire could feel Timmy's eyes on the back of her head and tried to sound natural. "Can you come?"

"You can't make it to HICEM?"

"No."

"The park is too far. Let's meet on the avenue itself. You walk down, I'll walk up."

"Okay." Claire replaced the receiver, her heart plummeting. No place was more public.

"Is everything all right?" Timmy asked from behind her.

"Everything's fine." She managed another smile and left. The shaded sidewalks running down the center of the Avenida da Liberdade offered relief from the sun, but Claire hardly noticed. In her head, Uncle Vincent's voice told her to look around, stay alert. But she hadn't, and the unthinkable had happened.

Ahead, she saw Gina approaching at a determined pace. Claire broke into a run and threw herself into the woman's arms, finally giving in to her sobs. Gina guided her to an empty bench and sat her down, smoothing her hair and making soothing noises. She sounded so much like Claire's mother that Claire cried even harder.

When her tears finally eased, Gina pushed her to arms' length. "What happened?"

"I lost my boat ticket. We're supposed to leave tomorrow." Claire sniffed and wiped her eyes. "Uncle Vincent's going to be so angry."

"What? How?"

"A boy stole it. Down by the river. I don't know what to do."

"Have you told anyone? Gone to the police?"

Claire shook her head. "You think they would help?"

"Probably the opposite. You haven't told your uncle?"

"I can't bear to. I've messed up everything. He has to go to America. But what if he feels like he can't leave me behind? And what if he does?" Claire heard her voice getting shrill. She no longer knew what she wanted.

Gina touched a quick finger to her lips, then put a reassuring arm over Claire's shoulders. "Calm down. Please."

Claire took a deep breath. "Can you help me? Maybe Uncle Vincent won't mind going if he knows I can stay with you." Her words rose in a question, but the nod she hoped for didn't come.

"You need to start by telling him," Gina said firmly. "You still have a few hours. Maybe he can find another ticket."

"There are no tickets. The ships are full, for months to come."

"Vincent has been here a while. He must have connections, someone who can help."

Connections. Those he had, but not what Gina was thinking. Reflexively, Claire put a hand over her pouch. "He could make me a ticket," she murmured to herself. "He might have time." She looked up and noticed the strange expression on Gina's face. She'd spoken out loud.

Gina held her palms out, as if warding away bad news. "I don't want to know." She stood abruptly and walked away.

Claire followed, frantically trying to backtrack. "It's nonsense, Gina. Forget what I said."

Gina kept walking.

Claire struggled to keep up. "Of course my uncle will try to buy a ticket."

From behind them came a deep voice. "Good day, Miss Becker. Might I have a word with you?"

Gina went very still. Claire turned. The man who had spoken was gaunt, his cheeks as hollow as the skeletons in Claire's old schoolbooks.

"Of course," Gina said tonelessly. Pulling Claire away from the man, she kissed her on both cheeks and gave her a shove. "Go," she whispered. "Get out of Europe. Now."

Claire left, but not without glancing back. The man was leaning over Gina, talking into her face. Who was he? Gina shook her head. The man took her arm. Ladylike, Gina tried to shake him off, but he didn't let go. The man hadn't been near enough to hear when she'd mentioned making the ticket, had he? When she looked again, they were already far down the sidewalk. She directed her heavy steps toward the boarding house, and her uncle.

Antonio

"Child, sit down."

Antonio stopped pacing around the small, stuffy living room. Avó meant well, but right now he wanted to strangle her. They'd been waiting for an hour, and there was still no sign of the healer.

Across from them, a middle-aged man slumped in his seat, chin on chest. He was a model of patience. The mother holding a wailing baby, less so. Antonio would've taken off long ago if his grandmother wasn't there, bolting him in place with her eyes. His insides churned. From now on, he'd have to be on his guard constantly, second-guessing everyone he saw.

Antonio stood up and started pacing again, ignoring Avó's disapproving glare. Gray was dropping him from the network just as he was starting to prove himself. Antonio went to stand in the doorway, looking out into a dingy hallway. Behind him, the baby cried piercingly.

If there was a way to frustrate Hitler's plan for Portugal, he wanted to be in on it. For Thomas and Claire, and for the courage and loss they represented. For the bodies – and spirits – broken by this stupid war. Antonio lifted his hand and saw his bandage was coming loose. Neutrality was useless. But now Gray considered him a risk. Antonio kicked the doorframe with his foot. And then there was Claire. He wanted the time to know her better. And she wanted to find her parents. But he doubted she'd dare stay, especially after her experience in Lisbon so far.

Finally the old healer bustled in with a wooden box full of greenery. "Who's first?" she asked.

"You go." Antonio's grandmother waved at the flustered mother. Antonio stifled an impatient sound. Avó looked at him sharply and said, "You're a man. You can bear it."

"Sure," he said irritably. He was tired of bearing it.

The mother emerged with the baby fifteen minutes later. He was snoring.

"I'll take what he had," Antonio said under his breath. Avó pushed him forward with a little smile. "Go."

In a small back room that smelled of herbs, the healer unwound the bandage and prodded his hand, clucking her tongue. Antonio winced.

"You're lucky. It's broken but the bones seem to be in place." She began mashing up something he couldn't identify with a mortar and pestle, adding ingredients bit by bit. "This will take down the swelling." Antonio clamped his jaw shut as she packed the damp mash around his fingers, then bound his whole hand tightly. "But if you don't rest it, it won't heal."

Antonio tried to flex his hand. He didn't have much choice. The hand was so snugly bandaged he could barely bend his wrist, much less his fingers. Even if Mr. Silva let him back into the Chave d'Ouro, working with it was going to be a trick. He pushed the thought aside and let his body relax as she held some of the poultice to his bruised face. The concoction was already drawing out the fire.

He and his grandmother were outside before Antonio thought to say, "Avó, how did you pay?" The healer wouldn't demand a doctor's fee, but nothing was free. "You haven't been singing, have you?"

A flap of her hand waved his question away. "That healer and I go way back. We help each other out." Avó kept her eyes on the street ahead.

"So what do you owe her?"

"I'm sure she'll think of something. Are you coming home?"

"Uh, not right now." She'd fuss and ask more questions. Besides, he had to find Claire.

His grandmother frowned. "You heard what she said, didn't you? About resting?"

Antonio gave her a one-armed hug. "I will. When I get home tonight."

"Boys." She snorted. "Not an ounce of sense in them." But her skinny arms encircled his waist and squeezed as hard as they could.

Antonio watched her move away. Avó had always drawn her energy from singing, even when her audience was only a wide-eyed grandson who came up to her knee. And now she was bouncing away as if she had springs in her heels. Antonio sighed and headed towards Rossio. At least she wasn't coughing.

At Claire's boarding house, he raked his fingers through his hair before tugging the bell pull. This time the concierge couldn't say he wasn't presentable. But the old man stopped him on the stairs before he'd gotten a word out.

"The young miss has gone out," he said. "You can't go up."

Merda. He had no idea where else to look. "Do you know when she'll be back?"

"I can't help you."

The man was minimally polite this time. Antonio nodded and took a roundabout route to the waterfront. Boats steamed up and downstream, crisscrossing the ferries taking passengers to the far bank. He ached for the release of drawing, but Claire had his materials. Or he hoped she did. He closed his eyes. In quick succession, the wind whipped away a clanging bell, a horse neighing, and a car horn. Across the water were unknown opportunities. But not for him. For Claire maybe.

He wondered suddenly if she'd asked her uncle about the baby in Thomas's diary. Maybe she hadn't. Then they could just drop it, before Claire got pulled further into this mess. Antonio shook his shoulders loose and headed to the Chave d'Ouro. He had to get the diary and drawings back. And Claire and her uncle had to get out of Portugal.

Claire

Vincent stared at Claire. He'd gone as pale and frozen as a wax figure. "I can't believe you'd be so careless." He could barely get the words out.

"I'm sorry. I…" Claire's whole world had shrunk to this nightmare of a room. She wanted to curl into a ball and never move again.

"Our ship sails tomorrow." Vincent circled the table like a caged rat. "We have to be on it. This is impossible." He dropped into a chair and put his head in his hands. "*Mon Dieu.* How I wish your family were here."

So did Claire, with all her heart. "I'll stay and wait for them." She saw Vincent's incredulous expression and faltered. "Esther and Gina can help me. I'll find work."

"You've seen what's happened. You know the danger. How can you consider such a thing?"

"You're the one at risk. Not me."

"We all are. You can't stay." He stood up and pulled on his jacket. "I'll see what I can arrange."

Looking around, Claire saw that the room was unusually neat. "You started packing?"

"Yes. We only have a few hours. I didn't expect to need my equipment again."

"I'm sorry," Claire repeated.

"I have one last batch of documents to deliver before we leave." Vincent's voice was tight. "I'll go by the printer's first. Then I'll come right back."

"I'll come with you."

"It's better if you stay and pack." He slung the satchel over his shoulder. "Don't leave these rooms while I'm gone, all right? And don't open the door."

Impulsively, Claire hugged him. His arms tightened around her for a brief moment. "I'll be back soon." The door closed behind him.

Claire went to the window and leaned her forehead against the glass. No matter what happened, this was her last night in Rossio Square number 59. She wouldn't miss it.

Antonio

"Hey Scrappy," Antonio said. The shoeshine boy was in his favorite spot near one of Rossio's fountains, waiting for his next customer. "How's business?"

"Booming. I have reasonable prices and I help people look good. Makes me a popular man."

Smartass. "You're performing a public service, is that it?"

"Something like that. Now leave me alone. Customers won't like your ugly mug. You've got one hell of a black eye." Scrappy nodded at the boarding house. "Go see your lady friend. She's home."

She was home? Antonio turned, then realized what Scrappy had said. "Who?"

"Come on. Everybody knows. You haven't exactly tried to hide it."

Merda. Scrappy practically lived on the square, and saw everything. But he might not be the only one.

The shoeshine boy glanced at the boarding house again. Its door had opened. "Go on," he said with a cunning smile. "Now's your chance. Her uncle's leaving her home alone."

Claire

It was hot. Claire opened the window. Even after a week, she couldn't look down at the buzzing cafés and shops without aching for lively, pre-war Marseille. She watched idly as a black car cut in front of a tram. The tram driver clanged his bell long and angrily as the car stopped in front of the boarding house, blocking a lane. Passing vehicles honked. Below, Vincent exited the building and turned right, in the direction of the printer's. The doors of the black car opened. Four men got out and in seconds had surrounded him.

"What's this about?" Vincent's impatient voice projected up to the fifth floor. "Let me by, if you please. I have business to attend to." Claire heard the fear behind his bluster.

They didn't budge. One of the men leaned forward and said something.

Her uncle pulled back abruptly. "Under arrest? For what?"

Claire couldn't hear the answer, but her uncle shook his head vehemently.

"No. Certainly not. You've made a mistake." He clasped his satchel under his arms and lunged toward a gap between two men. One of them shoved him backwards. Vincent staggered. The others caught him and held him upright. The man who had spoken yanked the satchel out of his arms. He pulled out a newspaper, then a handful of small booklets, and waved them in Vincent's face.

Claire caught Vincent's stricken expression and slumped against the wall. They'd found the fake passports. Below her, the men muscled Vincent into the back seat of the car. Two of them climbed in with him and the car drove off. Claire stared, unbelieving. They were taking away the only person who'd always been in her corner, even when they argued. Claire saw Vincent twist around, his gaze locked on their window. He was mouthing something, but she couldn't make it out.

A movement below caught her eye. The other two men were crossing the sidewalk, on their way into the boarding house.

The United States provides Great Britain
with 10 coast guard ships

Diário de Notícias

CHAPTER 15

"D AMN," SCRAPPY SAID. "That isn't good."
Antonio stared frantically at the window,
ignoring him. Claire had been there, but now she'd
disappeared. She couldn't have picked a worse time to be home.

He looked at Scrappy, his gut churning acid again. "What now?
Do I go in?"

"Man, this is way out of your league."

"What if they take her too?"

"You think you could stop it? Forget it."

"Don't let them take Claire," Antonio whispered, speaking to
himself and to whatever gods might be listening. "Please, not
Claire."

Scrappy sat back. "What'd she do?"

"Nothing. She hasn't done anything." He'd been right. He was
sure of it now. The PVDE wanted whatever Thomas had given
Vincent. The question now was whether they'd gotten it when
they'd arrested the uncle. If not, and they suspected Claire was
involved, they'd arrest her too. Antonio leaned against the hard
stone of the fountain, his eyes on number 59. He'd find out soon
enough.

Claire

Claire turned in a circle in the middle of the room, her mind
frozen. She put her hand on the doorknob, then hesitated. There

was only one staircase, and the men were coming up it. The neighbors wouldn't let in a frightened girl. On the contrary. The men would check the bathrooms, the kitchen, knock on all the doors. She tried to breathe, and felt like her chest was encased in thick glass. She rotated again. There was no place in Vincent's rooms to hide.

Her glance fell on the cabinet. The German plans. Those were a prison sentence for sure. Even worse than the forgeries. Kneeling down, she clawed the pile of papers out and onto the floor. The envelope was still there. She grabbed it and made for the door, then stopped again. Their documents. She could feel the seconds ticking by, tapping out their rhythm on her skin.

She rummaged frantically on the shelf by the dishes. Tucked in with Thomas's diary were their passports and Vincent's boat ticket. Claire stuffed it all into the envelope and opened the door cautiously. No one was in the hallway, but loud voices echoed up the stairs at the end of the corridor. Claire slipped out, pulling the door shut behind her, and ran to the kitchen. In the patio beyond the glass door, lines of laundry hung, barely moving in the heat. The kitchen itself was empty. Thank heavens. Claire stepped into the patio. The door squealed as she tried to pull it shut, and she released it as if burned. Already, the noises in the hallway were closer.

"See who's on this floor."

"Yes, sir." Footsteps, then the sharp rap of knuckles on wood. No one answered.

Claire heard the concierge's alarmed voice. "Wait. Please. There's no need to break down the door." Metal jingled.

Not waiting to hear more, Claire wove through the moist sheets to the far side of the patio. She was cornered. She imagined the men going through Vincent's mounds of papers, and their anger when they didn't find what they wanted. She tucked the envelope under her blouse so the waistband held it snugly in place, and set to work adjusting the sheets around her so they almost touched the floor. Standing still and quiet wouldn't do much good if someone saw her feet. When she was done, she gathered some stray clothespins in her hands. If they came, she'd be a normal tenant hanging laundry – unless the concierge gave her away.

Above her, a seagull landed on the edge of the roof and cawed. Otherwise, there was no sound. If only they'd left. Something clanged in the kitchen. Claire tensed. There was more clanging, then the rhythmic thump of chopping.

The first voice came again, clearer now. "Madame, do you know the tenants of the corner room. Vincent Lemoine?"

"No."

"You don't know who lives with him?"

"No." The chopping continued.

"You're alone in here?"

"As you can see." *Chop, chop. CHOP.*

"Is there anyone outside?"

"Not that I've seen."

The woman's answers were just at the borderline of contemptuous. Claire almost smiled. Then the glass door squeaked, followed by steps on the patio. Clotheslines near the door drooped and bounced as someone pushed the fabric aside. Claire lifted her clothespins and grasped the edge of a sheet. Another few steps and he'd be right in front of her.

"*Chefe?*" a voice called from inside. "Seems no one was home with him."

"Son of a bitch." The man on the patio batted his way back through the laundry to the door. The glass rattled when he slammed it.

Claire dropped the clothespins and sank to the floor.

Antonio

Someone passed close to Claire's windows a couple of times, but Antonio couldn't make out who it was. He waited and fidgeted. The men still hadn't left the building.

"I have to go," he told Scrappy. "I'm in enough trouble with Mr. Silva already. Signal me if she comes out, ok?"

"So you can do what?"

"Do it, all right?"

"Yeah," Scrappy said without enthusiasm. "If I see her."

Antonio hightailed it to the Chave d'Ouro. Making his boss angry again was a gamble he didn't want to take.

"You think you can work like that?" Mr. Silva looked irritated the moment he saw Antonio's bandage.

"Yes, sir." He'd eat humble pie if he had to. Without giving his boss time to answer, Antonio went into the back and got his uniform on, swearing at his own awkwardness. His hand was throbbing again. But that didn't bother him nearly as much as not knowing what had happened to Claire.

Claire

Shadows inched across the patio. The chopping in the kitchen stopped, a chain rattled, and the woman hummed a few bars of a song. Claire didn't move. What if the men were still in the building, waiting for her and Esther? Bit by bit, the square of sky above her darkened. How many hours had passed? The noises in the kitchen stopped, started again, accompanied by the slightly burnt smell of over-cooked meat, and finally stopped for good. Claire climbed stiffly to her feet. She had to get out of the building.

From a clothesline, she pulled down a well-used apron, one a washerwoman might wear. She tied it around her waist, then searched until she found a dark shawl. She wrapped it around her shoulders, bunching it at the neck so her face and hair were partly hidden. At least it was dark outside. That would help. She crossed the empty kitchen and peered down the hall. The door to their rooms was closed, the hallway empty. She reined in her relief. There was no way of knowing if a guard was waiting outside.

Quietly, she walked to the bend in the corridor, wondering where Esther was. All was silent. At the top of the stairs, she listened again. Still nothing. She started down, avoiding the creakier steps. Halfway there, the front entrance opened. Claire stopped on the third-floor landing. It was the concierge, talking with another man. Claire peeked over the banister, ready to race out of sight down the corridor. But it was only the Polish tenant, climbing the stairs with his heavy tread. Claire flew past them both, averting her head. The concierge called out, but she didn't stop. She'd never come back here again.

On the ground floor, Claire cracked open the front door. No one was stationed at the entrance. Maybe they'd gotten what they wanted after all. She damped down a flicker of hope. Either way, it didn't bode well for her uncle. Outside, she put her head down and walked away at an even pace, hunching her shoulders like a tired old woman. The envelope rustled beneath her blouse. She'd never been out this late alone. Another turn, and she was away from Rossio Square. But she couldn't escape the crawling sensation that someone was right behind her, groping for the back of her neck.

Antonio

"Antonio! Customers!" Mr. Silva barked.

He turned around too quickly and bumped into a table. A glass tipped and fell, shattering on the floor. *Merda.* He apologized, then found the mop and cleaned up the mess one-handed, not looking at Mr. Silva. He was never this clumsy. Antonio put the mop away in a back room. He stayed there a moment in the dark, holding his hand above his head to ease the swelling. Back in the café, a couple at a table outside signaled him. He went to take their order. Scrappy was nowhere in sight.

Claire

The American Legation was on the Avenida da Liberdade, Claire was sure of that. It had to be around here somewhere. She searched for the U.S. flag, praying she'd picked the right side of the street. Weaving back and forth would just attract attention, and she already felt like she had a *Wanted* sign on her back. Uncle Vincent might have been arrested because of the forgeries, but what if the secret police forced him to tell them about the war plans? Keeping them with her was folly.

Night had fallen completely by the time she spotted the U.S. seal on the façade of a two-story building. All of the lights except one were off inside. She knocked. A lamp came on over the front entrance, and moments later the door opened.

"Yes?" The guard didn't step aside.

"I need to see the ambassador. Please. It's urgent."

The man sighed. "It always is. Why do you want an audience with the ambassador?"

"I can't say. I can only tell him."

The guard reached for a ledger lying on a table inside the door. "You could see someone…" Squinting, he ran his finger down a page, then turned to the next one. "On Friday, April 18. It won't be the ambassador, but I'm sure they'll do their best to help."

Claire drew in a sharp breath. April 18 was six days from now. "You don't understand." What had her uncle said? "It concerns the national security of the United States. Please. I need to see the ambassador now."

Even in the dark, Claire could make out pity and fatigue in the man's gaze.

"He's not here," he said gently. "No one is but me." He held up the ledger. "Shall I make the appointment or not?"

"What if I come back in the morning?"

"You'll get the same answer, I'm afraid."

"I'm American. I have my passport." She felt like she was sinking down, down. "Doesn't that make a difference?"

"This is the best I can do. You must understand. There are so many of you."

Claire eyed the doorway, only half-listening. If she could make it over the threshold, she'd refuse to leave. They'd have to let her see the ambassador. As the guard stepped back to shut the door, Claire dashed through it and past him. For one heady second, she thought she'd made it. Then the guard's hand clamped onto her arm, and he swung her around and right back out the door. It shut in her face, the lock turning with a heavy thunk.

Claire dropped down onto the top step, unable to believe it. Despite her uncle's warning, she'd been sure the Americans would help. Now she was a girl on a dark street at night, alone. Leaving the Legation felt like swimming away from a life raft. She shivered and tried to think.

Gina. Surely she'd give Claire a place to stay until she found Esther and they decided what to do. Her parents were already missing. She couldn't lose Vincent too. She just couldn't. After one last glance at the Legation, she pushed herself to her feet and began walking.

At Gina's building, slats of light glimmered through the shutters of three second-floor windows. Hoping against hope that Gina was home, Claire rang the bell. Once, then again, more insistently. A shutter squeaked above, and Gina's head appeared.

"I'm sorry, Claire," she said. Her voice was so quiet it hardly carried. "I can't see you now." She started to close the window.

"You've got to let me in."

"Go away."

"I can't. I don't have anywhere else to go."

"Why not?" Her voice was even quieter than before.

 "Please, Gina. It's urgent. Hurry."

"I…I'm coming." Moving very deliberately, Gina shut the window. When she opened the front door, her eyes were red and she drooped as if she hadn't slept in days.

"What's wrong?" Hours ago, Gina had been fine. Claire leaned forward and sniffed. "Are you drunk?"

Without answering, Gina turned and shuffled up the stairs. On the threshold of Gina's room, Claire halted. The bed was unmade and piled with clothes. An empty suitcase lay open in a corner. On a small table sat a glass and a bottle of red wine. It was almost empty.

"What are you doing?" Claire couldn't hide her panic. "Where are you going?"

Gina went to lean against the window, her eyes on the street below. "To hell," she said tiredly. "In fact, I'm already there."

"What happened? Is it your sister? Where is she?" Claire looked around. There was no sign another person lived there.

"You really should go. It's not safe for you here."

"Nowhere is safe." Claire shut the door behind her. "The secret police arrested Uncle Vincent."

Gina followed her movement with dead eyes.

"Don't you understand?" Claire wanted to shake a reaction out of her. "They caught him with forged passports. They searched our rooms. They might still be there, waiting for me and Esther."

Gina pressed her forehead against the window and didn't answer.

"What is wrong with you?" Claire grabbed Gina's shoulders and pulled her around. "Say something."

Gina pushed her back. "Just leave."

"I won't."

"You don't want to be near me."

"I need your help. I'm not going anywhere until you talk."

"I need a drink." Gina poured, splashing some of the red liquid onto the floor. She made no move to clean it up.

Claire grabbed the bottle. "You've had enough."

"It'll never be enough." Holding the glass with two hands, Gina sank into a worn armchair.

"You're scaring me." Claire pulled up a chair. "What happened?"

"My friends and I thought we could change the world." Gina's voice and gaze were far away. "After Hitler came to power, we saw the persecutions. When people started fleeing Germany, years before the war began, we swore we'd help them." Gina repeated the phrase bitterly. "I helped people then."

"Like you are now," Claire said. Like Vincent had. And look where it had gotten him.

A tear slid down Gina's cheek. "We hid them, or got them as far away from Germany as possible."

"That was…good, wasn't it?" Where was Gina going with this?

"It was the most fulfilling time of my life. Until…" Gina's voice trailed off.

"Until?"

"Until Germany invaded the Netherlands. The Gestapo had us all within days. We'd been so naive. They knew where we lived, who our families were." Gina's voice trembled. She took another gulp of wine. "They took my husband and Sarah. My little girl. She was two."

"I'm so sorry. I didn't know." Claire reached out to squeeze her hand, but Gina pulled it away. "Do you know where they are?"

"The Gestapo said we'd be reunited if I followed their orders," Gina said tonelessly. Her eyes didn't leave the frayed carpet. "They lied."

"Orders?" Claire heard her own shocked voice at a distance. "What orders?"

"I was to supply them with information on refugees of interest. In Lisbon."

The words took a moment to register. "You didn't. You couldn't."

Gina bit her lip and nodded.

"You betrayed the people you'd sworn to help?"

"They had my family," Gina said dully. "Would you have done differently?"

"At the aid agency, you were working for the Nazis?" Claire felt like all of the air had been sucked out of the room.

"I helped those I could. I hid what I could." Without her bright red lipstick, Gina's face was naked, imploring. "But sometimes, when the Gestapo wanted something – or someone – there was no hiding."

Their last conversation flashed through Claire's mind. "The man we saw this afternoon," she whispered. The pieces were coming together in a horrible puzzle. "You didn't tell him about Vincent, did you?"

Gina picked at a seam of her chair. "They already knew. Or suspected. When he saw us talking – with you so upset – he was sure you'd told me something important. And you had."

"That Vincent was forging documents."

"Yes."

"But you didn't have to tell him." Claire jumped to her feet and backed away, almost yelling. "He's my uncle. You could have lied."

"I thought it was Vincent or my husband and daughter." Gina choked over the words. "But today, he said the deal was off. My family was gone." She leaned forward and covered her face with her hands. Her body shook. "My baby is gone."

Claire opened her mouth, then shut it. No words could make this right. Blindly, she pulled the door open and stumbled down the stairs. Somewhere inside, she registered Gina's pain, but she couldn't deal with it now. She didn't have pity enough for both of them.

English and German armored units engage in close fighting
at 2 places along the line of resistance in northern Greece

Diário de Notícias

CHAPTER 16

REFUGEES OFTEN STOOD outside the Chave d'Ouro, rooting through their pockets for change, happily anticipating a drink. Claire's face, when Antonio saw it through the window, looked nothing like theirs. She was plaster-white, standing with her arms wrapped around her chest. Her eyes bored into his desperately.

Antonio set his tray on the counter with a thud. "Cover for me, will you?" he asked.

The bartender followed his gaze to the window. "Watch it. You're on a thin rope already."

"One minute." Antonio held up a finger, then pushed through the tables and out the door.

"They arrested Uncle Vincent," Claire said without preamble.

"I know. I saw." She'd gotten out of the boarding house safely. But she was clutching her stomach. "Are you all right?" He reached out to touch her.

Claire pulled back and brushed his question aside. "What will they do to him?"

Antonio slid his bandaged hand behind him. "I don't know." Nothing good, that was sure.

"They might be looking for me too. I can't stay out in plain sight. Especially not here."

"Antonio." Mr. Silva was at the door. "Back to work."

Merda. "One minute. Please."

Mr. Silva scowled and went back inside.

Antonio turned back to Claire. "Where's Esther?"

"I don't know. She wasn't at the boarding house this afternoon."

"And Gina?"

Claire made a harsh, unrecognizable sound. "It's her fault Uncle Vincent was arrested." She shuddered, once, violently. "I need a place to hide. Will you help?"

She looked so fragile and lost. With effort, Antonio kept his arms at his sides. "Walk toward Praça da Figueira. I'll catch up with you."

"Promise?"

"Yes. But I have to get out of this uniform." And face the consequences of leaving hours before his shift ended. He touched Claire's shoulder. "Now go."

She turned away as if numb. Antonio went inside. Mr. Silva looked like a furnace about to explode.

Before he could start yelling, Antonio said, "I have to leave. I'm sorry. It's urgent." He was already unbuttoning his vest.

"Go now, and you won't work here again," Mr. Silva spat. "Your choice."

"You know I want this job. I'll make it up, I promise. But it's…it's an emergency." He was struggling to unknot his apron.

"You think I don't have eyes? You're dismissed."

"Mr. Silva, no. You know I work hard. I always have. Just let me go, this one time."

Mr. Silva yanked the apron from his hand. "I don't need your kind of help."

Behind Antonio, a woman coughed. Deep in her chest, like his grandmother. He was crazy to leave, with her depending on him. People lined up for jobs like his. But Claire was in danger and it was partly his fault. He'd shared his ideas about Thomas and her uncle with her. He'd told her about the diary – then left it for her to take care of. Antonio ran to the back room and fumbled his way into normal clothes. Dozens of eyes watched him leave the café. Discreet, he wasn't. At least Gray wasn't there to see it.

After a zigzag route that revealed no one behind him, he caught up with Claire on Praça da Figueira. "We'll go to my grandmother's. No one will look for you there."

"Then what?" She was still folded around herself, as if she was trying to make herself smaller.

"We'll figure out a plan." Carefully, Antonio slid his good arm around her waist, covering the hand she held to her stomach with his own. She trembled, then slowly relaxed.

"Do you know why your uncle was arrested?" Antonio asked as they walked.

"He was forging documents for refugees. They caught him with them."

Antonio swore under his breath. Salazar didn't tolerate foreigners who broke the law. Especially when it antagonized the Germans. "Did they take anything else?" he asked.

"I think they searched our rooms, but I wasn't there. I couldn't see what was happening." She hugged herself even more tightly. "I have the diary."

Antonio felt a surge of relief. Brave, brave girl.

"But not your drawings."

"Where are they?"

"In our rooms. The tube was too big to take."

Merda. He hadn't signed them. But if they fell into Mr. Black's hands, he'd make the connection. And Antonio had lost his paper and all of his pencils. It shouldn't matter, but it did.

"It's okay. I'll draw more." They were already in Mouraria, climbing a long flight of stairs that opened onto a cobblestone square. Antonio started to lead Claire across it, then jerked to a halt.

"Turn around." He pulled her back toward the stairs so abruptly she missed the top step and almost fell. He steadied her and picked up the pace.

"Antonio?"

"Shhh. Just hurry."

Claire caught his tension and increased her speed, running down the steps with him. At the first landing, he took a left into a small street, then a right, into an alley that led downhill. Only then did he slow down and pull her to him protectively. They were both breathing hard.

"Change of plan," he said. "We're not going to my grandmother's."

"Why not?" Claire leaned back in his arms, trying to see his face. She didn't pull away, and he was glad.

"I think she's going to have other company tonight, and it's not someone I want to meet."

"Why? Who is it?"

"My cousin Rita has a new boyfriend. They were on that square, heading toward my grandmother's."

"And?"

"I thought I hadn't met the boyfriend. Turns out he's the thug who did this." He held up his bandaged hand. "At PVDE headquarters. Just after I told him Thomas hadn't given me anything."

In the lamplight, Antonio saw Claire swallow. He traced her cheekbone gently with his thumb, wishing again that they'd met at a different time and place.

"Not to you," she said faintly. "He gave them to Vincent."

"So we were right." He wished they hadn't been. "What was it?"

"Stolen German war plans. And now I have them." She nodded down at the arm that was still tightly pressed against her middle.

Antonio stared, incredulous. "You took them? When you know the Gestapo wants them?" That was more crazy than brave.

She tilted her chin up. "If they'd found them in our rooms, it would go even worse for my uncle."

"Yes, but..." It was too late to argue about it now. "What are you going to do with them?"

"Uncle Vincent was going to hand them over to someone when we got to New York."

"But he's not here. The safest thing for you would be to get rid of them."

"Is that what you'd do?"

Antonio thought for a minute. He'd bargain with Gray, use them to get back into the network. "We'll figure it out later. Now we need a place to hide. Come on."

"Where?"

"The art gallery."

"Mr. Gray's gallery?" Claire took a step back. "He already got me in trouble once. Why would we go there?"

"It's inside. We'll be safer. And if the plans are real, he'll know what to do with them."

"Of course they're real. And I'm not giving them to anybody. Not after my uncle took such risks to keep them safe."

"They knew each other. They worked together."

"Whether they did or not, I'm not taking that chance."

"Claire…"

"No. I have to do this my way." She paused. "You're going to help me, aren't you?"

"Yeah," Antonio said, without enthusiasm. He pushed aside the whisper telling him to just haul her off to Gray, for both of their sakes. "But that was my good idea. What's…?"

Claire clapped a hand to her mouth. "Oh no!"

Antonio looked around wildly, ready to run again. "What is it?"

"We have to go to Belém."

"Belém? What's in Belém?"

"I'll tell you on the way."

Claire

The Travessa do Páteo das Vacas was quiet, but Claire still jumped at every shadow. Would they never open up? She knocked again on the door of the darkened safe house, waited, then rapped on a shutter. The tapping echoed around the street. She cringed.

"Are you sure this is the right place?" Antonio had his back to the wall and was scanning the road.

"It's late. They're not expecting us." She knocked again. "Vincent didn't say anything about moving the children. They have to be here."

"No, they don't."

Claire ignored him. "Open up," she pleaded, as if the people inside could hear. "You know we'd break this door down if we were the secret police." She took another careful look around. All of the houses on the block were equally closed and dark, but that didn't make her feel any less vulnerable. They had to get inside.

Desperately, she thumped the door with the butt of her hand. Seconds later it opened. The boxer man cursed and jerked her inside. He tried to shut the door in Antonio's face. Claire grabbed his hand and pulled him in behind her.

In the entrance hall, the man barred their way, hands clenched at his sides. "I should strangle you, young lady, before you get us all killed," he rasped. "And you brought a stranger here. You have no sense."

"He's a friend." Claire gauged the distance between them, making sure she was out of reach of his fists. "Are the children still here?"

"Why did you come?"

"Uncle Vincent's been arrested."

At the top of the stairs, something moved. The woman was making her way down, her head bent forward to catch what they were saying.

"He knows Serge and Alicia are here. If they force him to talk…" She paused, trying to control her voice. "I had to come. I had to warn you."

"We already know."

"You do?"

"Yes. They have Esther too."

The floor tilted, and Claire felt herself sway with it. Antonio pulled her against him. So everyone – truly everyone – she thought she could depend on was gone. Except Antonio, and what could he do? She struggled to gather her thoughts. "You have to move the children. It's not safe here anymore."

On the street a truck slowed, its brakes squealing. No one moved. The truck accelerated away and silence returned.

"You're reckless and I don't trust you." The man spoke deliberately, stressing each word. "But you're here and Vincent isn't, so what we do with the children now depends on you."

"Me?" Claire asked. "Why?"

"You're a Lemoine, are you not?"

Claire nodded.

"The children have boat tickets and new passports. In the name of Serge and Alicia Lemoine, two young American citizens. Vincent was planning to take them with him."

"And now?" She barely managed to get the words out.

"You'll have to take them."

"To America? Alone?" She folded her arms across the bundle under her blouse and leaned back, pressing harder against Antonio. He was the only solid ground she had. The couple looked at her, waiting.

"I can't do this," she said. No uncle, no parents, no Esther. When she'd offered to help, she'd never imagined it might mean ferrying two children she hardly knew across the Atlantic. "What would I do with them? I don't even know where I was supposed to go in New York."

The woman spoke for the first time. "If Vincent or Esther talk, the PVDE will know that Serge and Alicia are alive and in hiding. They'll never be out of danger in Portugal."

"But how can I? I don't even have money. Everything is at the boarding house."

"Vincent left money for the children. If you're careful, you could manage with that." The man's eyes slid to the side. For the first time, Claire noticed two small suitcases in the corner of the entry hall.

"They're already packed?" she asked faintly.

The woman nodded. "One way or another, they're going to take a trip very soon."

Claire wanted to burrow into Antonio's chest and stay there. There was no way she could make a decision like this.

"Could you leave us alone please?" Antonio said. His tone didn't allow for a refusal, but the couple still hesitated.

"For a moment," the man said. "Then come up. We need to talk." They climbed the stairs and disappeared into one of the rooms.

Claire turned and buried her face in Antonio's shoulder. His arms encircled her, holding her safe. But nothing was safe. To go or to stay. No matter what she chose, it would be wrong.

"I feel like I'm just getting to know you." Antonio's breath on her ear was warm. "I wish you could stay in Lisbon."

Claire lifted her chin, savoring his nearness. He pushed her hair away from her face and looked down at her.

"I had decided to. I couldn't give up on my family." She tightened her arms around him, hoping he'd understand that he counted too. "I was going to tell my uncle. Then my ticket got stolen and I thought I had no choice."

"You can't stay now," he said quietly. "Serge and Alicia aren't the only ones at risk."

Claire closed her eyes, willing tears not to come. They wet her lashes anyway. Father and Mother. Frédéric. Her grandfather. Vincent. Esther. The war was robbing her of too much. Even the possibility of something, someday, between her and Antonio.

"You have passports, and tickets, and money."

His reasonable voice came from far away. She didn't want to hear it.

"You'll find your uncle in New York. He'll take you in. Then you'll hand off the plans and put this behind you. You can do it."

"But…with the children?" Claire wasn't even sure she could take care of herself. She burrowed further into his arms. "How will I see you again?"

His eyes looked into hers, their green so close it was hard to focus. Then she felt his lips, soft, exploring. Claire pressed upward into the kiss until she was almost on tiptoe, not wanting it to end. Finally he drew back. Claire felt her face flame. He kissed her again, lightly.

"This is ours to keep," he said. "This, and hope."

A door opened above them and the woman appeared on the landing. "Are you coming? There's a lot to discuss."

Claire and Antonio stepped apart. If she wanted to leave, to refuse what they asked of her, now was the time. She searched inside, hoping for an answer. None came, but some of the horrible churning had subsided. She took Antonio's hand in a bone-crushing grip and climbed the stairs.

Antonio

Antonio watched silently as the man spread the passports, tickets, and money on the table in a room with tightly covered windows. What were the chances he'd make it to America, or Claire would return to Lisbon? He'd told her to go when he wanted exactly the opposite. Head over heart. If Gray knew, he'd be pleased. Antonio just felt hollow.

"This is all false?" Claire asked.

"Not the money," the man said.

In the next room, Serge and Alicia slept quietly. They'd peeked in on them a few minutes ago.

"Do the children know what's happening?" Claire asked.

"Just that they'll be taking a trip." The woman handed her a small satchel.

Claire packed the travel documents and money into its front pocket. "And their parents? What have you told the children about them?"

"Not much. That they had to go away and we don't know when

they'll come back. But that the children will be safe with us until they do."

"Do you think they'll be willing to come with me?"

Claire sounded so uncertain. Antonio started to put his arm around her again, then stopped. So much depended on her now. She had to be strong on her own.

"The choice isn't theirs," the man said gruffly.

"Maybe not, but if they start wailing for their parents, it's a problem," Antonio broke in.

The man turned on him. "It's bad enough to have one reckless adolescent involved. Who are you, anyway? This isn't your business."

"Claire told you. I'm a friend. And her safety is my business." Antonio tried to keep his voice neutral. If this was to work, Claire needed their help. "The police – and the PVDE – will be watching people get on that ship. The children can't make a fuss."

"We'll talk to them," the woman said. "We did that when they came here. They know to behave."

"But you haven't taken them out, have you?" Claire asked.

"No, but…"

"Sit down," the man interrupted. "Everyone. We need to go over what happens tomorrow, step by step."

Under the table, Antonio took Claire's hand.

"You'll have to go alone," the man said. "We can't be seen with the children."

"I'll get them to the dock," Antonio said. Helping her leave was the last thing he wanted to do. "What time do you need to be there?"

"Boarding starts at nine," Claire said.

"We'll get there just before nine then," Antonio said." It'll be crowded, but the less time you wait, the better."

Claire's hand tightened in his. "You think someone will be looking for us, don't you?"

"If they've interrogated Vincent and Esther, we have to suppose someone will be trying to find you," the man said. "But maybe they won't expect a woman traveling with two children. Or maybe your uncle will manage to keep your secret."

Antonio flexed his left hand, and winced. No one could keep a secret if the PVDE went all out.

"Do they know what you look like?" the man asked Claire.

"I don't know. Maybe, if they saw me with Antonio or Uncle Vincent."

Or if they'd taken a look at the contents of the drawing tube. Her portrait was in it. "We should probably assume they do," Antonio said.

"Can we disguise her?"

"We could put up her hair," said the woman doubtfully. "I don't know what else."

The man pushed back his chair. "We should get some rest. Tomorrow will be a long day."

"We're not fitted out for guests," the woman said. "All I have are extra blankets." She went into the hall and came back with an armful.

"Thank you. That'll be fine." Claire piled them on the table, then sat down and cradled her head in her arms.

"We can't leave two..." the woman began.

"Yes, we can," snapped the man. "Good night."

"Good night." The woman's disapproving gaze followed Antonio as he shut the door. At the table, Claire was still, as if sleeping, but her eyes were open and stunned. Could he ask her for more? He ran a hand gently down her back. "May I see the plans?"

She jerked upright. "Why?"

"I want to tell Gray about them."

"No."

"He's on our side. Against the Nazis. I know he is. Didn't you say your uncle wanted to get the plans to someone who would know what to do with them? Gray would know."

"I won't give them to you. I can't." She sounded exhausted.

"I know. But I'll memorize what I can. I have an eye for pictures, remember?"

She sighed. "Can you lock the door?"

Antonio checked. "No key."

"Do it quickly then, all right? No one else can see them." Claire pulled the envelope from under her blouse. "It's not all drawings. There's writing too."

"I'll get what I can." Antonio spread the pages out. America's coastline was clear, but he didn't recognize many of the other markings. This would be hard to remember. On the windowsill, he saw some drawings the children had made. Antonio turned them over, grabbed a pencil, and began copying. Claire watched him silently.

Antonio paused. "Are you all right with this?"

She nodded. "Don't give them to anyone before I'm gone."

Antonio started drawing again, working as quickly as he could. "Do you know what these mean?"

"Uncle Vincent said they showed where the Germans would attack if America entered the war."

Antonio studied the map. "That makes sense. See how they've marked some of the big cities? And these must be German ships or U-boats."

"I hope none of them are in position now." Claire ran her finger in a line from Lisbon to New York. "Look how many are on our route."

"These are plans for something that hasn't even taken place. Don't worry." Claire didn't look reassured, and Antonio didn't blame her. He finished the map and started on the text, concentrating hard. If he started thinking about the U-boats, he might not let her board that ship at all. His hand cramped. He shook it out and started copying again.

Somewhere in the house, a door opened and shut. With flying fingers, they folded the papers and spread the blankets on the floor in the corner of the room. Claire lay down, the envelope with the plans between her and the wall. Antonio turned off the light. Soft footsteps paced the corridor, but no one came in. Silence fell again.

"Stay with me?" Claire asked softly.

Feeling his way in the dark, Antonio found the blankets and lay down beside her. With his finger, he traced her face, from her eyebrow down her cheek to her chin. She sighed and laid her palm against his chest, then snuggled in closer.

"Thank you," she said, and he felt the soft pressure of her lips on his. Then she rolled over, curled so the length of her back was against him. Antonio curved his bandaged arm around her waist. The envelope rustled.

Why this? Why now? Everywhere she touched him was alive, aching with wanting and holding back. Did she know how hard it was for him? Slowly her breathing evened out, and she slept. If ever he'd had a chance to be with her, he'd lost it now.

CHAPTER 17 – SUNDAY, APRIL 13

LAYER BY LAYER, Claire emerged from the deepest sleep she could remember. The floor was hard, but soft blankets cocooned her. One of Antonio's arms cradled her head and the other lay across her hip. She relaxed into the warmth of him against her legs, her back, her shoulders. Within the curve of his body was shelter. Claire wasn't ready to leave it.

She'd slept with a man. She repeated the sentence in her head, each word punctuated by an exclamation mark. What the children's caretakers would think didn't matter. Antonio had been a gentleman, as she'd trusted him to be. Claire trembled, ever so slightly, imagining what could have been.

Behind her, Antonio shifted. She rolled to face him. His eyes were open, smiling.

"Sleep well?" he asked.

"Surprisingly so. It must have been the company." Claire felt the heat rise in her cheeks. What kind of answer was that?

Antonio grinned and pulled her closer. "May I?"

Claire didn't have time to say yes before he brought his lips to hers. This time his caress was rough and exciting and full of promise. Finally she pulled away, dizzy and breathless.

"This is how you say you want me to leave?" she asked. "You're making it so much harder."

"There's nothing easy about this," Antonio said. He sat up. "If we'd met when life was normal..."

"I know." Claire took his good hand and explored it with her fingers. They might've had time to find out if there was a future for them together. Instead she was leaving Europe, smuggling documents, and hoping to keep two young strangers safe. The way ahead terrified her.

Beside her, Antonio rummaged among the blankets. He handed her a folded piece of paper. "Don't lose this."

"What is it?"

"The address of Gray's gallery."

"I really don't want…"

"I know you don't like him. But I'll make sure he knows how to find me. You have to write, to tell me where you are."

"Then will you…?"

A knock interrupted them.

"Morning." The woman put her head around the door. She looked relieved to see them properly dressed and sitting apart. "We need to get some food into the children. Then you must leave. Can you get them?"

Reluctantly, Claire released Antonio's hand and went to wake Alicia and Serge.

"Today, you're going to take a trip," the woman told them at breakfast. The children caught something uneasy in her tone and started crying.

"They're making too much noise," the man warned.

"Shush. Shush," the woman told the children. They continued to sob uncontrollably.

"Serge. Alicia. Listen to me. Maybe your parents will be waiting for us when we arrive," Claire said.

That got their attention. Serge hiccupped and looked up. Rubbing her face, Alicia did too.

"You want to go see, don't you?"

The children nodded uncertainly. Claire breathed a sigh of relief and gave Antonio a resigned shrug. Now to get them on board before they started questioning her story. "Well then, let's get ready. Go wash your faces. You need to be presentable or they won't let us on the ship."

Serge and Alicia ran to the bathroom.

"You're making it worse," the woman said reproachfully.

"It worked, didn't it?" She'd deal with that problem later, once they were safe. In America. The woman didn't answer, and Claire regretted snapping at her. She was only trying to protect them.

"We have a better chance of getting on that boat if the children look reasonably happy, right?"

The man grunted. Claire couldn't tell if it was in agreement or not.

The woman went off to help the children dry their faces. After herding them back down the hall, she eyed Claire critically. "Do you want to put your hair up? You'll look older."

Claire nodded. The woman twisted her hair into a severe bun at the back of her neck, then tied a scarf around her head. Claire winced but stood still, watching Antonio's mouth turn down. It didn't become her, but she knew what he really didn't like was the reason she had to wear it.

On the tram to the docks, Serge and Alicia huddled together, their faces apprehensive. But they were quiet, for now. Standing beside them, Claire and Antonio swayed together with the tram's movement. She wasn't proud of the lie, and felt a headache coming on where the woman had pulled the strands of her hair especially tight. She teased them loose with her fingers.

The facades of Lisbon spooled by, luminous in the golden light of morning. Not far to go now. Could she still change her mind? Claire ruffled Alicia's hair. The little girl grabbed her hand and held it to her chest. She noticed Antonio looking at them thoughtfully. Only a few days ago, Claire had been pushing so hard to be allowed to take care of them. She'd had no idea what that meant.

What had the man told her? To keep the children still. To say as little as possible if questioned. To remember the story they'd invented. She would – they'd gone over it five times before he was satisfied with her answers. Claire wasn't so sure about the children.

She leaned down to their level. "Shall we play our game?"

They nodded.

"What is your name?"

"Serge Lemoine."

"Alicia Lemoine."

"Do you have any brothers or sisters?"

They pointed at each other.

"Anyone else?"

Alicia shook her head.

"Yes we do, silly," Serge said. "Claire is our big sister now. Remember?"

"Oh. Yes." Alicia didn't sound too certain.

Claire saw her own worries reflected in Antonio's eyes. "You'll stay with us until we're on the ship, won't you?"

"I'll go as far as they'll let me."

"To America? Someday?" Claire had given him her uncle's name and all the information about him that she could remember. She refused to believe seeing him again was just wishful thinking. He slid his arm around her, offering her his safety for a few moments more.

"The next stop is yours," he said.

Warehouses, their metal roofs a series of wide, upside-down Vs, lined the street where they got off. Claire took Serge and Alicia by the hand and walked to an open space where hundreds of people had massed against a barrier. Antonio followed with the children's suitcases and the satchel the woman had packed for Claire.

Off to one side were stacks of boxes and chests and suitcases. Claire's own possessions had dwindled to an ill-fitting old lady's coat the woman had given her, the satchel, and her pouch. In America, she'd really be starting from nothing. It didn't bear thinking about.

On the other side of the barrier was a long table that had been placed at the bottom of a steep gangway. Towering above it all was a huge gray ship, the *Excalibur*. Big red letters on its side spelled out REFUGEE. Seven letters that were supposed to ward off enemy fire.

"What do we do now?" she asked Antonio.

"Wait, I guess. Until they open the gate. It shouldn't be long."

It felt long.

Serge tugged on Claire's hand. "I'm tired of standing," he whined.

"I want to go home." Tears brimmed again in Alicia's eyes.

"Why don't you sit on your suitcases?" Claire suggested. They couldn't act up now, in the midst of all these people. Anyone could be looking at them — or for them. She rifled through the satchel and found a sausage roll. She broke off two small pieces. "Here." The children chewed pensively.

Antonio put his good arm around her waist. Claire leaned into him. If only he was coming with them. She folded both hands over his and kept her head high, determined not to show her fear. A ripple went through the crowd. Antonio released her and rose onto his toes to get a better view.

"The ticket-takers have arrived," he said. "They're opening the gate."

Everyone surged forward, almost overrunning the children. Claire pulled them to their feet and gathered them in front of her.

"Do you have everything ready?" Antonio asked.

"Yes." Claire pulled their tickets and passports out of the satchel, her palm suddenly sweaty. She hoped the ink wouldn't run. "Serge, Alicia, hold hands. Alicia, take mine. We don't want to get separated."

Silently, they obeyed. Antonio picked up the suitcases again, and their little group inched forward with the crowd.

Antonio

Ahead, passengers were filing through the gate in clumps, two, three, four at a time. At the table, two uniformed men examined their documents, asked a few questions, and waved them onto the ship.

There were a dozen people between Claire and the ticket-takers when Antonio saw them. Rita's boyfriend, the hand-breaker, and the other man who had hauled him off to PVDE. They stood beside the gate, scrutinizing the faces of the passengers. If they were there, Mr. Black might be too. Antonio couldn't let them see him anywhere near Claire.

He caught Claire's arm. "You're ready with your story, right? No hesitations?"

She nodded. "Why?"

"Just keep your head down and your scarf on, all right?" He didn't want to make her more nervous than she was. The line moved forward again. Closer to the men. "I have to go," he whispered. "Stay safe."

He moved to the side, searching for the path of least resistance. Then, over a sea of shoulders, he saw Mr. Black. Their eyes locked. Mr. Black surged forward to plant himself between Antonio and the gate.

"Get him!" he yelled, an arm high, pointing in Antonio's direction. "He doesn't get on this ship."

Antonio whipped off his beret and ducked away in the opposite direction. They thought he was trying to leave Lisbon. He prayed they hadn't realized he wasn't alone. As he got further from the gate, the press of people lessened. He skirted a small wooden outbuilding and stopped, panting. From the far side, he looked cautiously around the corner. Mr. Black hadn't broken free of the crowd. Yet. Antonio saw his head pop up, disappear, and pop up again. The man was hopping up and down, trying to locate him.

Antonio managed a grim smile and shifted his attention to the ship. Claire was on the gangplank, herding the children before her. She'd made it past the ticket-takers. Antonio waited, hardly daring to believe it, as they neared the top and found a place along the rail. Holding Alicia in one arm and shading her eyes with the other, Claire scanned the crowd. He hadn't said goodbye – again – but she must have understood why. And she'd kept her calm.

Carefully, keeping the building between him and the PVDE agents, Antonio moved into her line of sight. It took a moment, but she saw him. He raised his good arm high above his head and held it there, a final salute.

Claire

High on the deck, Claire sent a wide, slow wave to the tiny figure below. Then she turned her head away, not wanting to risk betraying him to anyone who might be watching. On the wharf, hundreds of white handkerchiefs fluttered. Beyond them rose the hills of Lisbon, the city that had offered, and taken, so much. When she looked for Antonio again, he was gone. Claire caught her breath and hugged Alicia. Too hard. The child struggled and Claire put her down, then touched her stomach. The envelope was there, to be delivered into the best hands she could find once they got to America; her precious pouch was around her neck; and she and the children were, for the moment, out of harm's way. Antonio, too, was free. As for the others she held dear, her search would continue.

In her pocket, the note Antonio had given her rustled. She pulled it out. *Edgeway Galeria de Arte*, it said, with the address on the Largo do Carmo. And three words. *Until next time.* It was signed "*A.*"

Antonio

Antonio ran far downriver, stopping only when his legs and lungs gave out. No one would find him today. Not way down here. He flopped onto the bank. In little more than a week, his world had been turned on its head. He'd solved the mystery of Thomas's death, but his friend was gone. So too, most likely, was his job. He'd joined and been dismissed from a sabotage ring. His hand had been broken, his drawings praised, and his convictions about Portuguese neutrality shredded. He'd witnessed courage that had humbled him in the service of others. Claire had come and gone too quickly, leaving him raw and longing for what he'd had no chance to fight for.

Antonio slid his hand around the diary she'd returned to him, now safe in his jacket. Between its pages were his copies of the German plans. Gray would surely want them.

Soon, he'd have to salvage what he could from the remnants of his life. But now nothing mattered more than watching the ship Claire was on steam down the river toward the Atlantic, bound for a safer harbor on the other side.

ᴆ ᴆ ᴆ ᴆ ᴆ

If you enjoyed this journey into Portugal's past, start reading **The Filigree Master's Apprentice** to see what happens to Henrique, a young man who flees the dusty vineyards of the Douro Valley in 1877 for a new–and precarious–life in Porto.

ᴆ ᴆ ᴆ ᴆ ᴆ

And please help other readers find **Rossio Square N.° 59** by leaving a review on Goodreads, Amazon, or wherever you bought the book. Thank you so much!

HISTORICAL NOTE

Claire, Antonio, and the other main characters in *Rossio Square N.°59* are fictional, but their stories are set against the backdrop of actual events in Lisbon and elsewhere in April 1941. After France was occupied, Portugal was Europe's last open exit route, and thousands upon thousands of refugees made their way there in hopes of traveling onward. It was not an easy journey. As Claire would have known all too well, "obtaining a transit visa, valid for three months, required an exit visa from France, a transit visa for Spain, a visa from the destination country, and a passage by sea that was confirmed and already paid for," writes Christina Heine Teixeira in an article entitled *Lisbon, Symbol of Hope and Liberty.*

Many refugees gave up – or knew they'd never be given visas – and decided to escape over the Pyrenees, as Vincent and Eleanor's family did. Some were caught, detained, or turned back. Others got help, and made it to Lisbon successfully. Lisa Fittko's *Escape Through the Pyrenees* describes her perilous attempts to guide refugees across the mountains. Esther's flight from Belgium bears some resemblance to a story told in 2013 by then U.S. Secretary of State John Kerry: "(A)s the Germans were marching into Paris, my mother got on a bicycle with her sister and a couple of friends and biked out of Paris and forged her way across France, got to Portugal, where she got help to get on a ship to come back to America."

Once in Portugal, some wealthier refugees did go to the resort town of Estoril, where they might have stayed in the opulent Hotel Palácio and frequented the casino. In Lisbon, a number of humanitarian agencies, including HICEM, JOINT, the USC, the Red Cross, and the Quakers aided the less fortunate with food, the legalization of documents, boat tickets, hotel bills and more. One of the boarding houses open to the new arrivals was located at Rossio Square number 59, "the Pensão Colonial, where hundreds of refugees stayed during this period," notes the wonderfully informative map and guide that accompanies the book *Lisbon: A City During Wartime*.

Newcomers flocked to cafés in downtown Lisbon, and the multi-story Chave d'Ouro was one of them. On the ground floor was the café, which had an open gallery above it. The upper floors housed a restaurant, a tearoom, a barbershop, and a billiards room. Like Claire, refugees coming from war zones were amazed by the lights permitted in Lisbon even after night fell, and by the ready availability in stores and restaurants of everything from fish, fowl, meat, cheese, fruit, vegetables, chocolate, coffee and cakes to butter.

In contrast, on April 5, 1941, the *Diário de Notícias* newspaper reported that in Paris people were eating sandwiches of mushrooms, tomatoes, mortadella, and sardines, along with nuts and dates. Refugees also spent their time in line at the post office in the Praça do Comércio, at the consulates of destination countries, and at shipping company offices, where tickets could be in desperately short supply. On March 15, 1941, *The New York Times* wrote that "(t)he last remaining regular passenger service on which refuges by the thousands have escaped from Europe direct to the United States has been indefinitely closed" because of a backlog of bookings exceeding an estimated 10,000 tickets. For refugees like Vincent and Claire, it would have been almost impossible to modify their departure date or replace a lost ticket.

Under Prime Minister Salazar, Portugal remained a conservative society. Foreign women might – as Antonio noticed – frequent cafés and smoke, and they didn't always wear stockings. Cultural clashes were inevitable, as Claire discovers in Estoril when – as shown in a 1941 photograph from the *Vida Mundial Ilustrada* – a member of the Beach Patrol Police berates a couple for wearing "inappropriate" bathing suits.

Despite Portuguese neutrality, a German invasion was considered probable in April 1941. Unbeknownst to Portuguese authorities, J.G. Beevor, a member of Britain's secret Special Operations Executive (SOE), had been sent to Lisbon in January to organize a resistance movement prepared to destroy the oil installations along the Tagus river if this happened, as Gray is trying to do in this novel.

The *Polícia de Vigilância e da Defesa do Estado* (PVDE), created in 1933, was responsible for borders, immigration control, and counterespionage. Spying by all countries involved in the war – whether carried out in cafés or brothels or hotels or by using radio transmitters to report on ship movements on the Tagus – was a given. As Antonio witnessed in the Jolly Roger, British seamen "were one of the Abwehr's best sources of information in the U-boat war. The Abwehr [Germany's military intelligence service] financed or controlled a few brothels, where the girls were briefed on extracting and memorizing the details of routes and dates of convoys," Beevor notes in his memoirs. The fictional story of the coal bomb on the *Serpa Pinto* – a ship that actually did ferry refugees to the U.S. during this period – was inspired in part by the adventures of a British double-agent called Zigzag, who convinced the Germans to hand over an example of this revolutionary technology by telling them he would use the bombs to sink a British merchant ship.

The plans carried by Claire to New York about specific attacks on America's east coast did not exist. However, U-boats arrived off the poorly protected eastern seaboard very soon after the United States entered the war, where they proceeded to sink hundreds of ships in a matter of months.

The timeline of this novel owes much to the Lisbon-based *Diário de Notícias*. Between April 1 and 14, 1941, the newspaper ran articles on the invasion of Yugoslavia; Josephine Baker's part in an elegant *festa brilhantissima* in support of victims of a cyclone that had caused devastation in Portugal earlier that year; the announcement of America's Lend-Lease aid plan for allied countries; Benfica's championship win; the sinking of ships in the Atlantic and Mediterranean (along with some amazing rescues); bombing raids over England, Northern Ireland, Calais and Dunkirk; and Portuguese neutrality.

On a somewhat lighter note, we also learn that during this period Alfred Hitchcock's film *Mr. and Mrs. Smith* was playing in Lisbon, English lessons were on offer, and women in Paris were reportedly lining up at pharmacies ahead of a possible shortage of lipstick and perfumes.

ACKNOWLEDGMENTS

Many bits and pieces of this book owe their existence to people who were unbelievably generous with their time and expertise. If Claire and Antonio come alive on these pages, it is in great part due to the advice and sometimes painful honesty of Phyllis, my mentor, and Dina, Sabrina, Olivia, Mayra, Monica, Laurie, Katie, Lisa, Michelle, Karen, Marcy and Amy, my wonderful critique group partners and writer friends. Thanks also to Anne D, Graça, Paulo M, Rita, Elisabeth, Hilde, Jose C, John S, Antonio, and Allison, who gave me feedback and information on everything from Portuguese traditions to U-boat movements off the U.S. coast. José M, who patiently corrects my Portuguese when we go walking, lent me his sharp eyes when it was time to review the Portuguese version. Paula, you jump-started my journey to publication, and I am eternally grateful. I'm also thankful for assistance that came from unexpected quarters. One day, when I was standing on Rossio Square wishing I could see past the scaffolding then covering number 59, a kind builder named Rui appeared unexpectedly with a key in his hand. He offered me a tour of the gutted building, helping me solve a plot problem in the process. Laure, a child when her family fled Belgium at the beginning of World War II, spent an afternoon recounting her experiences to me. The staff in the archives of the *Diário de Notícias* let me spend hours in their offices on more than one occasion. A million thanks to Marta Ramires, the editor of the Portuguese version of this book, who believed in my story. Anne H and Lynn, your friendship keeps me afloat and (somewhat) balanced. I am incredibly lucky to have you in my life. And to Daniel, Mom, Dad, Mark, and David, I could never have gotten to this point without your support and love and encouragement. Thank you.

ABOUT THE AUTHOR

Before moving to Portugal, Jeannine Johnson Maia worked as a journalist in Belgium and Washington, DC. She served as a press specialist at the U.S. Mission to the European Union in Brussels; studied in the United States and Italy; taught English in France; and lived in Cape Verde. She has a Bachelor's degree in Foreign Policy from the University of Virginia (U.S.), a Master's degree from the Johns Hopkins School of Advanced International Studies (U.S.), and a Master's in Creative Writing from Lancaster University (U.K.). She lives in Vila Nova de Gaia, near Porto, a city she finds irresistibly photogenic. Jeannine is the author of two historical novels that take place in Portugal: *The Filigree Master's Apprentice*, a story of 19th-century Porto (published as *O Rapaz do Douro* in Portuguese), and *Rossio Square N.º 59*, a novel of WWII Lisbon (published as *Praça do Rossio, N.º 59* in Portuguese).

https://www.jeanninejohnsonmaia.com